KU-767-586

The Flying Squad

HOUSE OF
STRATUS

COVENTRY CITY LIBRARIES	
3 8002 01822 380 2	
HJ	03-Mar-2010
	£7.99
CEN	

Copyright by David William Shorey
as Executor of Mrs Margaret Penelope June Halcrow otherwise Penelope Wallace.

All rights reserved. No part of this publication may be reproduced, stored in a retrieval system, or transmitted, in any form, or by any means (electronic, mechanical, photocopying, recording, or otherwise), without the prior permission of the publisher. Any person who does any unauthorised act in relation to this publication may be liable to criminal prosecution and civil claims for damages.

The right of Edgar Wallace to be identified as the author of this work has been asserted.

This edition published in 2001 by House of Stratus, an imprint of Stratus Books Ltd., 21 Beeching Park, Kelly Bray, Cornwall, PL17 8QS, UK.

www.houseofstratus.com

Typeset, printed and bound by House of Stratus.

A catalogue record for this book is available from the British Library and the Library of Congress.

ISBN 1-84232-681-3

This book is sold subject to the condition that it shall not be lent, resold, hired out, or otherwise circulated without the publisher's express prior consent in any form of binding, or cover, other than the original as herein published and without a similar condition being imposed on any subsequent purchaser, or bona fide possessor.

This is a fictional work and all characters are drawn from the author's imagination. Any resemblances or similarities to persons either living or dead are entirely coincidental.

We would like to thank the Edgar Wallace Society for all the support they have given House of Stratus. Enquiries on how to join the Edgar Wallace Society should be addressed to: The Edgar Wallace Society, c/o Penny Wyrd, 84 Ridgefield Road, Oxford, OX4 3DA. Email: info@edgarwallace.org Web: http://www.edgarwallace.org/

3 8002 01822 380 2

Edgar Wallace was born illegitimately in 1875 in Greenwich and adopted by George Freeman, a porter at Billingsgate fish market. At eleven, Wallace sold newspapers at Ludgate Circus and on leaving school took a job with a printer. He enlisted in the Royal West Kent Regiment, later transferring to the Medical Staff Corps, and was sent to South Africa. In 1898 he published a collection of poems called *The Mission that Failed*, left the army and became a correspondent for Reuters.

Wallace became the South African war correspondent for *The Daily Mail*. His articles were later published as *Unofficial Dispatches* and his outspokenness infuriated Kitchener, who banned him as a war correspondent until the First World War. He edited the *Rand Daily Mail*, but gambled disastrously on the South African Stock Market, returning to England to report on crimes and hanging trials. He became editor of *The Evening News*, then in 1905 founded the Tallis Press, publishing *Smithy*, a collection of soldier stories, and *Four Just Men*. At various times he worked on *The Standard*, *The Star*, *The Week-End Racing Supplement* and *The Story Journal*.

In 1917 he became a Special Constable at Lincoln's Inn and also a special interrogator for the War Office. His first marriage to Ivy Caldecott, daughter of a missionary, had ended in divorce and he married his much younger secretary, Violet King.

The Daily Mail sent Wallace to investigate atrocities in the Belgian Congo, a trip that provided material for his *Sanders of the River* books. In 1923 he became Chairman of the Press Club and in 1931 stood as a Liberal candidate at Blackpool. On being offered a scriptwriting contract at RKO, Wallace went to Hollywood. He died in 1932, on his way to work on the screenplay for *King Kong*.

BY THE SAME AUTHOR
ALL PUBLISHED BY HOUSE OF STRATUS

TO MY YOUNG FRIEND
LADY PAMELA SMITH

1

Lady's Stairs was a crazy wooden house overlooking and overhanging the creek between canal and river. You saw it from the lock that marked the place where canal ended and the broad, muddy estuary began, a sagging barn of a place, supported on huge wooden piles, with a dingy façade which had once been painted white, and then not painted again. It was streaked and blurred by nature into strange neutral shades that would have rendered it invisible but for the fact that it was wedged between a high warehouse on the one side and the barrel-roof of an ironworks on the other. Beneath the main rooms the creek ran, rising to within a few feet of Li Yoseph's sitting-room in flood-time.

Lady's Stairs, whence it took its name, has vanished. Once this dark and oily waste had been a pleasant backwater to the Thames, and there was still evidence of its one-time pastoral character. Stock Gardens was a slum that ran parallel with the canal; Lavender Lane and Lordhouse Road were no less unsavoury; and where the tenements raised their ugly heads, and the squeals of playing children sounded night and day, was still called The Meadows.

Li Yoseph used to sit in his little room and watch the colliers tie up at Brands Wharf at high tide, and see the barges towed slowly towards the lock. He found cause for satisfaction that, by craning his neck through the window, he could also see the big Dutch steamers that went down Thames River to the sea.

The police had nothing against Li Yoseph. They knew him to be a fence and a smuggler, but they had no positive evidence, and did not expect to find more on this fatal visit of theirs than they had upon previous visits.

All the neighbourhood thought Li was rich, and knew for certain that he was mad.

He had a habit of holding lengthy conversations with invisible friends. As he shuffled through the streets, a strange-looking creature with his big yellow face as hairless as a child's, yet wrinkled and creased into a thousand criss-crossing lines, he would be talking and gesticulating and smiling dreadfully to his unseen companions. Mostly he spoke in a foreign language which was believed to be German, but was in fact Russian. He confessed to an acquaintance with fairies – good fairies and bad; he saw and conversed with dead men, who told him the strangest tales of unknown worlds. And he was a seer, for he foresaw the future surprisingly.

He was walking about the sloping floor of his room overlooking the creek, mumbling and muttering to himself. It was a strangely lofty room, and in the light of three candles, which served to accentuate the darkness of the apartment, was a place of terrifying shadows. The walls, which had once been lime-washed, were streaked yellow and green, and in wet weather the roof leaked, and little streams of moisture appeared on the walls. This was his living-room – he slept in a big cupboard, which had only this advantage, that it was in the one part of the house that was over dry land.

But the bigger apartment was office, store and recreation-room. Here he interviewed Dutch, German and French sailors who came rowing softly up the creek at high tide, and, steering their little boats through a maze of green piles that held up the overhanging out-thrust of the house, moored at last at the foot of the crazy ladder, down which the old man would climb and chaffer for certain articles they brought to him.

It was quite dark beneath the house, even in the daytime the forest of props and piles letting in the faintest twilight. Only at certain times could these water-borne negotiators come, for when the tide dropped there was nothing below but mud, the depth of two men – thick, watery mud, that moved all the while in great unease as though beneath its blanket some silurian monster was turning in his sleep.

Old Li always had a boat tied up here, fitted with a little motor which he had learned to work. In this he made infrequent excursions on to the river itself. He was contemplating some such trip that night; twice he had rolled up the discoloured square of carpet, pulled open the trap-door which the carpet covered, and, grunting and muttering, had gone down the rungs of the ladder, depositing something in the boat, which lay on its side in the mud. At last his work was finished, and he could devote his time to the shadowy host which peopled the room.

He talked to them, always in Russian, joked with them, rubbed his hands and chuckled at the amazing wit of their repartee. They had been whispering a thing all day – to a normal man a dreadful thing that would have made him cringe in fear. But for once Li did not believe the ghosts.

A bell clanged, and he shuffled out of the room, down the steep stairs, to a little side door.

"Who is it?" he asked.

He heard the low reply, and turned the key.

"You have come early or late – I don't know which." Li had a deep, husky voice, with only a trace of a foreign accent.

Closing and locking the door behind him, he followed his visitor up the stairs.

"Here there is no time," he chuckled hoarsely. "Days or nights, I do not know them. There is high tide, when I must make business very quickly, and low tide, when I may sit and talk to my beautiful little friends." He kissed his hand to a dark corner, and Mark McGill snarled round on him.

"Cut that out – you and your damned ghosts! His sister's coming here tonight."

"His?"

The yellow-faced man peered at him.

"Ronnie Perryman's – she's come over from Paris."

Li Yoseph gaped at the visitor, but asked no questions of the big man.

There was something about Mark McGill that inhibited a request for confidence. He was a commanding man, broad of shoulder. His coarse features had a certain handsomeness; yet the terror he inspired in his many subordinates had its origin less in his patent strength or the brutality of his big hands than in a pair of the palest blue eyes that ever stared from the face of man.

He rolled his half-smoked cigar from one corner of his mouth to the other, walked into the recess where Li had his bed, and eyed the darkening waters thoughtfully.

"High tide in an hour." He was speaking half to himself.

Li Yoseph, watching him as a cat would a mouse, saw him lift a violin from the bed.

"Been playing your fiddle all day, I'll bet — have the police been here again?"

The Jew shook his head.

"No more questions about Ronnie? Well, she'll ask you some. I tried to keep her away. You know what you're going to tell her, don't you?"

A pause; slowly he nodded.

"He was kilt — by the p'lice. They caught him in a boat wit' something he find in the ship. So they say 'Where you get this?' an' they beat him so he fell in the river and died."

"Good for you." Mark bent his head and listened. "That's Tiser and the girl — bring 'em up."

Li went noiselessly down the stairs. He came back, leading the way; Tiser followed — a twittering, nervous man with a big-toothed smile. His brow was perennially moist, his shining black hat and neat black tie added to his repulsiveness. Ann Perryman disliked him from the moment she saw him at the station — a clammy man, whose everlasting smile was an offence.

She came slowly into the room, paused for a second, and in that period of time took in, without perceptible emotion, the squalor of the place in which she found herself. Her eyes rested for the space of a few seconds upon Mark, and he grew strangely uncomfortable under her scrutiny.

She was a straight, neat figure of a girl. In some lights her hair was a deep gold, in others you saw a reddish tinge that almost changed her appearance. She had a high, wide forehead from which the hair was brushed back, and that gave her a certain old-fashionedness. She was straight-backed, held herself rather stiffly, and conveyed by this very poise her aloofness. She was not easily approached; men found her rather coldly austere, and said she was deficient in humour because she could not appreciate theirs. Her grey eyes, set wide apart, could be very hard. Ronnie had known how soft they could be, but Ronnie was dead and no other man had seen love shining there.

Ann Perryman had the stuff of martyrs in her; intellectually and spiritually she was made for grand experiences. Her will was inflexible, her courage sublime.

So this was Ann Perryman! He had never seen her before, and was struck dumb by her unexpected loveliness.

She put out a cold hand and he took it, held it for a second and then released his grip. He hardly knew where to begin.

"Tiser has told you, of course?"

She nodded gravely.

"I saw the account a fortnight ago. I am teaching in a school in Paris, and one has the English papers. But I didn't know that" – she hesitated – "Ronnie went under an assumed name."

She said this in a quiet, even, conversational tone.

"I might have told you before," said Mark, "but I thought I would wait till everything was over before I broke the news."

There was so much sympathy in his voice that Mr Tiser, whose restless eyes had been roving the apartment, brought them back to his confederate with a stare of genuine amazement. Mark was really wonderful!

"It was rather a difficult situation," Mark went on in the low, strained voice of one who is telling an unpleasant story. "You see, if Ronnie was breaking the law, so was I. One naturally hesitates to incriminate oneself."

She inclined her head at this.

"Of course, I know Ronnie wasn't – " She hesitated. "He has been rather unfortunate all his life, poor darling! Where was he found?"

Mark pointed towards the creek.

"I'm going to be frank with you, Miss Perryman. Your poor brother and I were smugglers. I suppose it's very reprehensible, and I'm not excusing myself: I'm being perfectly candid with you. The police were keen to trap us, and I think they regarded Ronnie as rather a weak vessel, and I happen to know that they had made several overtures to him – they hoped to induce him to betray the organisation. That sounds highly melodramatic, but it is the truth."

She looked from him to Tiser. The old Jew had crept behind the curtains of his recess.

"Mr Tiser has told me that the police murdered Ronnie – it is incredible!"

Mark shrugged his shoulders.

"There's nothing incredible about the London police," he said dryly. "I don't say they intended killing him, but they certainly beat him up. They must have caught him coming back in a boat from one of the ships that bring the contraband to us, and either he got a blow that knocked him overboard or else he was deliberately thrown into the water when they found how badly they had injured him."

She nodded again.

"Inspector Bradley?" she asked.

"That's the man. He always hated Ronnie. Bradley is one of these clever Scotland Yard men who have acquired a little education and an inferiority complex."

From behind the drawn curtains of the recess came a thin wail of sound. Mark started round with a snarl, but the girl's hand dropped on his arm. By a gesture she silenced him.

From the recess came the sweet, melancholy cadences of Tosti's "Adieu."

"Who is it?" she asked in a low voice. Mark shrugged his shoulders impatiently.

"It's the Jew – Li Yoseph. I want you to see him."

"Li Yoseph? The man who saw Ronnie killed?"

Mr Tiser found his voice.

"From a distance, my dear young lady," he twittered. "Nothing definite was seen; I think I explained that. Our dear friend merely saw the police officers struggling with our dear departed comrade – "

Mark's cold eyes fixed him.

"That will do, Tiser," he said. "Ask Li Yoseph to come out."

The music ceased. She became suddenly aware of a curious presence. Li Yoseph came forward, his shoulders stooped, looking at her from under his brows, his long hands rubbing over one another. He was a terrifying figure; her first sensation was one of revulsion.

"This is Miss Perryman, Ronnie's sister."

The Jew's face twisted in a little grimace.

"I haf just been speaking to him," he said. His voice was singularly low and melodious, except for the gutturals which occurred at rare intervals.

The girl stared at him.

"You've been speaking to him?"

"Don't take any notice of Li." Mark's voice was sharp, almost peremptory. "He's a little…" He touched his head significantly. "Sees ghosts and things."

"And things," repeated the Jew, his eyes opening wider and wider. "Queer t'ings, t'ings no man sees but me – Li Yoseph!"

She saw his face crease into a grotesque smile. He was looking at something that stood between them.

"So you are there!" he said softly. "Ah, you would come, of course, my leetle Freda."

He stooped and patted the head of an invisible child and chuckled.

"You been goot girl since you was drowned in canal, eh? Ach! you look so happy – "

"Shut up, Yoseph," interrupted Mark roughly. "You're frightening the lady."

"He does not frighten me," said Ann steadily.

7

Li Yoseph was walking back to his little room, his shoulders shaking with laughter.

"Is he often like this?"

"Always," said Mark, and added quickly: "But he's perfectly sane in all other respects. Yoseph, don't go away. I want you to tell this lady what you saw."

Li Yoseph came slowly back till he was within a few paces of the girl. His hands were clasped at his breast; it was almost a gesture of prayer.

"I tell you what I see." His tone had become suddenly mechanical. "First de boat mit Ronnie, she pull from the sheep. And den Ronnie he pull and pull, and den de police launch she op-kom. Den I see dey fight and dey fight, and I hear de splash in do water, and presently Mr Bradley's voice I hear. 'We got him; say nodings about it.' "

All the time he was speaking he was looking at her, and she almost thought she saw in his eyes a mild defiance, as though he were primed for the challenge to his story which she might offer at any moment.

"You saw this?"

He bowed his head, and she turned to Mark.

"Why wasn't a charge laid against these men? Why did they allow it to go under the cases of 'Murder against some person or persons unknown'? Are the police in this country sacrosanct? Can they commit with impunity any crime...murder, and never be charged?"

For the first time he realised something of the volcano that was smouldering in her heart. Ann's voice was vibrant, almost electrifying.

"Bradley – who is Bradley? He is the man you were speaking about. I shall remember him."

She looked at the old man again. He stood with closed eyes, his hands still clasped, swaying to and fro.

"Did he make a complaint to the police?"

Mark smiled.

"What is the use? You've got to understand, Miss Perryman, that the police are a law unto themselves, not only in this but in every other country, I could tell you stories of what happened in New York – "

"I don't want to know what happened in New York." She was a little breathless. "Will you tell me this: is this man to be relied upon?" She nodded to the Jew.

"Absolutely." Mark was emphatic.

"Absolutely, my dear young lady," said Mr Tiser, too long held outside the circle of conversation. "I can assure you he is a highly respectable man. His unfortunate origin is, of course, all against him. But why should we despise Jews? Was not Moses a Jew? Was not Solomon the wisest of all ages, and that same interesting – "

He met Mark's eye and passed through an incoherent stage to silence.

She stood for a moment, her head bent, her finger at her lips, her wide forehead wrinkled in a frown. Mark had offered her a chair, but this she had ignored. He waited for her to speak.

"What did Ronnie do for you?" she asked at last. "You can tell me everything, Mr McGill. He has often spoken to me about you, and I gathered that you were engaged in something…illegal. I suppose I've got a curious moral outlook, but I'm not so shocked now as I was then. Was he valuable to you? And is his loss a very…serious one?"

McGill did not answer instantly. He was turning over in his mind just what lay behind that question.

"Yes," he said at length, "he was almost indispensable. He was the type of boy who could go about the country without creating suspicion. He was a marvellous car driver, and that was extraordinarily useful, for just now the police have a Flying Squad – Bradley is at the head of it – which needs considerable evasion. Ronnie used to collect the stuff we smuggled, sometimes distribute it – and I trusted him. Why do you ask?"

"I was wondering," she said. "This man Bradley, what is he like?"

Before Mark could answer, she heard a little chuckle of laughter and spun round.

A man was standing by the door; how long he had been there she could not tell. Long enough to settle himself, for he was leaning lazily against the door-post. His soft felt hat was pulled rakishly down over one eye, and though the night was chilly he wore no overcoat. A tall, slim-built man, with a long, good-humoured face and sleepy eyes that were regarding her now with amused interest.

"I shouldn't be surprised if this was Miss Perryman," he said, straightening himself and taking off his hat leisurely. "I don't know whether you feel you'd like to introduce me, Mark?"

Mark stiffened.

"My name is McGill," he said harshly.

"Sensation," said the other sardonically. "It's been McGill all your life."

And then the humour went out of his face and left it a little sad-looking, as he lounged across to where the girl was standing. She knew him instinctively, and the eyes that met his were like steel.

"I'm terribly sorry you've had all this trouble, Miss Perryman," he said. "I wish I knew the man who killed your brother."

He bit his nether lip, a trick of his, and looked thoughtfully at Mark.

"I did my best to keep Ronnie out of bad company." He paused, as if inviting an answer, but she did not reply, and his eyes began to rove around the apartment.

"Where's that musical spiritualist?" he asked. "Hallo, Li! I see you've got company."

Li Yoseph came fawning forward, his yellow face tense and alert; shot one quick glance at the detective – a strange glance, thought Mark, and watched Bradley; but that man's face was inscrutable.

"I wonder why they brought you down here?"

He spoke to Ann, but was looking at Tiser, and in his agitation that oily man's eyes were blinking with extraordinary rapidity.

"They haven't been trying to stuff you with that story about the police killing your brother, have they? I should imagine you're just a little too intelligent to accept that kind of fairy-tale. Your brother was killed on land and left in the river."

Again he paused; he saw the tightening of her lips and realised that she was not convinced.

"Do you want anything?" demanded Mark aggressively.

Inspector Bradley's eyebrows rose.

"Pardon me," he said with exaggerated politeness. "I didn't know you'd taken over Li Yoseph's establishment and were acting as host. I shall be at the Yard tonight between ten and two."

A chill passed down the spine of Mark McGill. To whom were those words addressed? Not to him; not to Ann Perryman; certainly not to Mr Tiser. Why had Bradley called? Mark knew him well enough to realise that he would never have come had he known Ann Perryman was there. He had called to see Li! And the reminder that he would be at Scotland Yard was also addressed to Li.

He turned and loafed towards the door, swinging his soft-brimmed hat. On the landing which was immediately outside the door he turned and waved a cheery farewell.

"I'd like to have a little chat with you, Miss – er – Perryman. Perhaps I could call at your hotel tomorrow?"

She did not answer him. The eyes fixed on his were heavy with hate and loathing – Inspector Bradley was too sensitive a man to make any mistake about that.

They heard his footsteps going down the uncarpeted stairs, and the slam of the door. Mark turned to Tiser, showing his teeth.

"You left that door open, you – " He checked himself. "Go down and see that it's closed now, and locked. And stay at the bottom of the stairs till I call you up."

He banged the door after the man and left him to flounder down in the dark; then he came back to where Ann was standing.

"That was Bradley?" she said in a low voice.

"That was Bradley," he replied grimly. "The clever Alec of Scotland Yard. What do you think of him?"

She dropped her eyes to the ground and considered this question.

"Who is taking Ronnie's place in your – organisation?" she asked.

Mark threw out his hands.

"Who could take his place? That kind of man isn't found very easily."

"I could."

His mouth opened in shocked surprise.

"You?" incredulously.

She nodded.

"Yes, I. I drive a car quite as well as poor dear Ronnie."

He was staggered, momentarily thrown out of control. He had expected to meet a weakling dependent who would need a little help for her immediate wants. But for the desire to convince Ronnie's one relative, and to stop those persistent inquiries which relations sometimes make, he would not have seen her at all, certainly would never have brought her to Lady's Stairs.

A thousand possibilities flashed through his mind.

"You'll join us, eh?" He threw out his hands enthusiastically. "Little girl, you're the partner I've been looking for."

Her eyes met his.

"My name is Ann; you may call me that," she said. "And the partnership will be on business lines."

This was one of the few occasions in his life that Mark McGill accepted a rebuff without resentment.

2

There was no telephone at Lady's Stairs. Li Yoseph was a careful man, who never spent money unnecessarily. Long after his visitors had left he sat huddled up in a springless old armchair which he had drawn to the big round table. A lamp burnt at his elbow; before him were the five scrawled sheets of an unfinished letter which he had taken from a box beneath his bed.

He rose slowly and went into the tiny room, looked through the long window on to the creek. The green and red lights of a tug making for the lock gates fascinated him, and he watched it until it was out of sight. Then he took up his violin, cuddled it under his chin and drew the bow softly across the strings. For once the sound of his own music disconcerted him; he put down the violin, came back to the table, and after a while took up his pen.

It was not an easy letter to write, but it had to be done. Presently he would put it in an envelope and, stealing out, find old Sedeman, who occupied a frowsy room in the neighbourhood; and Sedeman, for a consideration, would carry the message to Inspector Bradley.

Though his spoken English was bad, he expressed himself well in the written language. He picked up one of the sheets at random.

...McGill knew that Ronnie was in touch with you. Ronnie Perryman was very untrustworthy when he drank. He drank a great deal. He had quarrelled with McGill and talked about getting out. He discussed it with me, and I also said that I wanted to get back to Memel, where my home is and my nephews and nieces live. I think that McGill must have found out, for he came down here on the night in question, having

followed Ronnie from London. Ronnie was rather drunk. It was one o'clock in the morning when McGill and Tiser arrived. They quarrelled. Ronnie said he would not have anything to do with murder. He said McGill was responsible for the hold-up at the Northern and Southern Bank, where a watchman was killed. He also boasted that he had only to lift his finger to have us all in jail. If he had not said that I think I should not be alive. It was because he brought me into it that way that McGill did not get suspicious about me. Ronnie was standing by the table with a large glass of port, which I had poured out for him. He was lifting this to his lips when McGill struck him with a life-preserver, and hit him again before he fell. McGill tied a sheet round Ronnie and lowered him through the trap into my boat. I don't know where he and Tiser dropped him into the water, but in half an hour they came back and said that Ronnie had recovered and had gone home. McGill told me he would kill me if I spoke a word. He did not then say I was to tell any story to Ronnie's sister. It was only later, when he sent for her, that he told me...

He put down the sheet. There was very little more to write; he finished his narrative on the next page, blotted the paper, folded it and put the letter into an envelope. And all the time he was doing this he was talking softly in Russian.

"...you see, my little pigeon, I must do this, or they will take old Li and put a rope round his neck, and I shall be with you, my little ghost!"

Sometimes he would turn and stoop to caress one of the strange little shapes that only his crazy eyes could see.

"So, so...this wicked McGill, it is better that he should die, eh? That nice young lady who came here, it would be too bad if she should become his friend – "

He heard the sound of a turning key and looked up, thrusting the letter inside his coat. It was Mark's step; he knew it too well; and Tiser was with him, he noted, before the door opened and they came into the room.

Mark walked straight across to the table. He looked down at the pen and paper.

"You've been writing a letter, eh? Posted it?" The old man shook his head.

"My dear friend!" Tiser's voice was an agitated squeak. "Perhaps you are wrong, dear comrade. Now, tell Mr McGill that his suspicions are not well founded. Tell him – "

"You needn't tell him what he's got to say." Mark's tone was deadly calm. "Let's see that letter. You haven't had time to post it – there's still ink on the table."

Li Yoseph shook his head. Then, before he realised what had happened, Mark lurched forward, gripped him by the coat and tore it open. The edge of the letter showed and he pulled it out. The superscription condemned the traitor.

"Bradley – I thought so!"

Mark tore open the envelope, glanced quickly through the contents.

"Going to put up a squeal, were you? That was why Bradley was going to be in his office from ten till two. Well, he'll wait a damned long time for this letter!"

The old Jew did not move; he stood at the edge of the closed trap, his hands lightly clasped before him, looking. All this was inevitable; perhaps the little ghosts that crowded round him were whispering encouragingly, for he smiled again.

"Now, Li," said Mark breathlessly, and Li Yoseph saw death in his eyes.

"Me you cannot kill, my goot Mark," he said. "I may die, yes, but I shall come back. The little spirits – "

Suddenly the old man stooped, flung up the trap, and twisting, dropped to the first rung of the ladder that led to life and safety. Mark whipped a revolver from his pocket; the silencer fixed to the barrel's end caught in the lining of his coat but gave the doomed man no respite.

Plop! Plop!

The second "plop" was louder; right between the shoulders the bullets struck. They heard the squelch of the body as it fell in the water below.

"Shut the trap!"

Mark's face was white; he spoke with difficulty. Tiser came forward, making strange, whimpering noises, and dropped the trap in its place gently.

"Now pull the carpet over it."

Mark walked to the window, tugged it open and looked out. It was a very dark night; a drizzle of rain was falling, and the tide was high.

Tiser was leaning on a chair, breathing heavily like a man who had taken enormous exercise. He was incapable of speech, nor did Mark McGill demand his approval. Tiser dared not look up until he heard the window close.

"That's all right. Come on, you...don't forget what you've seen tonight, Tiser."

The man's teeth were chattering as he followed his sombre master to the head of the stairs. They had reached the landing when there came a heavy knock on the door below. Tiser put up his hand to check the scream that rose. Again came the knock.

"Open the door!"

McGill reeled back into the room. In one wall was a small closed shutter, and, extinguishing the light, he opened this and looked out into the street.

Three cars were drawn up by the kerbside – the third arrived as he looked, and before it came to a standstill half a dozen men were jumping to the pavement. Tall, alert men, who moved towards the house quickly.

In the bright light of a head-lamp he saw a well-hated face – only for a second, and then it passed into the darkness.

"Bradley!" he said thickly. "The Flying Squad – the place is surrounded!"

3

Mark closed the trap and, reaching out his hand, switched on the light. He took one eagle-keen look around, walked quickly to the table, examined it carefully for any sign of writing, and then pointed to the door.

"Go downstairs and let them in," he said.

The knocking was resumed at this moment, heavier, more insistent.

"Wait!"

Tiser was in the doorway. Mark rolled back the carpet, pulled open the trap and flashed a lamp down. He saw nothing but the dark water. And then he remembered his pistol. He watched it strike, heard its faint splash, before he closed the trap again and pulled over the carpet.

"Let them up," he said curtly.

Bradley was the first in the room. One of the four detectives who followed him had an automatic in his hand.

"Stick 'em up!" said Bradley briefly.

Mark's hands went over his head.

"Where's your gat?" asked the detective, whose quick hands passed over the big man's frame.

"If by 'gat' you mean revolver," said McGill coolly, "you're wasting your time. May I ask what is the meaning of this piece of melodrama?" He addressed Bradley.

"Where is Li Yoseph?"

Mark shrugged his shoulders.

"That is exactly what I'd like to know. I was talking with him in quite the friendliest way when he told me that he had to see a man and went out, promising to return in ten minutes."

The detective's lips curled.

"Went to see a man – about a dog, I'll bet!" He sniffed and frowned. "Queer smell here, rather like cordite. Been having a little rifle practice, Tiser?"

Mr Tiser's face was pale, his teeth were chattering. But Bradley had seen him that way before. The man was such an arrant coward that his present agitation meant nothing except that he was terrified to find himself in contact with the police.

Bradley walked to the recess, looked round, and took up the violin and bow, regarding them thoughtfully.

"He didn't take the orchestra, I notice," he said. He tucked the fiddle under his chin, drew the bow across the strings softly and played a short aria. "You didn't know I was musical?" he asked.

He put down the instrument on the table.

"I only know you're theatrical; I suppose the artistic temperament has to find some expression," said Mark.

Bradley's eyes were fixed on his.

"Will you stop thinking you're addressing a public meeting, McGill, and tell me where I can find Li Yoseph?"

The man's face flushed a deep red; the hatred in his eyes was beyond hiding.

"If you want to know why I came here, I'll tell you. Tiser and I are trying to do a bit of good in the world, raising up the men you've crushed, Bradley – "

Again Bradley smiled.

"I know the Home of Rest, if that institution is the subject of your lecture," he said dryly. "A convenient meeting-place for useful crooks. A great idea. They tell me you preach to them, Tiser."

Tiser grinned dreadfully, but was incapable of articulation.

"You're not going to tell me that you made this journey to induce Mr Li Yoseph to join in the general reformation of the criminal classes? Because, if you are – "

A man called him urgently from the doorway. He went over, spoke to him, and Mark McGill saw the surprise in his face.

"All right, tell Miss Perryman she can come up."

Ann Perryman walked slowly into the room, looking from one to the other.

"Where is Mr Yoseph?"

"Exactly what I'm asking," said Bradley cheerfully. She ignored him and repeated the question.

"I don't know," said Mark. "He was here a few minutes ago, but went out for some reason or other – he hasn't been back since."

A hand closed over her arm and drew her round. She faced Inspector Bradley, trembling with fury at the indignity.

"Now, Miss Perryman, will you kindly tell me why you came to Lady's Stairs tonight? I'm asking you not as a friend but as a police officer."

The expression in her face would have abashed most men – Mr Bradley was not easily perturbed.

"I came because he wrote asking me to come!" she said breathlessly.

"May I see the note?"

Tiser was staring at her open-mouthed. From Mark McGill's face it was evident he was unusually concerned.

Ann Perryman hesitated, then, with a savage movement of her hand, she snapped open the bag and produced a sheet of paper. Bradley read the two scrawled lines.

"*I must see you at 10. It is urgent.*"

"Where is the envelope?

"I've thrown it away." She was breathing very quickly; her voice trembled, and Bradley had reason to believe that it was not from fear.

"It was delivered by hand, of course? He intended posting it. He meant tomorrow night – I also had an appointment with him tomorrow night."

Bradley's glance transfixed the big man, but McGill did not quail.

"Will you please tell me what is the meaning of all this?" she asked.

She had regained her self-control with an effort.

"The meaning of all which?" asked Bradley coolly. "This is the Flying Squad – or one of them. I am Inspector Bradley. I came to gather in Li Yoseph before something happened to him. He had arranged to send me a letter tonight; I had an idea that it would have come by hand through the same messenger he employed to communicate with you. I'm not betraying police secrets when I tell you that I was scared about Li Yoseph, and wanted to get him to a place of safety before he went the same way as your brother."

Ann Perryman's lips were trembling, but again she controlled her emotions.

"Before he died at the hands of the police?" she said, in a voice that was not above a whisper. "That is the way my brother went – did you expect to send that old man along the same road? When you held my arm just now and pulled me round as though I were one of your prisoners, I realised just what a brute you were!"

"Who told you I killed your brother?" he asked quietly, and was not prepared for the reply.

"Li Yoseph," she said.

He was silent for a moment.

"I think that's the maddest story I have ever heard," was his only comment. And then he became his business-like self. "I may want to see you again tonight, McGill, and you, Tiser. In the meantime you can go home the way you came. As for you, young lady, I will escort you myself – I particularly wish to see you in the morning."

"I don't need your escort; I will go with Mr McGill."

"You will go with me," he said calmly. "Let me at any rate have the satisfaction of keeping you out of bad company for one evening."

"What's the idea, Bradley?" McGill almost shouted. "What charge have you got against me? I'm just about through with your innuendoes and mysterious hints! Let's have it out!"

Bradley beckoned one of his men to him.

"See Miss Perryman into my car," he said.

For a second she looked her defiance, and then, without a word, turned and followed the detective down the stairs. It was after she had gone that Bradley answered the question.

"I'll tell you what I have against you, McGill. Up and down the country there has been a big increase of crimes of violence. For the first time in our history the gunman has appeared in our midst and is a considerable factor. A policeman was shot on the Oxley Road last week; and when that gang broke into the Islington jewellers and were surprised, they shot their way to safety. That's unusual; you know the English criminal doesn't carry a gun. And there's only one reason why he should. There's a new race of gunmen in this country – that is why I'm sore about you."

"Are you suggesting I run a shooting gallery?" sneered the other, and Bradley nodded slowly.

"That's just what I am suggesting – the worst kind of shooting gallery that the devil could invent! Any man who knows the history of the American gangster knows just what is happening in England. You've found a new avenue for supplying dope to the criminal classes – and that is what you're doing. And when I get you, I'll get you good! There will be a stretch of twenty years between the hour you leave the dock and the minute you leave Dartmoor."

He walked a little closer to the pallid man.

"And I'll tell you another thing. I don't know what you're going to do with Miss Ann Perryman, but you might bear in mind that I'll be watching you like a cat; and if there is any funny business, I'll find a way of getting you inside – without evidence!"

"Frame me, eh?" breathed Mark.

"An interesting Americanism which accurately describes my intentions," replied Bradley with mock politeness.

4

Ann Perryman scarcely knew during that ride to town that she was being subjected to a cross-examination, so skilfully was it conducted. They passed many cab stands, but not once did the tender check its pace. At the corner of Westminster Bridge and the Embankment it stopped.

"I will get you a cab, Miss Perryman," said Bradley.

In the little saloon attached to her bedroom she had an interview with Bradley on the following morning; he had phoned asking for this. By the time he came she had collected her thoughts, and was coldly normal. He noticed that she did not take her eyes from his all the time he was speaking, and in their clear depths he read an abysmal loathing of him and his profession.

"There is no trace of Li Yoseph," he said, "but I think he will be found, unless he has been got away. He used to keep a small boat fastened to a pile beneath the house: that we found in the Thames, but empty."

She was examining him cold-bloodedly. Ordinarily she would have thought him rather a nice-looking man. He had the face of an intellectual: large, deep-set eyes, and a trick of peering through half-closed lids. The trick of laughter, too; his lips twitched once when he was talking of the people who lived in that squalid neighbourhood where Li Yoseph had his house. He was refreshingly clean-looking; he had the shoulders and waist of an athlete, large, capable hands, outspread on the table over which he leaned – she did not ask him to sit. And her hatred of him grew in inverse ratio to the appreciation of his attractive values. So might one bereaved by the operations of Caesar Borgia have grown revolted at the sight of his handsome face. She had been silent during most of the interview – suddenly she dropped a bombshell.

"I don't think you need bother to invent theories, Mr Bradley," she said quietly. "Li Yoseph was probably killed by the police – as they killed Ronnie!"

The suggestion was so ludicrous that for a moment the quick-witted Bradley had no answer for her.

"He was beaten up – I think that is the expression – because he would not tell you what you wanted to know. Why should Li Yoseph escape? He was a witness to the crime."

The eyes were narrowed now to the thinnest slits.

"I see," he said. And then: "Do you know what your brother was doing before his death, or why he had this association with Li Yoseph?"

She did not answer this.

"I'd like to help you."

He leaned farther over the table and his voice dropped to a softness which, in any other circumstances, would have appealed to her.

"You're teaching at a school in Paris, I understand, and I am hoping that you are going back to Paris and that you'll try to forget this awful business. I liked your brother: in a sense he was a friend of mine. I must have been the last person who spoke to him."

He saw her lips curl and shook his head.

"It must be because you're not quite normal that you are thinking as you do. Why should the police hurt him? Why should I, of all people in the world? I would have gone a long way to give him help. I know his past, every bit of it. I know just how unstable he was – "

"I think we can spare ourselves this discussion," she said. "Whether I go back to Paris or not is entirely my own affair. I know you hated him – I believe you killed him. There isn't a man or woman who lives in that neighbourhood who doesn't believe that Ronnie was killed by the police. I don't say they intended murdering him, but they did."

He threw out his hands in despair.

"May I talk to you when you're not feeling the strain?"

And then she flared out at him.

"I never want to see you again. I hate you and men like you! You are all so smug and suave and so patently dishonest! You are liars, every one of you! You cover up your villainies with perjury and your mistakes with persecution. It is a beastly trade you're following. You live on human misery and you build up your reputations on the hearts you break and the lives you ruin – that is all I want to say to you."

He opened his lips to speak, but thought better of it and, smiling faintly, he took up his hat and went out of the room.

She repented of her outburst later, and despised herself for her repentance. Ronnie had been killed by that man…

She was not singular in her belief. The Meadows and the folk of Stock Gardens had their own views, supported by the evidence of their eyes. They knew Ronnie was in the habit of visiting Lady's Stairs, they knew that the police staged a raid upon the place and that a carload of detectives had descended upon Li Yoseph's house at one o'clock in the morning, and that Brad of the Flying Squad had been heard to say: "I'll get the truth out of this boy if I have to beat his head off!"

This was overheard by Harry the Cosh, who was up and about when the tender of the Flying Squad came on the scene.

"Take it from me," said Cosh – so called because he had been twice convicted for using a life-preserver on policemen – "they caught him and coshed him, and when they found they'd done him in, they dropped him in the mud – I know the police. Why, they bashed me something awful the last time they took me."

Nobody suggested that old Li had been the murderer. Not even the police. They simply said that he had disappeared. It leaked out that the night he went a big Dutch steamer had slipped down the river on the tide and it was believed that he had sailed on her.

Li Yoseph's house was shut up and the keys deposited with an agent. He had a banking account at Woolwich, and it happened that, because of his ignorance of forms, he had authorised his banker to pay rates and taxes, so that, his house being a freehold, his theoretical occupation was not disturbed.

"Brad said: 'I'll get the truth out of that boy if I have to beat his head off.' " Cosh repeated the story to many people – to Mark McGill, sombre and silent, to Mr Tiser of the Rest House, to Ann Perryman, dry-eyed, her heart hot with hate at the vision of Ronnie's end.

An hour after Bradley left her at the hotel came Mark McGill. He was very frank and open. He did not know then how much Bradley had told her, of what secrets she was the repository. He only knew that she was surprisingly beautiful and might possibly be the most useful recruit to his organisation.

"I'm not hiding anything from you, Miss Perryman. Ronnie and I and Tiser are smugglers. I've been in the game for years, and Ronnie was my best pal. You see, I can only trust Tiser up to a point – he drinks. He's – well, he's erratic. I'm not pretending that I'm a saint, but you know what the law is – it's death on the man who offends against property. A brute can kick his wife half to death and get away with three months; let him take a few shillings out of the till or rob a capitalist of a few hundred pounds, and he's lucky to get away with six."

It did not seem so terribly sinful to Ann; there was romance in it. He watched her as he spoke and saw resolve kindle.

There were lots of articles that paid heavy duties – saccharine, for example, was three and ninepence an ounce. He – and Ronnie, of course – had got as much as ten thousand ounces over in a week: nearly a thousand pounds profit at the rate they sold. And there were other articles and one or two sidelines – about these he was vague. Ronnie had told her all this before – she was reconciled to the "crime."

It was a clean method of lawbreaking: nobody was hurt but the Government. The common people were in point of fact benefited: they could buy cheaply.

"Naturally I'm not going to let poor Ronnie's death interfere with your position. If you've changed your mind about joining us – "

She shook her head emphatically; there was a light in her eyes that he could interpret, for she had told him how Bradley had so coolly returned her to Paris.

"I have not changed my mind," she said.

"Bradley will tell you that we're doing things – smuggling dope and all that sort of rubbish. Naturally he wants to paint us – and Ronnie – as black as he can. Dope! I'd rather cut off my right hand!"

She interrupted him.

"Does it really matter what Bradley says?" she asked.

That day she became a member of McGill's organisation.

It was curious that she thought no more of Li Yoseph and did not speculate upon the mystery of his disappearance. But Bradley was thinking a great deal, and day after day men sat in boats on the muddy waters of the creek and drew their grappling hooks through the mud, seeking the old man who loved to sit at the open window of his den and play Tosti's "Adieu."

5

Little more than a year later, on the evening of an early spring day...

The far-away drone of an aeroplane engine came to Ann Perryman at last. She closed her book, rose from the running-board of the little saloon car where she had been sitting, and glanced at the watch on her wrist. It was seven forty-five – the pilot was punctual, almost to the second.

Opening the door of the car, she took out a long-barrelled prismatic glass, and, walking clear of the bushes which obscured her view and screened the car from observation, swept the sky. There was the machine, already planing down. The engines were no longer audible.

She went back quickly to the saloon, and, groping in the interior, pulled a handle set in the dashboard. The black roof of the car was formed of lateral strips, and as she manipulated the lever each strip turned on itself like the slats of a Venetian blind. The underside was made of mirrored glass that caught the last rays of the setting sun. Three times she pulled the handle; three times the roof opened and closed. She left it with the mirrors exposed, and ran out again to watch the swiftly moving machine.

The pilot had seen; his signal lamp was blinking hysterically, and he had already banked over towards her. Now his engines were thundering again...

He was scarcely twenty yards above the earth when the package dropped. The silken parachute to which the parcel was attached opened instantly, but did no more than break the fall, for the wooden box struck the ground heavily. No sooner had she located it than the plane was rising steeply.

She did not wait until it was out of sight, but, running to the place where the parcel had fallen, she lifted it, carrying it back to the car, and placed it with the folded parachute in a deep cavity beneath the seat of the saloon. It was not heavy. Mark McGill never allowed her to collect the heavier stuff – he arranged it in some way – and only the lighter parcels which were brought unchecked across the sea frontiers of the kingdom were left to her handling.

It was growing dark, and she sent the car cautiously across the uneven ground of the forest-common. Doubtless there were others – belated picnickers who had spent the afternoon amidst the wild beauties of Ashdown – who had seen the aeroplane dip, but it was very unlikely that any would be close at hand, for she had followed one of the tracks which of itself was but a feeder to a subsidiary road.

The main road she came to after a jolting passage. Turning the bonnet of the machine toward London, she sent the car flying northward. The engines were more powerful than even an expert would suppose from casual observation. Mark, who was an engineer, had taken certain liberties with the design, and this light car of hers could hold the road at seventy.

Speed was a passion with Ann Perryman; to sit at the wheel of a racing machine and watch the indicator needle swing beyond ninety stood for her chiefest satisfaction.

The car came at a steady pace up Kingston Hill. A policeman shouted something, and Ann Perryman switched on the lights, though the dusk had hardly fallen and the man had no right other than his own officious sense of authority to order her lamps to be lit.

A year ago she would have smiled on, ignoring the request, and found a sense of pleasure in flaunting this arbitrary and insignificant man in uniform. But Mark had insisted upon submission to the law and its representatives, in all minor manifestations. She hated policemen. The sight of a white glove upraised at a cross road brought the colour to her cheeks and a hard light to her eyes. Policemen stood in her mind for cruelty and cunning, for treachery unspeakable; for murder, even.

She slowed at his signal, and he gave her a grin as she passed. She would have struck the red, stupid face if she had dared. And yet his appearance brought her a sense of satisfaction and triumph. If he knew! If, gifted by second sight, he had pulled up the car and pried into the contents of the box which was hidden beneath the seat!

She slowed, approaching Hammersmith Broadway, whose blazing lights definitely advertised the close of the day; and here she found the inevitable traffic block. Worming her car between a lorry and a bus, she came to a stop near the kerb. And then she saw the man standing on the edge of the sidewalk, and shrank back. But the lights of a grocer's shop were on her face, and there was no escaping the observation of that keen-eyed gentleman.

His attitude was characteristic: hands thrust deep into trousers pockets, shoulders and head bent forward; and, though the keen brown face was in shadow, it was easy to suppose from his attitude that his mind was miles away from Hammersmith Broadway. At first, he made no sign that he knew her; she thought that she was not recognised, and, turning her head, stared fixedly at the delivery van drawn up on her right. Out of the tail of her eye she saw him move, and now his elbows were resting on the sill of the open window.

"Been taking a joy-ride, Miss Perryman?"

She hated him, she hated his drawling voice, she hated all that he stood for. Mark preached the gospel of expediency, but she owed her acquaintance with this man to her own deliberate act. Deliberately and cold-bloodedly, she had manoeuvred a second and a third and many meetings. She was still bearing the smart of Ronnie's death, but she acted her part well, was volubly penitent for all she had said to him: he could not know the hate that still smouldered in her heart.

"Mr Bradley! I didn't see you."

"People seldom see me when they're looking the other way," he said pleasantly.

She imagined that his eyes were searching the dark interior of the car.

"All alone? That's fine! Speaking personally, I don't know anybody I'd rather be alone with than myself! I suppose you feel that way, too."

He saw the head of the traffic jam was breaking.

"You're not going anywhere near Marble Arch? – I'm trying to save bus fares; it is believed that I'm Scotch."

She hesitated. If he came into the car and sat by her side, she felt she would scream. But Mark had said...

"Do please come in! I'm passing Marble Arch," she said.

He seemed to open the door and sit by her side in one motion.

"This is where my stock gets a rise," he drawled. "If the Deputy Commissioner or the Chief Constable could only see me riding in such good company, I'd be promoted next week. What snobs we are!"

She loathed him for his calm assurance, for the undernote of superficial cynicism; she hated him worse because she felt he was laughing at her, that he knew just the part she had been playing in the combination, and, knowing, was rather amused than shocked. The insufferable hint of patronage in his tone was hateful.

She set her lips tighter as the car sped quickly through the tangle of lorries and tramcars and up the road towards Shepherd's Bush.

"Mr McGill well?" he asked politely – almost deferentially.

"I know very little about Mr McGill," was the prompt retort. "I see him occasionally."

"Naturally," he murmured, "living in the same block of flats you wouldn't see much of him. The Home going strong? There's a man who's doing good work! Give me the philanthropist! If I hadn't been a detective, I should have been a banker and given away money."

She gave him no further encouragement, but Brad did not need provocation.

"Will you be going to the theatre tonight, Miss Perryman?"

"No," she said shortly.

"To supper, perhaps?"

As a matter of fact, Mark had told her that he might need her.

"Were you thinking of asking me out to supper?" she asked, heavily sarcastic.

Bradley coughed.

"In a sense, yes."

For the second time she saw him glance over the seat to the back of the car.

"If I hadn't been a detective I should have gone on the stage. Did you ever read what the *West London Gazette* said about my performance in 'The School for Scandal' which our dramatic society put on?"

"It seems an appropriate play for members of Scotland Yard," she said.

He nodded.

"If I weren't amused, I'd laugh. School for Scandal – Scotland Yard!"

Then he relapsed into silence until the car drew up by the pavement opposite Marble Arch, and he alighted.

"Thank you very much for the ride, Miss Perryman," he said.

He would have lingered by the window of the car to talk, but before he could speak again she had moved on.

Mark employed a chauffeur-mechanic to look after the car – a lame man who lived alone in rooms above the garage; he was waiting for the girl at the end of the mews when she drove up.

"Good evenin', miss – you're a bit late."

She smiled at his anxiety. Mark found his servants in queer places. This man had come to his service by way of the Rest House.

"It is all right, Manford – I had a passenger who might not have liked fast driving."

A taxicab passed at that moment and turned the corner into Cavendish Square. When she herself walked towards the Square, she saw that it had stopped. Its passenger had alighted and was standing by the kerb. She had a glimpse of him as she passed...

Had she seen him before? She had a vague sense of acquaintance... Or had she evolved a mental picture of such a man as this? He stood motionless, silent, a grotesque figure in the formal and decorous setting of Cavendish Square. When, as she walked up the steps of the flat and looked back, he was still standing by the kerb, she imagined that he was watching her.

Mark, she knew, was in. There were two lights showing in the fanlight over the door.

Ann used her key and went in, and found him in the sitting-room, reading an evening paper with his back to a small fire.

She had applied to Mark the supreme test of propinquity, and he had not failed her. He was affectionate in a heavy, brotherly way.

"Back – good business! That fellow picked you up? Fine! He ought to – he was once a French Ace."

Ann had taken off her close-fitting hat and was arranging her hair before a mirror.

"I had a travelling companion from Hammersmith to the Marble Arch – I will give you three guesses."

He shook his head, reached to the silver cabinet on the table and found a cigar.

"I am too lazy to guess," he said. "Besides, I am not boy friends with your girl friends."

"Guess."

Mark McGill groaned and settled himself comfortably on the couch.

"Riddles I never attempt to answer. The riddle of a Customs authority which charges exorbitant duties upon saccharine is, I'm sure, the easiest, and I haven't even attempted to solve that. It was somebody interesting, I'm sure."

"It was Central Inspector Bradley."

He was startled.

"Bradley? What was the idea? Did he hold you up? Where was the stuff—"

She laughed at this staccato rattle of questions, and the relief which her amusement gave him was visible.

"He begged a ride and I gave it to him. I couldn't very well refuse. He asked after you."

Mark blinked at this.

"A comic fellow!" He smiled uneasily.

She stood before the mirror, pushing her hair into place with a little golden comb. He could see the oval of her face reflected, red lips and big grey eyes under the straight golden fringe.

"Every time I see myself I seem to be growing more and more like a Real Bad Woman, Mark! I think I'll dye my hair black!"

Mark did not answer, and there was a silence of a minute. He was sitting on the sofa-head, frowning down at the carpet, when she spoke again.

"Sometimes my resolution wants a lot of supporting. About Bradley – what do you call him – Brad? I couldn't somehow get the proper feeling about him as I drove him along the Bayswater Road. I ought to have felt sick and yet I didn't – it is a very wearing business, flogging up one's animosities. I kept saying to myself: here is the man who killed dear Ronnie – he did kill him? It may have been one of the other men – Simmonds – that brute?"

"Brad killed him all right." Mark was staring gloomily at the carpet. "And old Li, too, I expect – "

He brooded on this, walking up and down the room, his arms folded tightly, his usually placid face screwed into an expression of distaste.

"I hate to talk of Ronnie, but you've raised the question twice in the past month. What happened nobody knows."

He stopped in his walk at a desk, unlocked a drawer, took out a small envelope and shook the contents on to the blotting-pad. He sorted these out and found a newspaper cutting. He came back towards the fireplace, where the light was better.

"I've never shown you this before – it is an extract from the *South-Eastern Herald*, and gives a fairly accurate description of what took place."

Fixing a pair of pince-nez on his nose, he read:

"In the early hours of last Wednesday, the Flying Squad, under Inspector Bradley, paid a visit to Lady's Stairs, a ramshackle old house, the property of Elijah Yoseph, a Dutch or Russian Jew. It is believed that the activities of the police were connected with a complaint made by

the Customs that certain dutiable articles were being smuggled into the country. When the police arrived at Lady's Stairs they found the house empty, but the room in which Yoseph lived presented a scene of such extraordinary disorder that the police were under the impression that there had been some sort of struggle. On the sash of a window which opened on to the Creek were bloodstains, and on the floor about three feet from the open window. A search was made of the Creek foreshore, and the body of a man, who has since been identified as Ronald Perryman, 904, Brook Street, was discovered. He had been beaten to death by some blunt instrument. Li Yoseph had also disappeared. Scotland Yard has a clue which may lead to an arrest. Garage keepers who had the car of any stranger to the neighbourhood, and which was seen driving from Meadow Lane after the murder, are requested to communicate with Scotland Yard."

"That is their story," said Mark, folding up the paper. "Mine is a little different. Li Yoseph's house was what has been picturesquely called a smuggler's den. We had one or two deals with him, and Ronnie was usually the go-between. Li Yoseph liked him. On that night Ronnie was sent down to fix the passage of a large quantity of tobacco. There is no doubt that whilst he was there the police made their raid."

"What happened to Li Yoseph?" she asked.

He shook his head.

"God knows. He probably cleared out at the first hint of danger. He had arrangements with most of the Dutch and German ships going down the river, and we know that he had a rowing boat to get him to their side. He was an extraordinarily strong old man. The police surprised Ronnie and tried to make him talk; when he wouldn't, they beat him up. Somebody gave him an unlucky blow, and to cover up their story this yarn was invented. Where was the taximan who dropped these mysterious strangers? Whoever saw them? They have never been heard of. That part of the tale's a fake."

"Have you tried to find Li Yoseph?" she asked, and only for a second did he hesitate.

"Yes, I sent a man over to Holland and to Lithuania to make inquiries – he's dead. He died at Utrecht. Nobody knows this but you and I."

There was an odd look in her eyes. For one panic moment he thought she disbelieved him, that she had acquired some knowledge of what really happened at Lady's Stairs.

"What did he look like – will you describe him?" she said.

"Who – Li Yoseph? Don't you remember? He was about sixty – rather tall, with a stoop. A shortish grey beard that ran up to his cheekbones. He always dressed the same, summer and winter – a black coat almost like a kaftan, buttoned up to his neck, and a Russian fur cap of astrakhan – what is the matter?"

She was staring at him with wide-opened eyes. "I saw him – a quarter of an hour ago – standing outside this house," she said, and the face of Mark McGill went grey.

6

Mark McGill was like a man paralysed: he neither moved nor spoke. At last:

"You saw him – Li Yoseph?" His voice was thick. "You saw Li Yoseph in – in Cavendish Square? You're mad – phew!"

He shook himself as if he were throwing off the burden she had suddenly imposed upon him.

"Where – tell me?"

She told him of the man she had seen standing on the kerb by the waiting cab, and, running to the window, he wrenched back the curtains, threw up the window and stepped out on to the balcony.

"Where?"

She had followed him and pointed.

"He was there – at that corner."

The cab was no longer in sight, nor the man.

"Rubbish – God! you gave me a – a turn! Of course, I understand. There's a fellow lives at the corner house, a Russian prince or something of the sort. He often has visitors, Russians and people of that sort..."

The hand that went up to his lips was trembling; she had never seen him like that before, and could only wonder at the agitation into which the very possibility of Li Yoseph's existence had thrown him.

"He is dead – I know that he is dead – what the hell – ?"

He spun round with the snarl of a frightened beast as Mr Tiser came into the room. Mr Tiser was dressed in his tidy black. He wore frock-coats that were a little too long for him and a ready-to-wear black tie, and his linen was always spotless. He had large rabbit teeth, which he showed in a perpetual smile. Mr Tiser was a very happy man. He was happy that he was alive (and he had good reason for this), happy that he had the opportunity of helping his fellow creatures, mostly happy always to welcome any distinguished visitor to the Rest House. He was happy now as he danced into the room.

"Goodness gracious, my dear friends, I seem to have startled you! I really must knock in the future. Did I come at an inconvenient moment?"

His voice, his manner, the lift of his eyebrows stood for archness. Ann did not actively dislike him, but she found it difficult at times to offer the admiration for his disinterested services to humanity which they deserved. Being human, she discounted the virtues and resented the perfections which were too apparent in Mr Tiser.

"My good fellow, you look ill. Positively! Do you agree, Miss Ann? I am concerned. Perhaps I observe these signs because I live, move, and have my being in an atmosphere of rude health? Take old Sedeman, for example – my old man of the sea – wicked but well. Ha, ha! Ha, ha!"

He laughed mechanically at his own witticisms. All the time he was speaking he was employing himself usefully. There was a lacquered cabinet in an alcove, and from this he had taken a bottle and a tumbler.

"Look not thou upon the wine when it is red: when it giveth its colour aright, eh? But when it is yellow and tawny and smelleth of peat, eh? Another matter, I think."

He sipped the whisky; his pale blue eyes were smiling approval.

"All is well at the Rest House – "

"Ann thought she saw Li Yoseph today."

Mr Tiser's face contorted painfully.

"For God's sake don't be comic!" he said shrilly. "Li Yoseph... pleasant subject to talk about, eh? Let the dead rest, old boy. Li Yoseph – ugh!" He shivered and put down his glass.

There was perspiration on his face; little beads appeared under his eyes; all his jauntiness had left him. The shock of the announcement threw him off his balance, and Ann realised for the first time how near the edge this suave missioner lived.

"Li Yoseph...do you remember, Mark? All those bogeys and ghosts of his? By heavens, he used to make my flesh creep! And now he's a ghost himself – most amusing!"

He chuckled foolishly, filled the glass again and drank the raw spirit eagerly.

"Li Yoseph is dead, as far as we know." Mark forced his voice to a calm he did not feel.

Mr Tiser stared at him, his mouth working foolishly. "You bet he's dead! Very good thing for everybody. Do you remember how he used to see things, Mark...talked to them...it made my blood run cold!"

He shivered, and the hand that held the glass trembled violently. He was looking into vacancy as though he himself saw something. In his terror he was oblivious of his audience. Ann heard him as a man who was speaking his thoughts aloud.

"It was horrible...confoundedly so. I wouldn't go through that again. Can't you see him as he stood grinning at us and saying – he – he'd come back – hey?"

Mark was at his side, gripped him by the arm and swung him round.

"Wake up, will you?" he said harshly. "And shut up! Can't you see you're worrying Ann?"

"Sorry, sorry!" mumbled the quivering Mr Tiser. "Before a lady, too! Most awfully bad form."

Mark caught the girl's eyes and signalled. She needed no encouragement. Picking up her hat and her handbag, she went quickly out of the room. From the passage she heard Tiser's shrill voice.

"Li Yoseph – Li Yoseph...men aren't immortal. Mark, you know he's dead... Ten paces, old boy, what...?"

She was glad to close the door on the sound of his whining voice. Tiser stood for the ugly aspect of the game. He was always drunk, always talking wildly; his unctuousness and hypocrisy were alike unpleasant. Ann very rarely spoke to him: she could count their conversations in the past year on the fingers of one hand.

She crossed the landing and opened the door of her own flat, a smaller apartment. Her daily maid had left her a cold dinner waiting and the table laid. She was not very hungry, and she delayed the meal until she had had a bath and changed.

Ronnie had been done to death over a year now. She tried to recover from the past something of her blind, insensate hatred of this suave officer of the law, something of the bitter contempt, something of the old schemes of vengeance she had hugged to her heart, and which had made imperative the cunning re-introduction which Mark had manoeuvred. She had a portrait of Brad cut from a newspaper, and that her bitterness should not die of inertia she had placed it in a double frame, so that they looked at one another: Ronnie, with his clear-cut profile and the youthful smile in his eyes; Brad, his murderer, sombre, cynical, hateful. She had set out to make this man like her, and Mark had not only approved her plan, but given it encouragement. It had been a heart-breaking task; all the time she had to fight down the memory of that ghastly thing she had seen, and which they told her was Ronald Perryman; but she had schooled herself so well that she could sit vis-à-vis his slayer, and smile in his eyes as she tapped her ash into the saucer of the coffee cup.

He liked her very well, she knew that that bitter day when she heard about Ronnie; but he went no further than liking. He was interested in her, seemed genuinely sympathetic in her sorrow. Not until that very night had he ever mentioned Mark McGill, though he had often spoken of Ronnie.

"He got into pretty bad hands, that boy," he had once said. "I could see him drifting deeper and deeper, and I did my best to save him. If he'd only told me just how far he was committed I might have done it."

As she dressed she set the photo frame squarely on her dressing-table. There was a little frown on her forehead as she brushed back her shingled hair. Had she been as clever as she had thought? She had learned nothing, was no nearer to his confidence than ever she had been. Mark used to ask her, when she came back from these meetings, what he had said – she could tell him nothing more about his work and himself than Mark already knew.

Bradley was not of the gentle class: his father had been a country wheelwright whose hobby had been the study of bird life; his mother was a labourer's daughter.

The labourer's ancestry was, in the days of his childhood, a subject for whispering gossips. The lad started life as a stable-boy; he graduated to the police through a variety of employments, all of which contributed something to his knowledge of life.

To learn had been his absorbing passion. He might be imagined parading his midnight beat, muttering strangely as he murdered the French irregular verbs, or spending hours of leisure reading such elementary textbooks on law as were intelligible to him.

At twenty-two he was a sergeant, at twenty-three a war captain. He came back to Scotland Yard from Mesopotamia with a knowledge of Arabic, written and spoken, a small and uncleanly library of Oriental works, which he confessed he had scrounged, and two new methods of lock-picking that he had learnt from a shameless Arabian burglar who called himself Ali Ibn Assuallah. He might have held an important post in Bagdad: he preferred the sergeant's rank, which was grudgingly restored.

Ann had finished her meal and was brewing coffee when Mark telephoned through to her.

"I don't know what is the matter with Tiser – it looks to me like a nervous breakdown. He has been overworking at the Rest House and I don't think the company has too good an effect on him. I hope it hasn't worried you?"

He heard her laugh and was relieved.

"I haven't thought of it since. I don't like him very much. He drinks, and I don't like people who drink."

Mark said something about "over-strain" and added that he had sent him back to the Rest House. He made no further reference to Li Yoseph.

There were so many things about Mark that were altogether admirable. Who but he would have devoted some of his illicit gains to the moral uplift of less fortunate breakers of the law? Viewed calmly, there was something grotesque, something Gilbertian, in the idea, and yet the Rest House was an accomplished scheme. Mark had bought an old public-house that had lost its licence, and had furnished the hostel at a considerable cost for the use of old convicts. Here, for a minimum sum, the old lag could find a bed and food.

"My amusing hobby," Mark described it; and though it cost him five thousand a year he regarded the money as being well spent.

She thought it was wonderful of him, and would have given up one night a week to the work, but he would not sanction this.

"I don't want your name associated with mine," he said. "One of these days I may fall, and I'd like to keep you out of it."

That was so like Mark – her heart glowed towards him. "Bring your coffee with you – I want to talk," he suggested when she told him what she was doing.

He was waiting at the open door to take the cup from her.

"Tiser's getting more and more impossible – with the drink he takes he ought to be dead," he said. "We'll have to look around for another superintendent."

"I don't like him," she confessed.

"I'm glad you don't. I had a devil of a time with him after you left. He's got a new craze – the Flying Squad! Every car he sees in the streets he thinks is a police car. He wants to go out of the game, and I'm inclined to let him."

This was an opportunity.

"I realise that you must have all sorts and conditions of agents – I've met a lot of queer ones who didn't seem like saccharine merchants! – but I've never bothered my head about that side of it – the fetching and carrying is the fun! But I always thought Mr Tiser was – a sort of good man – I don't like him, but I'm so curiously perverse that good people aren't very interesting to me."

He was taken aback by her surprise.

"He's a good fellow all right," he said hastily, "but even the best people are ready to cheat the Customs. I've never regarded myself as a great sinner, and I don't suppose he does, either. Which reminds me that I shall want you to go down to Oxford tonight with a little parcel. I'll give you a plan of the road and show you where they'll be waiting for you."

"In spite of the Flying Squad!" she bantered.

But he did not smile.

"I'm hoping great things from your friendship with Brad. He'll never have the nerve to arrest you, and if he did — well, I trust you, Ann. There would be quite a lot of people who would go to prison if you talked."

She smiled contemptuously.

"If I talked! Mark, you have the Flying Squad complex too!"

The drawing-room was in half darkness except for two soft, shaded lamps, one of which stood on Mark's writing-table, the other on a cabinet near the door. The night was chilly, and the red glow of the fire was very welcome. She sat down on a low stool and stretched her hand to the warmth. For a long time she looked at the red coal thoughtfully.

"Isn't it strange that every time one mentions Li Yoseph — "

"Li Yoseph seems to be growing into an obsession," he said, and changed the subject, but only for a while. Again they came back to the old Jew who owned Lady's Stairs and to that tumbledown house.

"Are you sure Li Yoseph is really dead?"

He fetched a long breath. Nobody knew better than he that Li Yoseph was dead.

7

"I – " he began, and then he heard the telephone ring in his bedroom.

There were two phones there and a small housewire. Of the two, one rang with a deep, resonant note, and this was the one that Mark never liked to hear.

He had some excellent agents – excellent in the quality of their services, however deficient they might be in the qualities which are usually associated with excellence, and they invariably called him on a number which was not in the telephone book.

He went out, closing the door behind him.

Ann looked up as Mark McGill came back into the room.

"Will you want me to go to Oxford – or anywhere?"

"I don't know." His voice was sharp, and she looked at him with a little frown of wonder.

"Is anything wrong, Mark?"

"Nothing very much – only one of my people told me that the flyers were out and the police may be coming here."

Mark huddled up in a corner of the settee, his arms folded tightly across his chest, his head bent. He had the appearance of a man in pain. It was Ann who broke the silence.

"Can you rely on the man who phoned? Do you really think the police will come tonight?"

He nodded.

"I don't know where he gets his information," he said at last, speaking slowly, "but I never remember his being wrong." And then, as if he realised the urgency of the situation, he jumped to his feet.

"You left the stuff in the car, of course? I'll go down and deal with that – "

"Do you want me?"

He shook his head.

His flat was on the ground floor, and he was in the privileged position of having a private passageway to the garage at the back. Passing through a narrow passage which opened from the kitchen, and down a short flight of stairs, he opened a door and went into the big garage. He could afford to switch on the lights, for the windows were darkened.

Ann's car stood as it had been when it was backed into the building. With a key he took from his pocket he unlocked the back panel and removed it. He then drew out the square box and the parachute, and, detaching the fastening, rolled the parachute into a ball. He then turned his attention to the box. It had a sliding lid, which was also unfastened with a key. From the interior of the box he removed twenty-five little packets wrapped in thin blue paper. In one corner of the garage was a large galvanised steel receptacle. It was connected to ceiling and floor by a big iron pipe. He opened the steel door and looked carefully inside. To the lower end of the funnel was fitted a cone-shaped plug, which he removed carefully and examined. The plug was of salt, and, having tested this, he returned it carefully to fill the lower part of the funnel. On this he laid the twenty-five packets, very carefully, and re-fastened the door.

He bundled the parachute into a box and carried this back the way he had come, into the kitchen. In place of the usual kitchen range was a tub-shaped steel receptacle, and into the interior he dropped the box containing the parachute, and clamped down the steel lid. Pulling open a sliding panel, he lit a match, and thrust it amidst the shavings that showed through a grating. He waited till the furnace was alight, covered the bars again, slid the panel into its place.

Now let the flyers come!

When he returned to the sitting-room he found Ann sitting on a stool before the fire, her face in her hands. She turned her head, and he saw that something had puzzled her.

"Suppose the police came and found – things? What would it mean to us?" she asked. "I've been reading a few leading cases lately. Magistrates very seldom give imprisonment for first offences; usually it's a fine of a hundred pounds. Of course, it would be rather awful for you – I mean the publicity of it – but it wouldn't be terribly scandalous, would it?"

She waited for a reply, and when he did not speak, she went on:

"Mark, you must do a much larger business than I help you with. The packets are so small and the profits hardly seem to pay for the motorcar service. I'm wondering if I'm not more of a danger and a nuisance to you than I'm worth. I know that that isn't the whole of your" – she hesitated – "transactions, but even with a profit of two or three shillings an ounce I hardly seem justified."

For a year Mark McGill had been dreading this curiosity of hers, and for some reason his answer was not so glib as it could have been.

"You're only in on a small section of the business," he said awkwardly. "The organisation is a much larger affair than you can see. It isn't because I want you to fetch and carry – you're useful to me in a dozen other ways, Ann. There are so few people in this game that I can trust. My dear, you know my angle. I've been frank with you all through. Smuggling is as much a breach of the law as burglary. I am not pretending it isn't. I put that point to you – "

"Of course you did, Mark," she said penitently. "Poor Ronnie was a law-breaker, and so am I. You don't suppose I'm weakening – I glory in it!"

She gloried in it, but – He had not exactly answered her question. Before she could pursue the subject she heard the shrill sound of the house phone in Mark's room, and he went in. He had an arrangement with the hall porter whereby all unusual callers were announced to him. Though he kept a staff of servants, they went off duty after dinner, and he had found that the assistance of the hall porter saved him many useless journeys to the door.

She heard him talking in monosyllables, and then he said:

"Yes, all right; show him up."

On his desk were two little brass levers that looked like light switches, and when he heard a knock at the outer door he turned over one of these. She heard a deep, gruff voice ask if the owner might come in, and when the foot of the caller sounded in the passage, Mark turned back the switch.

"Come in," he snarled in answer to the loud rapping, on the panel of the sitting-room.

The man who swaggered into the room might have been of any age that was between sixty and eighty. His head was completely bald, and the polished dome shone as though it had been waxed. His beard was of a dazzling whiteness, and hung halfway down his waistcoat. Incidentally, it concealed the fact that he wore neither collar nor tie. He was unusually tall and straight, broad of shoulder, powerfully built. In one hand he carried what had once been a white top-hat, but which was now a patchwork of fadings that varied between the palest primrose and the richest brown. A long ulster, slightly ragged at the wrists, covered his massive frame from shoulders to shoes, which were enormous, odd and patched.

He looked round the room with a certain haughty condescension which should have amused, but only added to his awesomeness.

"A good pitch, my boy – I've never seen a better, except perhaps the palace of my friend the Marquis of Bona-Marfosio."

He looked at Ann thoughtfully and stroked his heavy white moustache.

"Do you know the Marquis, my lady? A rare man to hounds, and a deuce of a feller with the wimmin – "

Mark's impatience had not eased.

"What do you want?" he snapped.

Mr Philip Sedeman put his hat on a chair.

"The cicerone of our little community has been taken ill. A mere nothing, but the members, like the good fellows they are – "

"Taken ill?" asked Mark quickly.

" – deputed me to call upon our admirable patron with the sad information," continued the patriarch, as though he had never been interrupted.

"How long has he been ill?"

The old man looked up at the ceiling. "It may have been two or three minutes before I volunteered to come along and see you. The cost in omnibus fares was considerable, but that is a matter we will not discuss. A man of my training and experience would hardly wrangle over a question of eightpence, nor, I am bold to say, would a man of your attainments, birth and education."

He looked at the girl with the benignity of a saint.

"What is the matter with him – Tiser, I mean?" asked Mark, eyeing the old man with no favour.

Again Mr Sedeman sought inspiration from the ceiling.

"An uncharitable mind – and there are many – might describe his symptoms as indistinguishable from delirium tremens," he said gravely. "Personally, I consider it to be no more serious than a very simple souse."

"Souse?" repeated the girl, puzzled.

"Pickled," explained Mr Sedeman courteously. "He has climbed above the eight mark. I had my doubts as to whether it would be advisable to come to you or whether I should seek out the young lady with whom he is, I believe, on terms of the deepest affection. You may have seen her – she is a suicide blonde."

In spite of the anxiety which Mark's obvious perturbation induced, Ann laughed.

"And what is a suicide blonde?" she asked.

"She dyes by her own hand," said Mr Sedeman gravely.

Mark's harsh voice broke into her laughter. "All right, Sedeman, I'll come along," he said, and, walking to the door, jerked it open.

Mr Sedeman took up his hat, smoothed it very carefully with his greasy elbow, ran his long fingers through his white beard, and sighed.

"The expenses involved, not counting loss of time, are a mere beggarly eightpence," he murmured.

Mark put his hand in his pocket, took out a piece of silver, and almost threw it at Mr Sedeman; but the old man was in no wise distressed; he favoured the girl with a flourishing bow, strode to the door, and turned.

"Heaven bless thy comings and goings, fair flower!" he said poetically.

"Get out!" snapped Mark, but the patriarch left at his leisure.

"Who is he?" she asked, when Mark had come back from seeing their peculiar visitor to the front door. "Is Mr Tiser very ill?"

Mark shrugged his shoulders. "I don't know, and care less."

Then he went into his room, and she heard him calling a number. He came away from the instrument to close the door; this was unusual in Mark, who had, she imagined, no secrets from her, and yet had taken this precaution twice in one night.

Ann Perryman was uneasy, and she had tried unsuccessfully during the past month to find the cause for her mental unrest. It was not conscience that was working: she was sure of that. She had no compunction, gloried in her work, but – always there was that but – Mark's arrangement with her was on the strictest business footing; he neither asked nor expected favours; her salary was regularly paid, the bonuses which came her way were modest. Only the cold-blooded regularity of their relationship made this strange life of hers possible.

In many ways Mark was a careful man: he checked petrol consumption, would spend an evening debating the problem of new tyres, and when, as she sometimes did, she went to Paris for "the firm," bringing back with her quite a number of little packages concealed in specially designed pockets, her expenses were in the friendliest way audited, and she was expected to account for all her movements. This latter arrangement she rather resented at first, until he explained that until he knew where she was and what she was doing, he could not be sure that she had escaped the shadowing detectives.

Mark came out of the room, his face as black as thunder.

"There's nothing much the matter with him," he said harshly. "Sedeman saw him come in and thought it was an opportunity for tapping me – I suppose Tiser looked a bit green."

He looked at her thoughtfully.

"I don't know…about that police visit…"

She saw his jaw drop, and he went quickly to the wall. Pushing back a panel, he revealed the green face of a little safe, which he opened, taking out an oblong package.

"I had forgotten this," he said breathlessly. "It ought to go in the container, and yet it can't!"

He looked at the package helplessly, and then at her.

"I ought to get this out of the house."

"What is it?" she asked quickly.

"It's the stuff for Oxford. There's a man there named Mellun, who will be waiting, anyway." Again he looked at the package irresolutely.

"I don't like to run the risk."

"I'll take it," she said promptly, and before he could protest she was out of the room.

In five minutes she was back in her leather driving coat. Yet he was reluctant to surrender the package.

"It may be a plant… Sedeman… Bradley – they may all be in it. I don't want you to take the risk."

Yet she knew instinctively he did want her to take the risk, and wanted very badly to have that package out of the house.

"You might slip into your coat and make your way to the Thames Embankment…throw it in the water."

She laughed at his nervousness.

"How stupid!"

She almost wrenched the package from his hand and dropped it into her deep inside pocket.

"If anything happens – I shall be brought into this. Naturally I shall stand by you, and if you bring me into it – "

She stared at him, hardly believing it was he who spoke.

"Of course I shall not bring you into it, Mark. If I am caught it's entirely my own affair."

He turned to relock the safe; she thought it was to conceal some emotion which was expressed in his face – apprehension or –

Mark was puzzling her tonight. Something had happened which had thrown him completely off his balance.

8

She made her way down to the garage, put on the lights and examined the petrol tank before she threw open the doors and, knocking away the chocks, let the car roll of its own volition down the gentle incline to the mews. She closed the doors and took one quick survey left and right. There were two ways out, that which led into New Cavendish Street and that to the street that ran parallel. She decided on the latter route, sent the car quickly over the uneven paving of the mews, turned back to Portland Place and ran steadily and without check into Regent's Park.

She followed the Outer Circle, making the widest detour, until she came to Avenue Road, and a few minutes later she was speeding up Fitzjohn's Avenue to the Heath. The straight road to Oxford, which would take her through Maidenhead and Henley, she avoided, and came by a little-used road to Beaconsfield and Marlow.

Henley was more difficult to avoid. She ran through the wide main street at a leisurely pace, and, as she believed, unobserved; had reached the foot of the long, wide, tree-lined Oxford Road, when she heard a voice shout at her. She turned her head quickly. Drawn up in a side lane was a big car, its lights burning dimly. She saw three men standing at the end of the lane rush for the machine as another jumped towards her footboard.

He missed, and almost at the same moment she saw the other car swing out of the lane and the men who formed its crew scramble aboard. She stepped on the accelerator and the machine leapt forward. There was need for haste. Somebody in the pursuing car was signalling with a red lamp to "stop." Police obviously – she knew by its drone the new type of car they were using.

She had a clear road and only one crossing to chance – she came in sight of this at eighty miles an hour, ignored the frantically waving danger lamp and flashed across the bonnet of a swift Rolls that was coming at right angles with not more than a foot to spare. Behind the Rolls she saw, out of the tail of her eye, the flickering lights of a big lorry – that would block pursuit for a minute. The mirror fixed at the side of the windscreen showed her the lights of the police car (now ablaze) swerving – skidding, probably, under a sudden application of brakes. A distant "plop" – a burst tyre; nothing else could make that sound.

Now she had careened round a sharp bend of the road. Half a mile away were two rows of cottages flanking the road, and she knew that beyond there was a crossing, and in the daytime a policeman. Short of the cottages a side road ran northward, and this was only safe if she could negotiate the little village which she knew lay midway. She always thought of this village as a bead through which ran the narrowest of threads. Her speedometer was down to forty-five, and, looking back, she could see or hear nothing, though she might well be deceived, for the narrow road twisted and turned. Here was the village ahead of her – she dropped to twenty.

Yet another policeman appeared out of the darkness – a mounted man, whose horse grew restless in the glare of her head-lamps. He had heard nothing apparently – and waved her on. And then she heard the shrill of his whistle and increased her speed. On the farther edge of the village the road ran straight and the surface had been recently made up. She stepped on the pedal and flew. It was pitch dark; the lamps turned the road and the fringing hedges into a lane of gold.

There was a bridge over a deep stream. She slowed for the hump of it; and then, right ahead of her, she saw two blazing lights appear, and above these the little green lamp which advertised the profession of its passengers.

She had to decide quickly. There was no room to turn the machine – if that mounted policeman's whistle meant anything, it meant that she was being followed and that he had received some signal to hold her. She knew that the Buckinghamshire police had a code of rocket signals to meet the depredations of motor bandits.

Switching off her lights, she stopped the car dead on the crest of the bridge, took out the package she was carrying, and, peering into the night, flung it into the swollen river. Then, restarting the car, she went on at her leisure.

The car coming towards her was moving as slowly and keeping to the crown of the road. Turning her head-lamps on full, she sounded her klaxon, but the machine ahead did not budge. There was nothing to do but to stop. Both cars halted together, their bonnets within a few inches one of the other. She saw two men approach and come running towards her, and heard a hated voice.

"Why, if it isn't Miss Perryman!"

He could not have recognised her, and his simulated surprise was all the more offensive.

"You slipped us rather nicely, and I'm afraid there's going to be a little trouble."

It was the voice of Sergeant Simmonds.

"Now, young lady, perhaps you'll explain what you mean by driving to the common danger?"

The stout man with his bristling moustache she had not met since the day he brought her the dreadful news of Ronnie's end.

"I'm not aware that I was so driving," was her answer.

He snorted at this.

"You're under arrest," he said gruffly, and called one of his men to take charge of her car. "Get down, please."

He gripped her firmly by the arm, and she went hot with fury.

"Let me go! There's no need to hold my arm."

She struggled to free herself, and he released her. But she was now visible in the light of the electric lamps that were focussed on her.

"Get into that car." He pushed her into the tender, sat on one side of her and another detective on the other.

The man who had taken charge of her machine backed it almost into the hedge to give them a clear passage. As they passed, Simmonds shouted:

"Bring that car back to the station-yard. I want it searched thoroughly."

Mr Simmonds' manner changed once they were on the way to London.

"A sensible young lady like you ought not to give the police all this trouble, Miss Perryman," he said reproachfully. "You might have killed somebody running your car at that rate! I don't suppose you knew what you were doing, or else you've been led into this by others."

A very sententious man was Sergeant Simmonds of the bristling moustache; but he was not a good actor. He was in truth the most obvious of kidders.

"You tell me where you were going and all about your little game, Miss Perryman, and I'll make things easy for you. I'm going to mention no names, but I know you're doing something which you wouldn't do if you knew what it was you were doing."

"That sounds rather involved," she said coldly, and he chuckled in the most genial manner.

"Ah, I haven't had your education, Miss Perryman! You know, a young lady like you oughtn't to be running around the country at this time of night; you're liable to meet all sorts of unpleasant people – "

"I have," she said grimly, and this time he was really amused.

"Sharp, eh, Walters?" He addressed the other detective. "Like a needle! We're not so bad, Miss Perryman – we're doing our duty. We're here for the protection of the citizen, his life, property and personal belongings. A lady like you ought to give us all the help you can, instead of – "

"What law have I broken?"

Mr Simmonds considered this.

"Well, you've driven to the common danger for one thing," and she smiled contemptuously in the darkness.

"It is a little difficult to prove, isn't it? I don't remember a case of a driver being summoned for speeding at night."

Sergeant Simmonds was well aware of his difficulty. Magistrates are chary of accepting evidence of identification. Cars on that part of the road where she had been chased were fairly frequent and difficult to identify; besides which, she was coming in the opposite direction to that she had been following when he had chased her.

"That won't be any trouble," he said, with spurious confidence. "But I don't want to charge you with anything. All I want is five minutes' talk with you. Just tell me who you were going to meet and what you had to deliver, like a sensible young lady, and you'll never see the inside of a police court." He added under his breath: "Except to give evidence."

Ann was unimpressed.

"I don't know what you're talking about – you've certainly no right to cross-examine me. You're not beating me, are you?" she demanded sarcastically.

Sergeant Simmonds emitted sounds of protest.

She answered no further questions, and after a while Simmonds sank back into the corner of the car and dozed for the remainder of the journey to London.

They took her to the little police station which lies in Scotland Yard. Ten minutes later a cell door clanged upon her.

9

Mark McGill was pacing up and down his sitting-room. The clock at which he glanced every few minutes pointed to two. No message had come through from Ann; he had been on the phone to one of his agents at Oxford and had learned that she had not arrived. That was hardly alarming. Ann was clever, and would make a long detour, avoiding the points at which the Flying Squad might pick her up. But he ought to hear from her soon. The Oxford man had promised to telephone again, but the instrument had been silent for an hour.

Ann was getting a little difficult. He knew that her faith in him had been shaken. Try as he did, he could not flog her into the old enthusiasm for vengeance. Many causes were operating against Mark McGill. The pitiable cowardice of Tiser was one of these; the fear of the man seemed to translate itself into doubt; and he had noticed that the girl was never brought into contact with that shivering confederate of his but she became a little more sceptical.

He looked up quickly. There was a buzzer in the hall and it had sounded three times. Walking to the window, he peered out. Cavendish Square was deserted and no car was in sight. It must be Ann – she always pressed the second button concealed beneath the ordinary bell-push and invisible to the casual visitor.

He passed into the hall, opened the door, and took a step backward at the sight of his callers. Bradley was there, and behind him two of his bulls.

The detective's cold eyes were fixed upon the big man.

"Expecting somebody?" he asked.

In a second Mark had recovered himself.

"Of course. I was expecting news about Tiser. He was taken ill tonight."

"Is your telephone taken ill too?" asked the other in even, deliberate tones.

"There's nobody at the Home who can use a phone," replied Mark with a smile. "You know what an ignorant lot of devils they are. I really must put in an assistant to Tiser. Did you want to see me?"

Bradley opened his pocket-book and took out an official-looking document.

"I have a warrant to search your place," he said. "I can only hope I haven't come too late!"

McGill's self-possession was amazing, he thought. It was also a little disappointing. Obviously he had come too late. He would not smile if he had any fear that this visitation would be followed by unpleasant consequences.

"Come in," he said, almost genially, and the detectives followed him into the sitting-room.

Mark walked straight to the desk and turned one of the two switches that were affixed to the table.

"Take your hand away from that!" said Bradley sharply. "What is the idea?"

McGill shrugged his broad shoulders.

"It is merely an automatic arrangement to close the front door. You gentlemen left it open, and I'm rather susceptible to draughts."

"The door was closed," said Bradley curtly. "What is the other switch?"

"That opens the door," was the glib reply.

The detective put his hand on the little lever and nodded to one of his men.

"Go into the hall and see what happens."

He turned the control lever, and the man standing in the doorway verified McGill's statement. Bradley turned the other.

"Anything happened?" he asked.

"No, sir."

"It doesn't close the door, eh? What does it do?" he demanded.

McGill met his eyes without flinching.

"The mechanism is probably out of order," he said. "Try the first switch. Either of them operates the door."

Bradley turned back the lever and heard the thud of the door closing.

"Now you can sit here while these men make a tiresome search of your rooms," he said, and obediently Mark McGill sat down on the sofa and reached for a cigar.

"There is no objection to my smoking, one presumes?" he asked sardonically.

"One day you'll roast," said Bradley.

For an hour and a half the detectives searched and probed, turning every article out of every drawer, inspecting wardrobes and cupboards, turning back mattresses, sounding panels. McGill watched with amusement the search of the room in which he was sitting. After a while he put his hand in his pocket and took out a key.

"There is a small safe behind a panel on the left of the mantelpiece," he said. "This is the key of it."

Bradley took the key without a word, opened the safe and inspected its contents. When he had finished:

"You have a garage, haven't you? There's a door leading from the kitchen?"

"Let me show you the way," said McGill politely, and, rising, walked before them.

In the kitchen Bradley saw the iron furnace. It was still warm. He opened the little steel door and prodded amongst the still glowing embers.

"Useful," he said.

"Very," replied McGill. "I burn my love letters there."

Inspector Bradley's lips twitched: he was not without a sense of humour, and the reply tickled him momentarily.

"You're something of a Lothario, they tell me?"

Though he did not appear to be, he was watching the man narrowly as he spoke.

"And who is your latest conquest – Miss Perryman?"

He saw McGill frown and was relieved. Before he could make a rejoinder, Bradley pointed to the door leading to the garage.

"Unlock this," he said.

He followed McGill down the stairs, waited till the lights were switched on, and then looked around. There was a sound in the little building – the sound of rushing water. Presently he located it. It came from the interior of a cigar-shaped container of galvanised iron.

"What is that?" he asked.

"A new system of ventilation," said McGill airily. "I have a scientific mind."

The detective unfastened the steel panel and pulled it open. He could see nothing in the light of his hand lamp except the glitter of falling water. Pulling up his sleeve, he reached in his hand till he came to the bottom of the container, where he found the place of egress: a round aperture through which the water was gurgling noisily.

"Anything there?" asked McGill pleasantly.

In a corner of the garage was a big cylinder of brown paper. Bradley tore the paper cover and drew out a white crystalline slab. It was round and perforated at regular intervals with holes as big as a sixpence. This he smelt, and, wetting his finger, rubbed it along the top and tasted it.

"Salt!" he said.

He pushed the disc into the container and laid it on the bottom. In a few seconds it had dissolved and disappeared.

"May I reconstruct this little scheme of yours, McGill?" he asked. "You put in there a disc of sugar or salt – I have an idea that the sugar is safer – and on this you put your illicit possessions and close the door. At the first hint of danger you start water running – the switch, of course!"

He nodded smilingly, and for the first time McGill showed some sign of uneasiness.

"When the police visit you, you turn the switch, the water washes away the support of your 'coke,' and before the police can reach the spot the evidence has vanished! Rather ingenious."

He tapped Mark McGill on the chest.

"Don't try that again – I shall probably raid the garage first, with very unpleasant consequences to you. Where is Miss Perryman?"

He asked the question abruptly, so abruptly that Mark was taken aback.

"Miss Perryman doesn't occupy this flat," he said.

"But you were expecting news of her, eh? She is the person you were waiting for?"

McGill's laugh was not very hearty.

"Really, my dear inspector, you have the most fantastic ideas – where do you get them from? It is, I admit, a relief to find a police officer with sufficient imagination to invent stories, but it is also rather trying – "

"You're expecting Ann Perryman, and you may have to wait some time," said Bradley. "She was arrested tonight on the Oxford road!"

Mark stood absolutely still, not a muscle of his face moved, by not so much as the lowering of his eyelid did he betray his concern.

"I'm sorry to hear that – what is the charge against her?"

"Being in possession of dangerous drugs," said Bradley.

Ordinarily, Mark McGill would have been suspicious, but for the moment he was rattled and did not even consider the possibility that Bradley might be bluffing.

"I know nothing about it," he said loudly. "If she was carrying drugs it was without my knowledge. If she says she got them from here, she is lying – where did you find them in the car?"

He had hardly spoken the words before he realised his error. Ann would have thrown away the package at the first sign of real danger. He was telling the detective what even the girl did not know – that the car contained something more than Ann Perryman realised.

10

To give him what credit was due, Mark McGill had, in a half-hearted way, endeavoured to minimise the risk which Ann so often ran. In nine cases out of ten she carried an innocuous package of common salt in her journeys to the country. The real "cargo" was hidden in a specially constructed cupboard let into the side of the car and concealed behind the leather lining.

Ann had certainly carried a dangerous load to Oxford that night, and he trusted her native wit to get rid of it if there was the slightest danger of detection. In the presence of Bradley, he recalled an alarming circumstance. A week before he had sent her to Birmingham, and the hollow side of the car had contained a fairly large quantity of cocaine.

There was always a man to meet Ann at her destination and garage her car. It was then, unknown to her, that the real cargo was removed. But something had frightened the Birmingham crowd; she had not delivered the package she carried, nor had the car been met. Neither Mark nor his lame mechanic had removed the stuff: it was still there when Ann had gone out to meet the aeroplane.

He had not been greatly troubled by the fact; the car was as good a hiding-place as the container. Some time after Ann had left it had occurred to him that the Oxford crowd might relieve the car of its contents, and probably be surprised to find such quantities on their hands. But that was a matter which could easily be adjusted.

He saw Bradley's eyes searching his, and forced a laugh.

"What I meant to say was – " he began.

"What you meant to say," said Bradley, "was that Ann Perryman was carrying something in the car besides the packet she threw into the river."

Mark McGill blinked at this.

"I know nothing about that," he said quickly. "There's no reason why she should throw anything in the river. She was taking a trip to Oxford – where is she?"

For a little time Bradley did not answer.

"She is at Cannon Row Police Station. I presume you wish to offer bail, and I'm telling you in plain English that I shall oppose the bail. I've tried my best to save that young lady, but she's in the limelight now and I can do nothing."

He stroked his chin thoughtfully, still looking at the man he hated.

"There's only one chance, and it is that she will give me evidence to get you, McGill. If she will oblige me in that respect I'll undertake to draw a red line under all her troubles."

His tone lacked the vehemence that Mark expected; it was almost mild in comparison with the nature of his threats. And Mark, who had a knowledge of men, realised that he had before him one whose mind was occupied with another problem. He was talking of one thing, and his mind was groping in an entirely different direction.

Mark saw him to the door, stood on the pavement whilst the police tender drew up noiselessly to the kerb, and watched it till it disappeared in the direction of Oxford Street.

There was a solicitor, a creature of his, a man whom he had promoted from the precarious livelihood he gained at a South London police court. Him he had installed in a respectable suburban villa, and had almost completely cured of his reprehensible habits. He spoke to the man on the telephone.

"I'm sending my car down for you: I want you to come up at once."

Mr Durther arrived at half-past three, a hollow-faced man, whose hands everlastingly trembled.

"They have a friend of mine inside. I want you to see her in the morning, brief the best counsel to defend her, and see that she has everything she requires. She will probably be charged at the Southern police court. When you see her, tell her that there is nothing to fear if she keeps quiet and refuses to answer questions. Another thing you can rub in is the fact that Bradley will move heaven and earth to get her convicted."

"What was she carrying?" asked Mr Durther, in his tremulous voice.

"Coke," was the laconic reply. "I'm not so sure they found it – you'll have to watch that, and if there's a remand, I want counsel to ask for bail and, if necessary, apply to a Judge in chambers."

After the solicitor had left Mark brewed himself a strong cup of coffee, took a cold bath, and sat down to wait for the hour that would bring the report of the solicitor.

11

Bradley went back to the garage where Ann's car had been deposited. He dismissed his men after the machine had been wheeled out into the yard, and alone, with the aid of his hand torch, he began a careful search of the car.

It was not difficult to find the box under the seat, or the method by which the contents of that box could be removed from the outside. The receptacle was empty. He searched the tool-box, with no better result.

He had almost finished his inspection when it occurred to him that the leather upholstery along the sides and the roof was a little more elaborate than was usually to be found in cars of this type. This he probed inch by inch. There was a pocket on each side of the door, but he had already felt in these without result. He felt again, and this time he realised that the door was thicker than seemed absolutely necessary.

Lifting the pocket which hung loose, his lamp went up and down the leather. There was a distinct square patch here. He looked under the pocket of the other door and found the same feature. There was no necessity for a patch in the middle of the door, unless it represented an opening of some kind. He prodded with a pocket-knife, and the point struck steel.

And then, quite by accident, he found the hiding-place. He was raising up the covering pocket, and must have exercised more than usual pressure, for there was a click, and the square of leather opened like a trap. Inside he saw a dozen flat packages packed tight. These he removed carefully before he made an attempt on the second door.

He wasted little time here, for he had learned the trick. The upward jerk of the pocket released a spring, but this time the hidden cupboard held nothing.

He tried the front doors of the driving space, but evidently the secret receptacles were confined to the saloon portion of the car.

Carefully he stowed away the packages in his pocket, re-closed the trap and pushed the car back into its lock-up garage.

He had a queer sense of thankfulness which he could not quite understand. Why should he be so pleased with his discovery – a discovery which would hopelessly incriminate the woman who occupied his thoughts day and night? It wasn't that at all, he discovered: his gratitude was for having had the intelligence to send away his men so that there were no witnesses to the finding of the packages. He was shocked to realise this.

He did not return to Scotland Yard, but hurried to the modest flat he occupied. Letting himself in, he switched on the lights in the dining-room and locked the door before he removed the small parcels from his pocket. One of these he opened – there could be no doubt as to what that crystalline powder was which sparkled under the overhead light. He wetted his finger and put some of the stuff to his tongue. Cocaine!

For a long time he sat staring at the deadly drug, and then the phone rang. The sound of the bell made him jump. He hurried to the instrument, more to stop its continuous ringing than with any eagerness to learn who was at the other end.

He recognised the voice of his superintendent.

"Is that you, Bradley? We've just had a squeak in from Oxford – one of these coke merchants says that we'll probably find a parcel of the stuff hidden in that girl's car. There's a secret pocket in one of the doors. I'll send Simmonds down – "

"No, sir, I'll go myself," said Bradley quickly.

He hung up the phone, came back to the table and eyed the packages. Whatever decision he made must be made quickly.

He went out into his little kitchen and had a look round. A woman cook-housekeeper came daily; she was a methodical and frugal person, and he knew she bought articles in large quantities. The flour bin was half full. He could substitute this for the stuff... And then the absurdity of the exchange struck him and he laughed. And in that laughter he took his decision; went quickly back to the sitting-room, gathered the packages, brought them into the kitchen, and poured their contents into the sink.

For ten minutes he stood, watching the water dissolve the white powder. When it had all disappeared, and he had burnt the paper, he put on his coat and hat and went back to the garage to search for something which was not there.

An hour later he went to report to his chief, and found that that wise man had left the office for his home.

It was no exaggeration to say that John Bradley stood aghast at his own amazing dereliction of duty. If anybody had told him that night that he would have wilfully destroyed evidence in a most serious case for the love of a prisoner, he might have laughed, had it not been that always at the back of his mind was the uneasy conviction that sooner or later Ann Perryman would come within the purview of the law. She hated him: he had no doubt on that question; less doubt that her hatred was inspired by Mark.

She had made some faint attempt to be pleasant, but she was a bad actress. He never met her but she strove vainly to hide her loathing, never left her but her face openly expressed her relief.

He went back to his office at Scotland Yard and dozed in his chair till a messenger brought him a cup of hot coffee and the realisation that in a few hours he would be prosecuting the woman he loved.

At eight o'clock that morning Ann was removed to the South London Police Court. She had the distinction of riding in a taxicab accompanied by a matron and a detective; sure evidence, if she could but read the signs, that the charge on which she was held was regarded by the police as being more than ordinarily serious.

She had hardly been locked in the cell attached to the police court when the matron came to her.

"Your solicitor has arrived – Mr Durther. You had better see him in my room."

Although the matron was present, the interview was obviously to be more or less private, for the quivering solicitor led her to a corner of the room near the window. At first she was a little alarmed by his apparent nervousness, and this he must have seen.

"Don't take any notice of my hands shaking," he mumbled. "Suffer from nerves."

He looked round past her at the matron.

"I've got a message from Mark," he said, lowering his voice still deeper. "There may have been a lot of stuff in the car...saccharine."

"In the car?" she said, amazed.

He nodded rapidly.

"There were a couple of pockets... If you are questioned about it...know nothing...understand?"

"What is going to happen?" she asked.

His thin shoulders went up and down in a gesture intended to express his ignorance.

"I don't know...can't get counsel down to defend you today... bound to be a remand."

She stared at him in consternation.

"Does that mean I shall go to prison for another week?"

Mr Durther avoided her eyes.

"Maybe. We'll try to get bail...do everything possible...police are bound to ask for a remand, especially if they found the stuff. Prison's nothing...get used to it."

Ann Perryman felt her heart sink within her. Prison was an experience to which she could never grow accustomed; and at the prospect she thought of Bradley, and hated him more bitterly than ever.

"How was the...saccharine packed?" And, when he told her: "How many parcels were there?" asked Ann after a long silence.

"Five. They were in the space let into the doors. Mr McGill says you are to deny all knowledge that they were there."

Another silence.

"What was in them?"

"Saccharine, my dear young lady – nothing more than saccharine," quavered Durther.

"What could happen to me?" she asked. "I mean, suppose they found them?"

The lawyer shrugged his shoulders. It was not an easy question to answer. Well he knew what would happen!

"Does one get imprisonment for smuggling?"

He shook his head.

"Not for the first offence. You would probably be fined a hundred pounds or so, which of course Mark would gladly pay."

He was rather relieved, and she wondered why. It was not easy to guess that Mr Durther wanted to forget what might follow the discovery of the cocaine, and was glad enough to discuss her hypothetical offence.

All Lady's Stairs were here today. She saw a majestic and bearded figure being pushed into a cell after his morning ablutions. Evidently Mr Sedeman had also fallen from grace. She smiled to herself, but as the door closed upon her she was serious enough. All that night she had turned on her hard plank bed, with a leather cushion under her head, thinking, thinking…

She was not frightened; the novelty of her position had sustained her for a while, but now that had worn off. This cell with the glazed brick lining, its ugly bench, set loose a train of tormenting thoughts. Ronnie had known the interior of such a place as this, had been familiar with the ghastly routine of servitude.

The matron brought her some coffee and two thick slices of bread and butter, and she was glad of these. Until now she had not realised how famished she was. She had hardly finished before the door opened again. At the matron's command she followed the woman into a smaller room than that in which she had interviewed the solicitor.

A man was standing by the window, staring out into the courtyard. He turned at the sound of the opening door, and she found herself face to face with Inspector Bradley. Her first inclination was to walk from the room. The matron, standing squarely by the closed door, made this course impossible.

He looked heavy-eyed, tired, slightly haggard, she thought. Some of his undoubted good looks seemed to have disappeared.

"Good morning," he said. His voice was sharp, peremptory, the voice of a police inspector rather than a friend.

She did not answer, but stood stiffly before him, her hands clasped behind her. He looked past her.

"You can go, matron. Wait outside the door; I have something to say to this lady."

Obediently the stout woman retired.

"Now, my young friend, you're in a very serious position. I'm taking a charitable view and am supposing that you do not know what you've been doing."

His old flippancy of tone had gone; his voice was grave but not unfriendly. She recognised this through the rising mists of her fury, although why she should be enraged by his obvious endeavour to help her she could not understand. Only she knew that at that moment she could have killed him.

"I know exactly what I've been doing," she said, trying to keep her voice steady. "I have been driving a car at night, and in some way I have made you hate me. You're anxious to do for me what you did for Ronnie."

"You are not going to say you're innocent?" he asked bluntly. "Or that you're the victim of police persecution? Will you say that you have not broken the law?"

He waited breathlessly for her denial, but she was silent, and his heart sank.

"Are you conscious that you have broken the law?" he repeated.

"I will tell the magistrate that," she answered coldly.

"Are you aware that you have been trafficking in noxious drugs?" he asked.

Her lips curled.

"Really, Mr Bradley, you're most unoriginal! That was the story you told me last year after Ronnie was murdered – that he was a dealer in drugs. Are you suggesting that I am doing the same thing?"

His very look was a challenge.

"Are you?"

She went white with anger, turned abruptly, walked to the door and flung it open. The matron was standing outside, her head resting against the doorpost. She might have been interested in the conversation which had taken place in the room, and probably was.

"Take me back to my cell," ordered Ann peremptorily.

"Has Mr Bradley finished with you?" asked the matron.

"I'm finished with him," said Ann.

She almost welcomed the solitude of the cell. She was shaking with anger, and, had there been occasion for speech, would have been inarticulate. How dare he!

To revive that old lie, and label her as he had labelled Ronnie! Whatever happened, whatever came, fine or imprisonment, no punishment would equal the humiliation this man had put upon her.

Bradley had followed her from the waiting-room, and none who saw his inscrutable face could have guessed the despair that was in his heart.

As he was going into the court, Simmonds took him by the arm.

"The doctor says that Smith ought to have some sort of sedative before he goes into court."

"Smith?" Bradley was shocked when he realised that he had forgotten that he had another case on his hands, one infinitely more serious than that of Ann Perryman.

There had been a murder a week before; a shop assistant had been killed, a jeweller's shop rifled, and the murderer had got away, later to be arrested. Bradley knew him at once as a drug addict, a nerve-tortured decadent who might well trace his ruin to the activities of Mark McGill.

"You hadn't forgotten Smith, sir?" Simmonds smiled at the absurdity of his own question.

"No, I hadn't forgotten him," said Bradley slowly. "He wants a sedative, does he? How long can we keep him going without?"

"Not more than an hour," said Simmonds.

Bradley nodded.

"I'll arrange for his case to be taken next," he said.

He was turning away when again Simmonds detained him.

"Steen wants to see you. He's been to the Yard, and they sent him down here."

Bradley stared at his subordinate in astonishment.

"Steen?" he said incredulously. "What is wrong?"

Simmonds shook his head.

"I think you'd better see him. He's got a Home Office letter."

Hurrying back to the small room where he had interviewed Ann, Bradley found a man waiting for him, sitting patiently on the edge of a chair, his big hands resting on his knees. He was a tall, angular, awkward-looking man, wearing a black suit a little too large for him, and round his neck a knotted handkerchief. He rose and touched his forelock.

"Good morning, Mr Bradley. They told me I'd find thee here."

He spoke in a broad north country accent.

"What's the trouble, Steen?" asked Bradley.

The man jerked his head in a gesture of deprecation.

"I want nowt of police protection, but tha knows what the fellows are at Home Office. It's over this man Libbitt — they say his friends talk of getting me. I'll get them first, I'm thinking." He chuckled at his mysterious joke.

"Go along to the jailer's office," said Bradley. "I'll see you after these two cases are over."

"Only two this morning?" said Steen, in astonishment.

"Two that count."

Bradley smiled to himself at the confession. Not even the case of Smith counted with him.

He was in court when Sedeman was brought in, jaunty and rather magnificent. He greeted the magistrate as an old friend; admitted certain errors of his on the night before; reminded the policeman witness, not once but many times, of the immediate consequences of perjury; and blandly awaited sentence. Not even the three weeks' hard labour he received affected him.

The clerk and a solicitor were in whispered consultation. Bradley recognised the lawyer as a friend of Mark McGill's, and when he heard the word "Smith" wondered exactly why McGill was interfering in that matter. It was the last case in the world he would have expected the big man to meddle with. Presently he was enlightened. Mr Durther went back to his table immediately after Sedeman had been removed.

In his proper environment he was no longer the timid and tremulous man Ann had met.

"Before your worship takes the next case," he began briskly, "I hope your worship will allow me to make an application. It has some relation to a case which is coming on later. Your worship will remember that I applied here a year ago for certain documents which were the property of my client, Mr Marcus McGill, that were in the possession of the late Elijah Yoseph, who was the freeholder of Lady's Stairs."

What was Mark's game? Why did he choose this moment to recall the disappearance of Li?

The magistrate nodded.

"I remember," he said tersely.

"The police took possession of his house, and I believe they still have a technical possession until his death is presumed in a Higher Court. We produced an affidavit by a man named Sedeman, who, curiously enough, came before your worship just now."

"I remember the affidavit," said the magistrate. "He swore that the documents had been left by mistake at Yoseph's house."

"They were quite unimportant – " began the solicitor, and the magistrate shook his head.

"That is not my recollection. The documents were lists of Continental chemists, and the suggestion was that these people had been supplying Yoseph or his principals with drugs," he said. "Isn't that so, Mr Bradley?"

"That is so, your worship."

"We can prove," said the solicitor, "that these lists had reference to a perfectly legitimate business."

Now Bradley understood. Mark had learnt that the police had found the hiding-place and was preparing a defence in advance. It was true that those documents which he had impounded on the night of the murder might tend to show that McGill was carrying on a legitimate business in chemicals.

"It is a matter entirely for the police," said the magistrate. "If they consider the documents vital, I will do nothing."

He looked at Bradley, who rose from his chair.

"We have as yet been unable to secure the evidence we want," he said quickly, "but I regard the documents as very important and I must oppose the application."

The man on the bench nodded.

"Very well. The application is refused."

Mr Durther was apparently not unprepared for this refusal. Bradley again rose.

"I would like to ask your worship if you would now take the case of William Charles Smith. I asked your worship if it could be taken this afternoon, but for a very special reason I wish the case to be dealt with at once. It will not take more than a few minutes."

The magistrate signalled his assent, and there came, through the door leading from the cells, a pallid man of slight build, a detective at each elbow. His wrists were held together by handcuffs, and this the keen-eyed stipendiary saw.

"Is it necessary that this man should be handcuffed?" he asked.

"Yes, your worship," replied Bradley. "He has given us a great deal of trouble."

The man stared at him, showing his teeth in a horrible smile.

The charge was read out – that he did wilfully murder Harry Bendon by shooting him with a revolver on the night of the 13th of April in Fellow Street in the Parish of St Martin's.

"Is he legally represented?" asked the magistrate.

Bradley shook his head.

"No, your worship. I only propose today to offer formal evidence of arrest and to ask your worship to remand him until next Friday."

The man in the dock strained across the rail.

"If I ever get at you, Bradley, I'll tear the heart out of you!" he howled.

What else he said none could hear.

The formal evidence of arrest was heard quickly, and the prisoner was hustled from the court.

"Has this man been seen by the prison doctor? He seems rather strange."

"I am informed," answered Bradley, "that he is to be kept under observation. He has shown an extraordinary craving for drugs since his arrest – that is half the trouble."

The magistrate shook his head sadly.

"The number of criminals who are coming in front of me who in some way or other are addicts is truly astonishing. Where are these people getting drugs? Usually that practice was confined to a certain type of undesirable man and woman. One never heard of people of Smith's class falling under its influence."

"It is being supplied systematically in every part of the country," said Bradley.

Durther came to his feet instantly.

"I hope this dreadful case is not being used to prejudice your worship in another matter which is coming up for hearing," he said, "the case of Ann Perryman."

"I had no such intention!"

Bradley almost snarled the words, but the solicitor kept his feet.

"The immediate effect of bringing Smith into court and this reference to drugs must create an atmosphere of hostility. I do not know what charge the police intend making against Miss Perryman – "

Somebody touched his elbow – Mark McGill had come into court and was sitting by his side. Bradley had seen him out of the tail of his eye.

"Leave it there," he said under his breath, and then, as the magistrate, the clerk and Bradley consulted in an undertone: "What will Bradley do?" asked Mark.

"If the stuff they found in the car was cocaine, he is certain to charge her with unlawful possession of dangerous drugs."

"But have they found it?"

"I haven't heard," said Durther. "All that I know is, Bradley made a search of the hidden pockets."

McGill pulled a long face at this.

"What will she get?"

"Three months – possibly six. It was cocaine, of course?"

Mark nodded.

"She didn't know it was there, though."

Durther smiled sceptically.

"Do you mean to tell me she doesn't know the stuff she's carrying?"

"No – and she didn't even know that she was carrying anything."

It was at this moment that the magisterial conference broke up, and the clerk called "Ann Mary Perryman!"

Ann walked into the court, nodded to Mark and stepped into the dock with a little smile. Bradley had seen that smile before on her brother's face; had watched him step with the same debonair unconcern into the pen of shame.

"Well, Mr Bradley!"

It was Ann speaking. He could hardly believe his ears.

"You've got me where you want me. This must be a very happy day for you."

"Don't address anybody in court except me, please," interrupted the magistrate testily.

She smiled sardonically.

"Good morning, your worship! I suppose I'm entitled to say something?"

The clerk looked at the sheet before him.

"You're charged with driving a motorcar to the common danger. Do you plead guilty or not guilty?"

Again the magistrate interposed.

"There was some suggestion this morning that a further charge would be preferred. I don't see this?"

To McGill's amazement Inspector Bradley shook his head.

"No further charge is to be preferred, your worship," he said. "Nothing has been discovered that would justify a further charge."

It was Ann who recovered first.

"You're not being merciful, are you? I'd hate that," she said.

The magistrate tried to stop her, but she went on. She felt strangely exalted; was afire with a sense of mastery. Bradley was lying! He was lying for her sake, and in his perjury had placed himself in her power – she thrilled at the thought. There was in her a fierce desire to hurt him – to maim as he had maimed; to bring him to ruin as he had brought Ronnie.

For the moment she lost all sense of personal danger – forgot Mark and his peril, remembered only that her enemy had delivered himself into her hands.

"My good friend Inspector Bradley, who is so anxious to help me! He's certainly helped me into a cell!"

Durther, in an agony of apprehension, tried to stop her.

"Miss Perryman, perhaps it would be best if – "

She arrested his speech with a gesture.

"Detective-Inspector Bradley has been very kind to me!" Her voice grew thin in her anger. "I don't know how many times he's tried to lead me to a better path. We've had lots of little meetings in restaurants for dinner, and I've danced with you, haven't I, Inspector? He rather likes me – he said he'd do anything in the world for me!"

Bradley stood motionless, his face a mask.

"Be silent, please."

The magistrate's attempt was vain.

"I'll not be silent!" she stormed. "When a man runs after me and holds my hand and goes on like a fool in love – and then catches me the first opportunity he gets and puts me in a filthy police cell, I'm entitled to say something, and I'm going to say it. Bradley searched my car last night – he said he found nothing. He is lying! He found five packages of saccharine!"

"Be quiet." Durther's voice was a wail.

"It was saccharine – and I was smuggling it!" she went on. "And he knows I was smuggling it, and he's got up there and lied – the poor, mushy fool! He thinks I'll fall on his neck in gratitude. I'm telling the Chief of Police just the kind of man he is – a detective who'll destroy evidence because he's crazy about a woman!"

Her voice broke; she stood breathless – amazed at her own fury.

"Keep silent, please!"

The magistrate was angry; he was also a little bewildered.

"I've said all that I want to say."

Durther stood up, facing her.

"Have you gone mad?" he demanded. "Don't you see what you've done?"

The magistrate was talking.

"I don't know what all this rigmarole means, and I'm not taking very much notice. No further charge is laid against you. Do you plead guilty to the charge of driving to the common danger?"

"We plead guilty to that, your worship," Durther swung round quickly.

"Very well. You will be fined twenty pounds and ten guineas costs, and your driving licence will be suspended for twelve months."

Mark heaved a sigh of relief; never did he dream of such an ending to the case.

For a moment Ann stood limply, clutching the rail of the dock.

"Can I go and get my coat?" she asked in a low voice. The matron beckoned her; she took Mark's hand as she passed into the passage leading to the cells.

"Why in hell did she do that? She must hate him!" said Mark behind his hand; but the solicitor was not in a mood to discuss the matter.

"Come along and fix up the fine," he said.

It was the last case on the list – close enough to the luncheon hour to warrant an adjournment. Almost immediately the court was cleared. The magistrate still fussed over some papers on his table. He saw Bradley and beckoned him.

"That was an extraordinary outburst, Mr Bradley?"

"Yes, sir." The detective's voice was spiritless. He was for the moment crushed and humiliated.

"This is the first time in my experience I have ever heard a prisoner accuse a detective of being in love with her."

His worship was considerably amused.

"I wish she had been lying."

The words came out before Bradley realised what he was saying.

"A very attractive girl," said the human magistrate. "Of course, it was a very stupid charge to make against you – but rather novel... extraordinary!"

Bradley was alone now in the deserted court, trying to straighten the tangle of his mind. He was there when the door opened and Ann came back. She stopped at the sight of him, and looked round for another way out. But she had to pass him to reach the little wicket that led to the body of the court.

"Is this the way out?" she asked, not looking at him.

"One of the ways."

He did not move; his back was against the wooden gate through which she had to go.

"Will you let me pass, please?" she asked.

And then she met his reproachful eyes.

"I never dreamt you could be so incredibly mean," he said quietly.

"Can I pass, please?"

"Certainly." He opened the wicket for her. "I hope you know where you're going?"

It needed but that to revive her resentment.

"On the downward path from which you have tried to rescue me – as you tried to rescue Ronnie!" she said.

He nodded.

"Ronnie's last words to me were: 'Thank God my sister doesn't know Mark McGill!' "

Her lips curled at this.

"Is that another invention – like the empty pocket in the car? You ought to be a novelist!"

"It was an invention," he admitted. "I threw away the five packages."

"Noble fellow!" she sneered. "And now I hope you're going to lose your job!"

He smiled.

"I hardly think so. Yet, if they knew the stuff I found in the car was cocaine – "

"It's a lie – it wasn't cocaine!" she said angrily. "It's a beastly lie!"

"A beastly traffic," said Bradley sternly. "There was a man in this court this morning charged with murder – one of McGill's victims, a dope! You may have carried the stuff to him."

She was white now.

"You're a liar – a damnable liar!" she gasped. "I've never carried such stuff in my life! I'm doing the work that Ronnie did!"

He nodded.

"That was just what Ronnie did – distributed the drugs that Li Yoseph and Mark McGill smuggled into this country."

"Even the dead are not safe from your slander." Her voice was tense. "Even the man you murdered!"

"What a dear fool you are!" he said sadly. "You tried to ruin me today – the papers will be full of this accusation of yours – 'A detective in love with a prisoner' – there's romance for you!"

She flamed round on him.

"I didn't say you were in love – I said that you were mushy! It's the sort of thing that passes for love with men of your class."

He nodded. That old bleak look came to his eyes.

"You can call it love – it is true."

Her laugh was hard and bitter.

"Love! I hope you do love me. I hope I am never absent from your mind day or night! I hope I am a torture to you and that your heart is one long ache!"

Her hopes were realised: she exulted in the thought. "I hate you and I hate your trade. You live on the miseries and sorrows of men and women. You step up to promotion on the hearts you break and the lives you ruin!"

She saw Bradley smile and was infuriated.

"That makes you smile too! It takes something like that to amuse you!"

He laughed softly.

"Go out of this court," he said. "There's a policeman to hold up the traffic for you and save you from accident. There's a detective to see that your bag isn't stolen. If it weren't for my trade, as you call it, there are men in this neighbourhood who'd kill you for a ten-pound note, who'd cut the fingers off your hands to get your rings! You sleep soundly in that flat of yours because there is a policeman patrolling your street, and the Flying Squad somewhere round the corner to chase the man who is after your jewellery. My trade is a good trade – it is the trade of the law."

"How very impressive!"

He ignored the sarcasm.

"As to *your* trade, you may go out and follow it. It is a trade that is bringing men and women into the gutter, into the dock – into the execution shed. A filthy trade, whether you know it or whether you don't. I love you as much as a man can love a woman, but I've given you your last chance."

Mark came into the deserted court at this moment and was a witness of what followed.

"Ronnie went his own way and died," Bradley went on. "You're going a worse way, if you haven't gone already!"

He tried to stop himself saying this, but it was out before he could curb his tongue. The next moment he felt the sting of her palm on his cheek. She looked at him, horrified at what she had done.

"I'm sorry – I shouldn't have said that," said Bradley, and here it was that Mark McGill made a mistake.

He came blundering forward.

"Serve you dam' well right! What do you mean by it, Bradley?"

Inspector Bradley looked at him through narrowed lids.

"You saw her strike me," he said slowly. "I'm passing it on – "

His fist shot out, and in another second Mark McGill was sprawling on the floor. He scrambled to his feet, his face livid.

"By God, I'll have the coat off your back for this, Bradley!" he breathed.

For a moment he thought that the detective would repeat the attack, but Bradley did not move.

"That's nothing to what is coming to you," he said. "I'm going to get you, McGill – before you get her!"

"Get me, will you?" McGill spat the words. "You think you can frighten me? I'm not scared of you, or Scotland Yard, or the best judge that ever sat on a bench!"

It was at that moment Steen came through the gaoler's door, an awkward figure in black. Bradley saw him and pointed to him.

"There's one man you haven't mentioned. That man! He's come here today to get police protection because he's got an unpopular job to do. Steen!"

Mark's face puckered up into an expression of horror.

"Steen!"

"Steen – the public hangman!" said Bradley. "Meet him! You'll meet him again!"

12

They drove home in silence, Mark McGill and the pale-faced girl, and came to Cavendish Square. In all their journey Ann had not spoken a word, although several times Mark had attempted to provoke her to speech. He was clever enough to give up his attempts when he found she was in no mood to discuss the events of the morning.

"Will you come in and have some lunch?" he said. "You must be hungry."

As he offered the invitation he expected a refusal. Ann had expressed her intention of going to her flat. To his surprise she acquiesced. She was listless; all the fire which she had shown in the court, that self-command which he had admired even as it terrified him, they belonged to another person. She had suddenly grown tired and a little peaked. There were shadows under her eyes which he did not remember seeing before.

He was about to ring the bell when she instructed him:

"Don't order lunch for me, Mark. I'll have a cup of tea; that will be sufficient. Then I think I'll go to bed."

"Poor old girl! That swine Bradley!"

She shrugged her shoulders and sighed.

"That swine Bradley," she repeated monotonously.

"Anyway, you've done him a harm beyond repair," said Mark with satisfaction. "He will be the laughing stock of London – what a pity there weren't any reporters in court to see you – "

"Don't, please." Her voice was sharp, peremptory. "I'm not terribly proud of myself."

"Then you ought to be," he said, with simulated heartiness. "If ever a man deserved – "

"He deserved nothing. He was doing his duty. It makes me sick to think about it."

"Reaction, my dear," said Mark cheerfully. "You were certain to feel like that. Bradley got what he deserved, or a little of it."

She looked up at him thoughtfully. She was half sitting, half crouching in a corner of the deep settee.

"Was that the hangman?" she asked. "That awful-looking man?"

He winced at the question.

"Ye-es, that was Steen. Bright-looking specimen, isn't he? I've never seen him, of course. One doesn't meet that kind of carrion crow. An ugly brute!"

"He was rather pathetic, to me," she said thoughtfully. "There was something sad about him, and something oddly dignified."

He opened his eyes wide.

"Dignified – a hangman? My dear, what on earth are you talking about?"

She sighed again and dropped her eyes.

"Nothing very much – I wish I hadn't done it! Oh, I wish I hadn't!"

He patted her on the shoulder.

"My dear, you've done a noble work! Didn't you see the evening newspapers as you came along? 'Amazing Scene in Court' – I'm looking forward to reading those. I'll send you the newspapers in when they arrive."

She came to her feet instantly.

"You'll do nothing of the kind. I don't want to see them! I don't want to be reminded. He was trying to help me."

She looked at Mark McGill long and earnestly.

"Why did he insist that it was cocaine I was carrying and not saccharine?"

"Because he's a liar," said Mark readily. "Because he wants to pretend that he's doing you a bigger service than he is. Don't you see that?"

She did not answer.

"I thought it was wonderful of you to bring out his mushiness. You never told me about those hand-holdings, little girl. All I knew was that you were getting next to him, and, of course, I knew you went to dinner and danced with him once or twice, but I didn't guess he was making love to you. If I had – "

"If you had?" she asked.

Mark McGill smiled.

"Well, I'd have let him know all about it, that's all."

"Why?"

The question took his breath away.

"Why?" he stammered. "Naturally, I wouldn't allow – "

"But why, Mark? Are you suddenly standing in *loco parentis* – do you feel responsible for my life and – morals?"

Mark McGill knew he was on dangerous ground.

"We're getting a bit too highbrow," he said. "Anyway, he's finished."

She shook her head.

"I know very little about the police, but I'm sure the authorities will take no notice of what I said. Why, there's hardly a case in court where the prisoner doesn't bring some accusation against the detective in charge of the case, and they'll treat me with the rest – I hope."

"You hope?" he gasped.

She nodded twice.

"Yes, I hope. It was a pretty foul thing I did – I wish I hadn't."

Mark chuckled.

"Ann, you're not in love with him, are you?"

The tea came at that moment, and she did not seem to think there was any necessity for an answer. Presently she put the cup down, gathered up her bag and her coat.

"I'm going to my room," she said, and, walking to the door, turned and stood for some time, her eyes downcast, thinking. "Why did he insist it was cocaine, both in my case and Ronnie's?" she asked again. "If that was the stuff we were dealing in, it would be ghastly, wouldn't it?"

Mark felt it was the moment for a little virtuous indignation.

"Do you imagine that I would do anything so horrible?" he asked. "Of course it wasn't cocaine! You've seen the stuff, you've tasted it yourself – good God! What is coming over you? Why, you'll distrust me next."

It was an unfortunate challenge, for, as their eyes met, he realised that she distrusted him already.

13

Mr Tiser sometimes invited a few fortunate inmates of the Home to attend him in his private room, which was also his bedroom. It was on the ground floor and the window looked out on to a noisy side street, so that the padded second door, designed, as he told visitors, to keep out the noises of the house, seemed a little superfluous. Perhaps it would be more accurate to say that the padded door retained sounds in the room, and not even the cleverest of eavesdroppers with the most sensitive ear glued to the largest keyhole could overhear the many interesting conversations that took place in this chamber.

It was very often necessary for Mr Tiser that he should discuss problems of the greatest moment, both to himself and to the ex-criminals whom the Home sheltered. That night he had three men who were particularly well known to the police, and two of them had the distinction, when they were badly wanted, of being described in the *Hue and Cry* as "dangerous – may carry firearms." One of these had only come out of prison that week for robbery and assault; and here he was fortunate, for the law makes a nice distinction between "robbery and assault" and "robbery with assault." If you steal a man's watch and follow this up by hitting him on the head, you are liable to all the pains and penalties of larceny; but if you hit him on the head and then take his watch, you have committed a felony, and have an even chance of being chained up to a steel triangle and receiving the agony inflicted by a whip with nine silk-tipped thongs.

Harry the Cosh – so-called because his favourite weapon was a life-preserver – a wizened little man, with a face which was distinctly simian, was one of the three; with him was Lew Patho – where he acquired his surname no man knew; and these, with the no less dangerous third, sat around Mr Tiser's loo table and drank free whisky.

It was ludicrously like a board meeting, with Mr Tiser in the chair.

"I am sorry for you," he was saying. "You poor, unfortunate people who are hounded by the police from pillar to post – who are never given a chance – who are, more often than not, because of your unfortunate convictions, arrested and jailed on false evidence, are deserving of every sympathy."

The three men looked at one another and agreed that they were.

"I have nothing to say against the police," said Mr Tiser. "They are often very respectable people. I have nothing to say against Mr Bradley, who, I am sure, may at heart be a Christian man. But I did not like what he said to me today."

Nobody questioned Mr Tiser, although he paused to offer the opportunity.

"He said: 'I wonder, Mr Tiser' – he always addresses me as 'Mister,' which is most respectful and proper – 'why you have such thugs' – that was his word – 'in your Home as Lew Patho and Harry the Cosh, and that red-faced brute who got three months for kicking his wife?' "

"That red-faced brute" stirred uneasily.

"If he's got anything to say to me – " he began hoarsely.

Mr Tiser raised his hand.

"I couldn't help feeling," he said, "in fact, the feeling amounted to a conviction, that this man will never be happy till he has you all in for a stretch. It is perfectly dreadful that the human heart, designed by the Creator as a nest of loving-kindness, should be so misemployed. I felt it my duty to warn you."

He leaned back in his chair. Harry the Cosh puckered up his face and made a little hissing noise.

"He'll get his one of these days," he said.

Mr Tiser shook his head.

"That is what I am afraid of. You see, I have studied the habits of Mr Bradley. I know exactly where he lives, what time he goes home;

I have often thought how stupid it is that a man, against whom the hand of all – unfortunate people are turned, should walk home alone at one o'clock in the morning through Bryanston Square, which is practically deserted, without an escort of any kind...very foolish – it is almost tempting providence!"

There was no response to this. The three men stared ahead of them.

"I do not say that it would be admirable in any aggrieved person to lay wait for this active and intelligent officer," said Mr Tiser; "but I do feel that it would be quite understandable."

He rose briskly, went to the sideboard and brought back a bottle.

"Now, boys, I'm going to let you hear the wireless," he said. "A dear unknown friend of the Home presented this set to us yesterday."

On the top of a bookcase were apparently two loud speakers, one rather smaller than the other. The workman who had installed the instrument had informed Mr Tiser that the smaller one acted as a filter to the harsher notes; and certainly, when he switched on the cabinet and stood in the corner, the sound of a woman's singing came naturally and without the slightest distortion.

It was the third member of the party, the red-faced beater of wives, who put the thought of the three men into words. Possibly the clear and harmonious notes that came from the loud speaker inspired him in his plan.

"What about waiting for this Bradley – that fellow's a bit too ikey."

"Hush, hush!" said Mr Tiser with a smile, and covered his ears playfully. "I mustn't hear things like that, you know!"

Evidently the music had no great charm for them. Before eleven o'clock they had shuffled out.

At a quarter to one o'clock that morning Bradley left Scotland Yard and was picked up by the red-faced man, who followed him at a respectful distance. All the details which Tiser had given of his movements were apparently accurate. He did not take a cab, nor board any of the night buses which would have carried him within a stone's throw of his flat. The red-faced man was close at his heels when he turned into Bryanston Square. Here, from the darkness, his two friends joined him. They walked noiselessly, for Mr Tiser had obligingly supplied them with three old pairs of tennis shoes – his philanthropy was unbounded.

Half-way up the deserted side-walk the three closed on their prey. They were within five paces of the inspector when Bradley whipped round.

"Stick 'em up, quick!" he said tersely. "And don't try to run, because it'll be a waste of breath."

Even as he spoke, two police tenders turned into the square, one from each end, drew up within twenty yards and disgorged their hateful passengers.

There was a quick search.

"Patho's got a gat," said a voice, as his groping hand withdrew, holding a pistol.

"That's ten years for you, Patho," said Bradley pleasantly.

When they were bundled into one of the police tenders he walked up to the side and addressed one of the sulky, handcuffed men.

"If I see Tiser I'll tell him that you carried out his suggestion," he said. "You had much better have waited for the rest of the broadcast programme. There was an interesting lecture on prisons to come. Not that the lecturer could have told you much that you didn't know or will not find out."

He went home, rather tickled. That night Mr Tiser, obeying an instinct which was stronger than reason, took down the smaller of the loud speakers, and, with the help of a skilled mechanic who was an inmate of the Home, traced the flex of it, not to the aerial, but to a telephone wire on the roof; and he went green with fear as he tried to recall the many incriminating conversations that had taken place in his parlour since the installation of the "wireless." For the smaller of the speakers was a sensitive microphone, and everything that had been said in that room had been heard – who knew where?

A week passed – a week of numb inactivity for Ann, a week of self-examination, which led to nothing more than a further confusion.

She had not read the newspapers – her mind was a news-sheet, black with staring, disagreeable headlines. The withdrawal of her motorcar licence deprived her of her greatest pleasure. Yet even this did not flog her hatred of Bradley into activity.

She saw him once when she was walking in the park. He went spinning past in a black car crowded with men, and she wondered what was his objective and who were the men who, unconscious of the approaching Nemesis, would be surprised to find their enterprise brought to ruin by his appearance.

Once she read some evidence he gave against a car-stealer; once it was a gang of pickpockets that had been shadowed from the East End and caught in a body near Hyde Park Corner.

Mark, in order to give her occupation, took her one night to the Home. It was not a pleasant experience for her. These frowsy men had neither grace nor humility. He told her about Sedeman, showed her his room.

"We dare not lock the old devil out, so the room is kept for him," said Mark. "Just now we've got very few people in the Home."

"You've reformed the rest?" she asked, and he thought he heard a note of sarcasm in her voice, and was a little alarmed.

She did not see Tiser. At her request, that oily man was absent the night she called.

"We don't really try to reform them," Mark explained as they were driving back in his car to her flat; "what we do try, is to find jobs for them."

"What kind of jobs?" she asked, and again he detected a tinge of scepticism in her tone.

They did not discuss smuggling any more. Mark had had a shock and had profited thereby. Not in his garage nor in the house did he keep a scrap of evidence which might one day bring about his undoing. He had even removed Ann's car to a garage, a little place off the Edgware Road which he owned, and which had been a very useful depot for him.

It was three weeks after the police court trial that Mark was to receive his second and more staggering shock.

14

Mark McGill strode up and down his big sitting-room, pausing now and then to look out of the window upon the gloomy square. A table was strewn with press-cuttings which had been supplied to him by an agency, and they all referred to the case in which Ann Perryman had figured.

He was interrupted in his restless prowlings by the arrival of Tiser. Things were not going well at "The Home"; there had been two police visitations, and one most promising inmate had been brought before a magistrate and sentenced to nine months' hard labour. Moreover, there had been certain activities among the provincial police which had made a very considerable difference to Mark's income. He had accumulated quite a considerable sum of money by his nefarious trafficking, but his expenses were heavy, and the suspension of the girl's licence had created difficulties which he had not foreseen.

He turned round with a scowl as Tiser came sidling into the room, closing the door behind him. Mr Tiser was blinking apprehensively, and by the twitching of his face and the nervous movement of his hands Mark guessed that his lieutenant was more badly rattled than was usual.

Tiser went straight to the cabinet where the whisky was kept, poured out a generous portion and drank it neat.

"What's the matter with you?" snarled Mark. "You give me the jumps – for God's sake don't let Ann see you in that state!"

"Ann, eh?" Tiser put up his hands to his quivering lips. He tried to screw the resemblance of a smile into his face, and succeeded only in producing a terrible contortion. "Notice anything about Ann, Mark – lately? She hardly speaks to me, hardly looks at me, my dear Mark. Surely she's nothing against poor Tiser?"

"She's never spoken to you, anyway," growled Mark McGill. "I don't see how any woman could talk to you and retain her self-respect. What's the trouble?"

"I'm rather worrying about her, Mark." Tiser lowered his voice. "She's been so quiet. Remember last night, when we were sitting here, she didn't talk all the time I was here."

"That shows her good sense. What had she got to talk about?" said Mark impatiently – more impatient since he also had noticed the disturbing symptoms in Ann. "What do you want?"

Tiser looked nervously left and right, drew up a chair near to the settee where Mark had seated himself.

"I've had a talk with one of those river rats," he said in a low, urgent voice. "He told me something that worried me, Mark. If I'd known at the time, I'd have died of fright."

"What is it?" demanded the big man. "Not that anything that would make you die of fright is necessarily serious."

"They've been searching for Li all the time," Tiser went on in a hoarse whisper. "They didn't give up the search when we thought they did, Mark. Every day they've been dragging and poking and probing round Lady's Stairs – this fellow told me that a fortnight ago they sent a diver down in a special suit that they got from Germany, to search the mud under the house. Nobody knew anything about it – it was done at night, but he was breaking cargo on one of the barges and saw the float come up and the diver dropped overboard."

Mark was silent. The news had taken him by surprise.

"Did they find anything?"

Tiser shook his head.

"No. This man of mine came ashore and found a little crowd of river police and Scotland Yard men, and got near enough to hear them talking. They've given up the search definitely."

Mark McGill fondled his big chin.

"They might have done that at the start. His body would have been washed out in the river and down to the sea."

Tiser was not convinced.

"I hope so, my boy. It would be terrible if he had got away unknown to any of us, and was nursing up some scheme for putting in a big squeak – eh, Mark? Do you remember what he said?"

He shivered, and again took a glance left and right.

"Just before he died? He said he'd come back, Mark. He said you couldn't kill him. I've heard him say that before. You remember his ghosts, his little children... Ronnie – eh, Mark?"

He peered anxiously into McGill's face.

"There was nothing in that, was there? You don't believe in ghosts...spirits walking about the earth? It's stupid, isn't it, Mark?"

Mark was regarding him in wonder.

"What in hell is the matter with you, Tiser? Have you gone gaga, or have you been smelling that white stuff?"

"No, no, no!" Tiser shook his head energetically. His voice was a wail. "I want to know, Mark...do you think that spirits can come back to earth?"

"You're drunk," said Mark roughly.

"I'm not, I'm not!" The pitiful thing by his side clutched his arm violently. "But last night, when I was in bed...I'd had a drink or two..."

He became incoherent. Mark walked to the whisky decanter, half filled a glass and almost pushed it into Tiser's hand.

"Drink up and let's hear what you've got to say, you poor, shivering jellyfish!" he sneered. "Ghosts! If I sniffed as you sniff, I'd see devils too."

Tiser gulped down the fiery rye – it was kept in the flat especially for his use; and then he became a little calmer and told his story. He had gone to bed earlier than usual, and admitted to having had several drinks, but protested he was not the worse for them. He was a light and restless sleeper, and remembered waking at one and at two. When he woke at half past two he was conscious that he was not alone in the room. There was a moon, and in the light of it, that flooded one diagonal patch of his sleeping apartment:

"He was there, Mark." His voice was a whine; his teeth chattered so that he could hardly articulate. "Sitting in a chair, with his hands on his knees, looking at me!"

"Who?" demanded Mark.

"Li Yoseph! He had that greasy old coat of his and the fur cap. I can see his yellow face now, Mark! Oh, God, it was horrible!"

He covered his face with his hands as though to shut out the memory of the vision.

"You were in bed, were you? And then you got up and found you had been dreaming?" suggested Mark.

The man shook his head.

"No, I wasn't dreaming. It was he. He just sat and looked at me, and said nothing for a time, and then I saw him talking to his children – I don't know what happened after that. I think I must have fainted. When I sort of woke up I was feeling terrible. The day was breaking – "

"And he wasn't there!" scoffed Mark McGill. "You'll have to change your brand of whisky."

"I saw him," insisted Tiser fretfully. "Do you think I could make any mistake? I know Li as I know the back of my hand – it was he!"

He heard Mark's harsh laugh and screwed up his face as though he were in pain.

"Don't do it, Mark! I wasn't drunk, I tell you. I saw him as plainly as I can see you."

"You're either inventing it or you were drunk, you fool," said the big man contemptuously. "Don't you think I know? Why should he go to you? He'd come to me, wouldn't he? Either it was your imagination, or one of those bright lads in the Home got into the room to see what he could find."

"The door was locked," interrupted Tiser.

"He could have got through the window. Your room's the easiest place in the world for a cracksman to burgle. No, you don't frighten me, my friend. Li Yoseph is dead, and that's the end of him. Do you hear what I tell you? You neither saw nor heard him. It was just a crazy dream of yours – "

Tiser had suddenly sprung to his feet, his face white, his eyes staring.

"Listen!" he gasped. "Listen, Mark! Can't you hear it?"

Mark was about to speak when he, too, heard the sound. It came from the street – the thin wail of a fiddle playing the "Chanson d'Adieu." With an oath he ran to the window, dragged aside the curtains, and, throwing up the sash, stepped on to the balcony. The sidewalk before the house was deserted; nobody was in sight, nor was there any sound of a violin.

He came back into the room and shut the window, and instantly he heard the tune again. It seemed to come from the wall.

"Did you hear it?" breathed Tiser.

At that moment there was a knock at the door, and, going out, Mark admitted the girl.

"Did you hear somebody playing the violin?" she asked.

"You heard it, too, did you? Yes; come in."

They went back to the sitting-room, the wall of which divided Ann's flat from his.

"I was sitting in my bedroom sewing" – she pointed to the wall – "when I heard it. Isn't it the tune that old Li Yoseph played?"

Mark forced a laugh.

"This crazy coot thinks he's seen the old man – the music's stopped!"

Tiser was blinking and mouthing like someone demented.

"You heard it?" he squeaked. "Li Yoseph… Nobody played that tune like he…he never kept the right time…like that always. Mark, it's Li – I'll swear it's Li! I'll swear it was Li I saw sitting in my room."

With an oath Mark McGill caught him by the shoulder and flung him down on the settee.

"Sit there, and keep quiet, you gibbering rat!" he said harshly. "Take no notice of him, Ann – he's drunk."

"When did he see Li Yoseph?"

"He never saw him – he dreamt he saw him. What can you expect from a man who never goes to bed sober?"

Feeble murmurs of protest came from the settee, but these Mark ignored.

"He's crazy – anybody can see he's crazy. It was some street musician. On a still night a violin carries a devil of a distance, and it was probably somebody round the corner. You're not going, Ann?"

She was already at the door.

"Yes, I'll go back. I wondered if you had heard it, that's all."

Before he could stop her she had disappeared. He heard his own and then her door slam. With one stride he was at the settee and, lifting Tiser to his feet, shook him as a dog shakes a rat.

"How many times have I told you not to frighten that girl, you poor dope? Be careful, Tiser! You'll go the same journey as Li Yoseph if you're dangerous to me. I can tell you that, because you dare not put up a squeak without hanging yourself. Go back to your bed and your booze."

He flung the man into the middle of the room, and only by a supreme effort did Tiser keep his feet. He stood there shaking himself, a look of bewilderment in his unpleasant face.

"All right, Mark," he said meekly, "I'm terribly sorry I bothered you. I had one over the eight, dear old Mark."

He sidled out of the room, fled down the stairs and ran along the pavement of Cavendish Square. He was out of breath by the time he reached Oxford Street, but his mind was a little better balanced; and by the time he reached Hammersmith most of his fears had dissipated.

The Home lay on the angle of two streets behind Hammersmith Broadway, and in neither of these thoroughfares were pedestrians to be found at this hour of the night. As he turned the corner he saw a man standing with his back to the lamp-post. From his attitude it might be supposed he was dozing; his head was sunk on his breast, his arms were folded. Tiser quickened his pace to pass him. The welcome light of the Home shone through the glass-panelled door, and his new-born confidence lent him a false sense of courage.

"Good night," he said jovially as he passed the man under the lamp-post.

At the words the stranger looked up... For a moment Tiser stared at the yellow face, at the fur cap and the untidy grey hair that fell from beneath it; the huge nose and the protuberant chin...

With a scream, Tiser turned and fled into the Home. He had looked upon the face of Li Yoseph!

15

Mark McGill had turned off the lights in his sitting-room and was preparing for bed when the telephone bell rang, and at the sound of the chattering voice at the other end of the wire he cursed softly.

"What's the matter with you now?"

"...I saw him, Mark...just outside the Home. He looked up at me...not a yard away from me."

"Whom are you talking about?" asked Mark harshly.

"Li – Li Yoseph – no, I'm not drunk! One of the men at the Home had seen him before – he wasn't drunk! And another fellow who came in after me saw him go round the corner and get into a cab. He was muttering to himself just like old Li always did. Mark, it's horrible! I don't know what to do."

"Who was the man who saw him? Send him to the telephone," commanded McGill.

He waited for ten minutes before a husky voice spoke.

"That's right, Mr McGill, I see the old chap – a yellow-faced man. He was standing under a lamp-post just before Mr Tiser came into the Home."

"Do you know Li Yoseph?"

"No, sir, I don't know him at all. Heard about him, but never seen him. But according to what I've heard, that was him."

"Tell Mr Tiser to come to the phone," said Mark, but when his lieutenant came he was so incomprehensible that Mark rang off.

He went back to the sitting-room, turned on the lights and drew a chair up to the dying fire. There must be something in this story of

Tiser's. It couldn't be wholly funk. And that music…where had it come from? From the wall? Sometimes memory is a better servant than observation. It seemed easier to locate the sound after the lapse of an hour. It came from the flat above. But the flat above was unoccupied; its owner had gone to Scotland a few days before, and had taken away the servants. Mark knew this because the hall porter had told him.

Li Yoseph? Why had the police suddenly stopped their search? Was it because they knew that the old man had come back to England? Bradley was one of those sly devils who would spring a thing like that on him; he was probably employing Li Yoseph as a stool pigeon.

Yet how could the man be alive? It was nearer five paces than ten when he had shot him. The bullet had struck him between the shoulders. Was it possible that by an accident it was a blank cartridge? Not two, at any rate!

He sat crouched up over the fire, his hands on his face, turning the matter over and over in his mind. Suddenly he heard a sound which made him sit bolt upright. It was the sound of shuffling feet and it came from the room above. The people who had gone to Scotland had taken their carpet up – he had complained to the janitor about the noise the workmen had made walking on the parquet floor.

Shuffle, shuffle, shuffle! It might have been slippered feet. Curiously reminiscent of old Li Yoseph. And then he heard the sound of a fiddle again, a little softer, a little more tender than the sound he had heard before. The man in the room above was playing the "Chanson d'Adieu."

Mark went back to his bedroom, put on his coat and, creeping softly along the passage, opened the door. A broad flight of stairs led to the flat above. There was a faint landing light to show him the way. At this hour the other tenants were sleeping. He crept up to the door of the apartment above his own and, stooping, pressed in the flap of the letter-box and put his ear to it. There was no sound.

Reaching up his hand, he pressed the bell and heard the loud shrill of it. Nothing followed; no footsteps sounded on the uncarpeted passage. He rang again, without any more interesting consequence.

There was a card fastened to the door with a drawing-pin:

During Sir Arthur Findon's absence in Scotland all letters and parcels must be given to the hall porter.

Mark was puzzled. He went downstairs slowly and returned to the sitting-room. The music had stopped. He waited an hour for the sound of shuffling feet, and then decided to go to bed.

He did not remember that he had closed the door communicating between the two rooms; he did not even consider the matter, till he turned the handle and found that the door was fastened. Mark came back from the door, breathing heavily, and his hand went to his hip. He turned out the lights, pulled aside the curtains and, raising the window, stepped on to the balcony. There were French windows to his bedroom, and he saw that these were open. There was nobody in sight.

He stepped gingerly into the room, his gun levelled, and, crouching low, made for the side of the bed and turned on the light. The room was empty.

Somebody had been there. Pinned to the pillow was a ragged-edged sheet of paper containing a few lines of sprawling handwriting. They began:

> *MEIN LIEBER FREUND MARK,*
> *Bald werde ich Li Yoseph zu Ihnen zuruck kommen.*

He read German fairly well. The message was short.

> *MY DEAR FRIEND MARK,*
> *Soon old Li will come and see you.*

That was all.

Turning to close the window, Mark McGill caught a glimpse of his face. It was a little paler than usual.

He did not go to bed that night, but dozed in a chair before the replenished fire. When daylight came he walked out on to the balcony and saw how simple a matter it was to gain entrance to his flat from a narrower balcony above. Somebody had been in the Findons' flat. Possibly the hall porter could solve the mystery.

The porter did not come on duty until nine o'clock, by which time Mark's servants having arrived, he sent one of them to fetch the man to him.

"No, sir," said the astonished porter, "there's nobody in the flat above. Sir Arthur never lets his apartment – and he's very particular about people looking over it."

Mark forced a smile.

"Perhaps he wouldn't object to my looking over it?" he said. "Do you know who has the key?"

The porter hesitated.

"Yes, sir, I have the key," he said, "but I'd probably lose my job if he knew that I'd let you in."

He departed through the basement to get the key, and Mark accompanied him up the stairs into the Findons' flat. It was a luxurious suite, most of the furniture shrouded in white holland covers. There were no carpets either in the passage or in the principal rooms. It was that which was above Mark's sitting-room that interested him most. But here there was no evidence of illicit occupation. The white blinds were drawn; the furniture had a ghostly appearance, wrapped in its coverings; when Mark tried the windows he found they were fastened from the inside.

"You must have been mistaken, sir. Nobody was in this flat last night. There are only two keys: I've one and Sir Arthur has the other."

"Who is Sir Arthur?" asked Mark.

Sir Arthur apparently was rather an important person, a permanent Under-Secretary of State, who lived with his wife and daughter and had very few friends.

"If he'd given anybody the key of the flat he would have told me," said the porter.

Mark examined the room more closely. It was larger than his sitting-room and, as he had suspected, must have overlapped Ann Perryman's bedroom. He opened the window and went out on to a small balcony, and saw how easy it would be for an agile man to reach the balcony below. LiYoseph was not agile – who, then, was with him? He examined the stone balustrade, but found no marks of ladder or hook.

Returning to the room, he was following the porter into the passage when he saw something on the floor and, stooping, picked up a tiny square object. It was familiar enough, but for a moment he could not place it.

"What is this?" he asked.

The porter took it in his hand and adjusted his pince-nez.

"That's resin, sir. I expect it belongs to Miss Findon. She plays on the violin."

"Is she in Scotland too?"

"Yes, sir; I had a postcard from her this morning, asking me to forward a parcel that arrived from Devonshire yesterday."

Mark was baffled; he was out of his depth. If the girl was in London, that would explain everything.

When he returned to his sitting-room he found Ann – an unusual circumstance, for he seldom saw her before the lunch hour, and not always then.

"I want to go shopping this morning," she said, "and I want some money. I don't think I have any right to it, because, whilst my licence is suspended – "

"Don't be stupid," he smiled. "You can have any money you like – fifty pounds, a hundred – ?"

"What is due to me?" she said. "If I am entitled to it – " And then, in the same breath: "Were you disturbed last night? Those people overhead were rather noisy."

"Did you hear too?" he asked eagerly.

"I heard somebody walking, that's all. I wish they would put their carpets down. Findon – isn't that their name? I thought they were in Scotland."

"Did you hear the violin?" he asked.

Apparently she had.

"Yes, I heard a violin," she said quietly. "Who was it playing?"

Mark shrugged.

"I don't know. Somebody's trying monkey tricks."

"But the old man – Li Yoseph – is dead, isn't he?" she insisted.

"I don't see how he could be anything else. It was a high tide, and if he fell in – "

Something in her face stopped him.

"But surely this was the police theory, that he fell into the river?"

He saw his error, and smiled.

"I've almost come to accept the police theory myself; I've had it dinned into me so often. My own view is that he got news of the police raid and cleared off to the Continent and kept himself hidden. In fact, I'm pretty sure he died there."

He tried to assume an air of confidence, but knew that he had been unsuccessful in imposing it upon her.

He recalled at that moment something which had happened on the night of her arrest.

"Didn't you say you saw Li Yoseph in Cavendish Square?"

She had almost forgotten the circumstance.

"Yes; I wasn't sure – you said there was a Russian prince living near here, and that it might have been one of his visitors. It could not have been Mr Yoseph; he would have called, wouldn't he?"

He did not answer this. She saw him frown, and presently he resumed his pacing up and down the room.

"Tiser says he's seen him – twice. I can't understand it, except of course that Tiser is a drunk who is liable to see anything."

There was a time when Mark pretended that Tiser was a really admirable person, but the time for pretence had long passed.

"Would it make much difference – to you, I mean, if he came back?"

It was an innocent question she asked, but Mark was in his most suspicious mood.

"What do you mean?" he asked harshly. "Why should it make any difference to me if he were alive? He was a handy old chap – but was getting rather past it. Besides, he was under police supervision, and he had about reached the end of his usefulness when he – disappeared. He was rather stupid too – all this ghost-seeing was a form of lunacy, and one never knew what he would be saying next. I kept friendly with him to the last, because he was the only man who saw the murder of Ronnie, and I wanted you to have the facts from an eyewitness."

"Did I?"

He walked slowly towards Ann and stared down at her.

"Did you what?" he demanded.

"Did I have the facts?" she asked. "You say he was a little mad; why should he have been telling me the truth? Why shouldn't that have been an illusion too?"

Here was an unanswerable question, and Mark's unease had another cause.

"I don't quite get you in these days, Ann," he said. "You say the oddest things and ask the queerest questions. You know what this fellow was – he was crazy in some ways. His ghosts and his children, for example. But in other respects he was the same as you and I."

He thought for a while.

"Of course, he may have been lying unconsciously – I'm no judge. I had to take the story and its inherent probabilities just as you have to take it. When he told me, it sounded true."

He paused again, and then came his challenge.

"If Bradley didn't kill your brother, who did?"

She shook her head and sighed.

It was more satisfactory to Mark that, in the weeks which followed, the depression which lay like a cloud upon the girl was partially lifted. She was cheerful, ready to smile at such small jests as the day and its doings provided. She stood for a double value in his eyes – the curtailment of her activities as a daring driver of cars removed for the moment one of these quantities. The other remained and, in the weeks of idleness which followed the police court scene, became intensified.

Women occupied no considerable place in his scheme of life. There had been two – one everlastingly requiring, whining, complaining, dissatisfied creature, who on a fortunate day fastened herself leech-like on a man who married her. The other... Mark always forgot what the other was like. More often than not he confused her with that fair-haired lady who had wailed for the moon.

Ann was different. He told her so once.

"All women are," was her discouraging rejoinder.

To say that he was in love with her would be to apply that expression as truly as it is usually applied. He admired her, and when he offered a closer friendship than she deigned to accept, he was prepared to take time as his ally. But time had been an undependable and uncertain friend. The new phase of his acquaintance, which began on the day they returned to Cavendish Square from the police court, demanded a new atmosphere. That he strove in vain to create.

There was much to occupy the mind of Mark McGill, for his business affairs were not prospering. In one stroke he had lost two lieutenants. The Home was no longer a home to Mr Tiser. He ceased to take any very great interest in its inmates or its humanitarian object. A man for whom Mark had been waiting nearly two years was allowed to leave Dartmoor without having the usual tout to meet him; and when, by the greatest of good luck, he turned up at the Home, Tiser allowed him to go away again. Mark was furious when he heard of this, and sent for his wretched assistant.

"What's the idea? Have we shut down business? What do you expect to live on? Or maybe you're not expecting to live at all?"

"I do my best, Mark," pleaded the unhappy man.

Mark's smile was not one of amusement.

"You do your best, eh? You did your best to put Bradley away, and draw the attention of the Squad to you and me! You sent out three left-handed wife beaters and naturally they were caught. You did your best to hide up what was happening at the Home, and allowed a microphone to be put there under your nose in the disguise of a wireless receiver. It was only by chance that I didn't call when that damned installation was working."

"Mark, I swear I didn't send those lads out – " began Tiser, but the other silenced him.

"What good to you and me is it if Bradley is coshed? There was only one way to get him, and that was to pick the right man, light him up with 'coke' and put a gat in his pocket."

Tiser was shaking like a leaf. He never ceased to shiver in these days.

"Let us get out, Mark," he begged. "We've made enough to settle down. What about South America? I've always wanted to be in a hot climate – "

"Wait till you're dead!" snarled Mark. "There are hotter places than South America!"

Tiser regained a little of his courage as the weeks progressed, for that weird apparition which had struck his heart cold made no reappearance. If he had occupied himself entirely with his partner's business he would have had no time to think of Li Yoseph or the dread possibilities which every morrow held, but he let business go and gave his horrid imagination a full head of steam. The actual running of the Home was in the hands of a steward, an ex-convict. There were a thousand other matters to keep Tiser employed; he gave up his hours to the consideration of what would happen if something else happened.

There were quite a number of callers who came in by the private way and not through the main entrance to the Home. They had short interviews with Tiser, and left as mysteriously as they arrived.

There was a man named Laring, a red-faced, bulbous-nosed man with faded blue eyes, who spoke with the voice of a gentleman – he had once held the King's commission in the old army. Laring was reputedly a well-off man, had a nice house in a southern suburb of London, ran two cars and always dressed well. He invariably had an excuse for calling at the Home, for he brought with him on each of his visits a large parcel of magazines and books for the use of the inmates. What he took back, nobody knew but Tiser and himself.

Such a man might easily have an interest in philanthropic enterprises. He had once been admitted to the exclusive home of Mark McGill. Ann had met him there – a very knowledgeable man, pleasantly spoken, who drank whisky without cessation from the moment he arrived till the moment he left, and seemed none the worse for it.

He called one night with a large package of literature and a gentle complaint. Tiser brought a bottle of whisky and a siphon and put them before him. Mr Laring had much to say.

"The business is going to pot, my dear fellow, and unless Mark is very careful he will find that American crowd cutting him out of the business. They have approached me, naturally, because my organisation is one of the best in the country. But I haven't had a consignment from you for two months! That won't do, Tiser, that won't do at all!"

Mr Laring's "organisation" was itself American. He was a very large exporter, had agents from New Orleans to Seattle, but was dependent upon such distributors as Mark, who acted as a sort of clearing house.

"The whole trouble is that you've got cold feet. Yes, yes, I know all about the police court case; I read it with the greatest interest. But business is business, my dear Tiser. It isn't my local connection that bothers me – I am thinking of giving them up, anyway."

It was at that moment that a little bell rang, which indicated that another visitor had come. Tiser, with Mark's injunction fresh in his mind, went twittering out to see the caller. It was Ann. He was so astonished that he stood gaping at her for a little time.

"My dear young lady, what on earth are you doing here – without an escort?" He shook his head. "That is very risky. I am rather surprised that Mark should let you come."

"Mark doesn't know," she said, and waited for him to invite her into his room.

His hesitancy was rather expressive.

"You have somebody with you?" she asked.

"No, no, only my dear friend Laring – he takes a great interest in the Home and never fails to supply us with periodicals. Will you wait one moment?"

He hurried back to his room and explained the identity of the caller. Mr Laring, a gallant man, greeted her with a little bow. But he was puzzled. Neither he nor any of Mark's agents was quite sure whether the girl knew exactly the kind of work she had been doing. It had been agreed from the first that no mention should ever be made in her presence of the traffic; but this was generally regarded as an amusing comedy, designed for her protection should the "busies" ever catch her.

Ann had left her flat and had come to the Home on the impulse of the moment: whether to escape trouble or to settle her own doubts she was not sure herself.

"No, Mark doesn't know I've come. I was bored. I thought I might see Li Yoseph."

She saw Tiser wince and regretted her pleasantry.

"Li Yoseph?" Laring lifted his grey eyebrows. "I thought our old friend was – "

"Abroad, old boy, abroad," mumbled Tiser. "Did you want anything, Miss Perryman – I mean, anything particular? It's rather late…"

It was in fact after ten, an hour at which young lady visitors were seldom to be met with in the Home.

"No, nothing particular – I needed a walk," she said, and knew how much of a lie he would think that if he had seen her getting out of a taxicab at the end of the street.

She was glad to see Laring – he was a link with reality. She had had some vague idea of talking to Tiser about the smuggling, and receiving from him a desirable relief from her perplexities. It was saccharine she had been carrying, of course…it was a common form of smuggling. Only last week she had read that a ship's steward had been fined a hundred pounds, and the police solicitor had enlarged upon the enormity of his offence and the amount of contraband that was coming into the country.

Bradley had been trying to frighten her. There was (she told herself) no doubt in her mind – Bradley's was an old police trick. He had wanted to disintegrate the gang, and set one member against the other. But suppose it wasn't saccharine? That was the "if" which had tortured her. And here was Laring, one of Mark's most important customers. She had once carried a small canister to him, and on another occasion had met him in Cardiff with a further consignment. Laring might tell her what this shivering partner of Mark's would be afraid to tell. He certainly would not tell her here; and when, after a quarter of an hour's amiable discussion on the weather, her unhappy experience of the police court, Mark's many good qualities – here he was fervently supported by Tiser – the red-faced gentleman rose to take his departure:

"I will walk back with you a little way, if I may," said Ann.

She saw a look of alarm come to Tiser's face, and was strengthened in her resolution.

Mr Laring had a car round the corner, and would be happy to drive her home, for he was not averse to the society of a pretty woman. Men seldom are so averse until they are dead. She gave Tiser no opportunity of warning him. Even his emphatic hint that there were one or two matters of business he would like to discuss with Laring was unheeded.

The red-faced man did not drive himself; his car was a small limousine, luxuriously upholstered, and he had a chauffeur of great dignity and reticence to drive him. As the machine glided through Hammersmith Broadway, Mr Laring made himself a little more comfortable in an unaccustomed corner.

"A curious fellow, Tiser. I fear he drinks too much."

She smiled at this criticism by one who only stopped drinking to eat.

"His nerve has gone, poor fellow!" he went on, and shook his head sorrowfully. "I'm afraid he'll be of very little use to Mark – it will be hard luck. I suppose you're not driving now, Miss Perryman? What a pity! The boys will miss you."

"Mark will manage to distribute the stuff," she said, and he grunted.

"He is not doing as much as he ought to do – I'm afraid he is losing his nerve too, and naturally. You gave us an awful fright, Miss Perryman. We thought you were going to prison. The whole thing was villainously planned by Bradley. He brought that man Smith into court before your case in order to emphasise in the magistrate's mind the iniquity of your proceedings."

And then he remembered.

"Not that saccharine smuggling is a very iniquitous thing," he added hastily.

"Saccharine?" replied Ann with a laugh. "Don't be absurd!"

There was a long silence after this, and she waited, her heart beating a little faster, for what was coming next.

Mr Laring sighed heavily.

"I often wonder whether I'm doing the right thing – whether I am not perhaps a force for evil." (He had never spent a second in wondering anything of the sort.) "But what is one to do? There is a very interesting novel published in the French language; it is called 'My Body is My Own.' You may have read it? It puts into concrete form my own philosophy. Has any person or corporation or country or society the right of telling you or me where and how we shall find our pleasures? Has anybody the right to say that I should not drink whisky, as I occasionally do, and thoroughly enjoy, or that you should not use perfume if its fragrance gives you pleasure?"

Here was her opportunity and she seized it.

"Or, for the matter of that, take cocaine?" she said, a little breathlessly.

He was embarrassed by the word.

To him it was "coke"; he never referred to it by any other term; more often than not he called it "the stuff."

"Exactly," he said.

And then, after a silence:

"Personally, it has never had any attraction for me. But I can well imagine that there are people who find the most intense pleasure – indeed their only pleasure in life – from its assimilation. I would not consider myself being guilty of a – um – reprehensible action, if I assisted them to such gratification. There are, of course, poor, weak-minded individuals who carry the thing to excess. But, then, there are people who smoke to excess and eat to excess…"

He might have added "drink to excess," but there were limits to his powers of self-deception. Ann listened with a sinking heart. She knew now, that if she asked him bluntly whether he was a trafficker in drugs, he would deny indignantly all knowledge of such a practice. And yet he had told her all that she wanted to know – more than she wanted to know.

The car, which had been held up at Marble Arch, slowed down and came to a stop in Cavendish Square. The gallant Mr Laring would have got out and assisted her to alight, but she would not allow this. She stepped on to the pavement and closed the door, and the red-faced man, settling himself in his more accustomed corner, drove off.

She stood on the edge of the pavement, watching the car, and then she became aware that a man was standing with his back to the railings less than two yards away. She saw the red glow of his cigarette, and would have hurried into the flat if he had not spoken to her.

"Nice night for a drive, Miss Perryman."

It was Bradley.

"Yes, very," she said awkwardly.

She could have walked past him into the house and said nothing, but her inclination was to linger.

"Have a good time at the Home? You ought to make a pretty useful impression on those thugs. In good little story-books, of course, you would. They'd go all soft and mushy – I like that word 'mushy'."

She made a wry little face as she heard the word she had flung at him across the court.

"Tears would come into their eyes, they'd give up all their evil ways and go chopping wood at fourpence an hour. But things don't quite work out that way, do they?"

He was as friendly and unconcerned as though he had never stood, white-faced and tense, under the lash of her scorn.

"I wanted to see you – in a way," he drawled. "There's a fiddle-playing ghost around here, they tell me."

"Why don't you arrest him?" she asked. After the first shock of the meeting she had recovered a little of her self-possession.

"Arresting ghosts is against regulations," he said. "You haven't seen old Li Yoseph?"

"Have you?"

"Not so much as a whisker of him," he said cheerfully, "and nobody else has, either."

There was a pause, but still she lingered. "Who told you I had been to the Home?"

"I followed you there," he said shamelessly. "Also I followed you back. You were held up by a traffic block at Marble Arch. I, being a licensed policeman, slipped through. You know my methods – Watson."

She smiled faintly.

"What have you been doing – since I met you last?" It was an inane but natural question. She heard his soft chuckle.

"Catching burglars, whizzers – you know what a whizzer is? He's a pickpocket and he's a dangerous thief – everything except smugglers of saccharine."

"I'm sure you've been very kind to them," she said maliciously.

"Kindness is my middle name," he answered with mock gravity. "Nothing gives me greater happiness than to put a burglar in a nice airy cell, tuck him up and hold his hand till he's asleep."

"And then you go out and throw away his tools and pretend you never found them?" she said, with amused scorn, and he laughed again.

"Quixotic – I'm all that. I've never got a man twenty years that I haven't cried myself to sleep!"

He was looking past her. She saw the headlights of a car moving swiftly towards them. It stopped before the house.

"I'll say good night, Miss Perryman. A little mission of humanity calls me."

He stepped on the running-board and swung himself into the police tender. Ann went back to her flat, feeling singularly light-hearted, and when she went in to see Mark before going to bed there was a light in her eyes that he had not seen before.

"Where have you been?" he asked.

"For a little walk," she said.
She made no mention of Bradley.

16

There were forces more potent than Tiser and his frowsy friends that were controlled by Mark McGill. The crude hold-up which had been attempted was the least disagreeable consequence of Mark's enmity. More scientific was the removal of a hub of the police car which Bradley used. Travelling at forty-five miles an hour on the Great West Road, one of the front wheels came off – only a miracle saved the crew from destruction.

It was no ordinary accident; even a superficial examination of the broken hub showed this. One night on the outskirts of London, when chasing a suspected car, the tender ran into a wire fastened between two trees across the road. The machine they were chasing was a sports car with a very low clearance – low enough for the driver to miss the stretched steel cord. Fortunately for the squad, its bright headlights revealed the wire just in time. The brakes were jammed on, but even then the windscreen was smashed.

Another night, as Bradley was going home, this time with an escort, a closed two-seater flew past him, and somebody from the interior fired three shots from an automatic. The public would have known nothing about this, but one of the shots went through the window of a room where a dance was in progress, and an innocent hired waiter, handing round refreshments, must bemoan the loss of a portion of his left ear.

What worried Scotland Yard was the increase in crimes of violence all over the country. The armed burglar is a rare phenomenon in England, and usually is the veriest amateur. Now he was appearing in the most unlikely places. Capital punishment is the greatest deterrent of murder – the knowledge that the scaffold inevitably awaits the man who takes life, not only keeps his finger from the trigger but keeps the pistol from his pocket. The old lag, who knows that his next lagging will be tantamount to a life sentence, yet hesitates to use lethal weapons. If he knew that he would receive the same sentence whether he shot or refrained from shooting, murder would be a pastime.

Only one thing strikes the fear of the rope from the criminal's heart – dope. There is no other deterrent. The habitual criminal is devoid of all human qualities. He is a liar, he is faithless to his kind, treacherous to those who help him, capable of any villainy from blackmail to murder. There is no salvation for him in this life. But the trap with the oiled bolt is a salvation for the law-abiding.

Bradley knew criminals as he knew the back of his hand. He knew them in all their ugliness; found no good in them; could be amused at times by the quaint angle of their humour, but knew that in their hearts there was neither gratitude nor grace. He had seen men stand up in the dock and threaten him with death and mutilation, and knew that when they came from prison they would shuffle up to him abashed and try to make friends with him. In the early days of his service he had helped their womenfolk and been rewarded by the basest calumnies.

He was entirely without illusions; he knew them all for what they were, neither despised nor hated them, but spent his life in a consistent effort to segregate them from normal humanity. He knew the whizzers – those innocent-looking men who crowd into omnibuses and rob the poor of their bitterly won earnings, who steal their bags, who would steal the very satchels in which working girls carry their lunch – not only steal them but glory in their theft. They worked in gangs, and had "minders," whose business it was to kick and disable the poor souls who found themselves robbed and attempted to recover their own.

One of the pleasant memories that Inspector Bradley carried with him was of an evening when he tackled one of these brutes who showed fight, and used his rubber truncheon on the bloated face of the man who tried to maim him.

They betrayed one another if it was safe to do so. There was no honour among thieves – expediency and self-interest dominated every criminal policy. Offer a sufficient reward, and a man would "shop" his own brother even if it brought him to the scaffold.

The police were very wary and sometimes obliging. They allowed receivers to carry on their nefarious calling without too close an investigation, so long as the receiver was prepared to supply information against the thief. Then one day he himself would go the way of the men he had betrayed.

There was a conference at the Yard, which Bradley attended.

"McGill has slackened off a little – he's doing no business at the moment. I think the case against Miss Perryman scared him."

"It is a pity you can't get one of these fellows to squeak," suggested his chief.

Bradley shook his head.

"There is no chance of a squeak against McGill. He is so well covered that you can't get at him."

"Could you do anything with that girl Perryman?" asked another officer.

Bradley stiffened a little.

"What do you suggest?" he asked coldly.

The grey-haired man who had put the suggestion laughed.

"Well, Brad, you're a pretty good-looking fellow – "

"Let's stop exchanging compliments and keep to the facts," snapped Bradley. "I'll get Mark McGill, but I don't want him for trafficking in drugs."

It was soon after this that Mark received from his agents the news that the police had ceased the inquiries they had set on foot, and which were intended to trace the centre of the traffic. Barrages which had been established outside the big towns were lifted; motors could go in and out without being subjected to inspection and search; and the strong forces of local detectives which had watched every railway station was reduced to one or two men.

Mark began to seek contact with his Belgian and German wholesalers. Much of the stuff came from the former country, and new methods had to be devised to avoid the Customs. Now that Ann was "disabled" and an aeroplane control had been established at the coast, his difficulties were almost insuperable. Li Yoseph had been a wonderful servant of the organisation; he was in touch with half a hundred avenues of communication; knew hundreds of sea-going men, and was favourably housed to receive contraband. There were legions of river thieves who pursued their illicit trade up and down the Pool. But they were utterly untrustworthy, until Mark found a reliable receiver, and that was a difficult person to come by.

He was breakfasting with Ann one morning – it was the meal at which they generally met – when he put a suggestion to her.

"I've been thinking of taking a house up the river," he said airily; "somewhere between Teddington and Kingston, with a nice lawn running to the river – how does that appeal to you?"

"It sounds very charming," she said, but did not raise her eyes from the table.

"The business is almost at a standstill," he said, "and I am losing money. You can't drive any more. I think the house on the river would be quite a good idea – but it ought to be below the locks."

She raised her eyes and looked at him straightly.

"Are you trying to find a woman Li Yoseph?" she asked, and in spite of his self-control he went red.

"I don't quite know – "

"What would you expect me to do in my house – with a lawn sloping down to the river? Or wouldn't it be better in some backwater that wasn't overlooked?"

He scowled angrily.

"I don't know what to make of you, Ann. Are you suggesting that I – "

He stopped, at a loss for an alternative explanation, and she smiled.

"I thought you might want a substitute for Lady's Stairs," she said; "a place where people could bring – stuff. I don't like the idea very much. I'm afraid I am a bad smuggler."

"There was no question of smuggling," he said sulkily. "You're an extraordinary creature! Whenever I try to do something for you, you find some sinister reason for my – " He hesitated for a word.

"Kindness," she suggested. "No, Mark, I don't think that would appeal to me. In the first place, I am what is known as a marked woman – I have appeared in court; I have annoyed Bradley. You may be sure that wherever I go I shall be watched. I don't want another experience like I had." She closed her eyes and shivered. "It was horrible, Mark...that awful cell!"

He dropped the subject, but was bitterly disappointed. It seemed a fairly easy solution to his difficulties. The stuff could be picked up in the Pool, could come up in the pleasure launch to the house, which he had already chosen.

It was sheer malice which prompted him to say, apropos nothing: "Bradley's in love with you, isn't he?"

He had the satisfaction of seeing her face go pink and scarlet, and from scarlet to white again.

"Don't be stupid," she said, but did not meet his eyes.

"You said as much in court," he went on remorselessly. "Queer that a fellow like that should be in love at all! I suppose he's recovered from that now? Anyway, he may have been kidding you along. These fellows would walk out with women tramps to get information. I should imagine that he loathes you."

It was on the tip of her tongue to produce evidence to the contrary.

"You were going to say – ?"

"Nothing," she said shortly, and in a minute or so left the table and went back to her flat.

She was facing facts bravely enough now. She returned to her room where the double portrait frame was – Bradley on the one side and Ronnie on the other – and she took out the newspaper of the detective and tore it into small pieces. Her animosity could not be stimulated any further. She did not hate Bradley; she did not believe that he killed her brother. She did believe that –

Here she came to the point where facts could not be faced. He had liked her; she was sure of that. And he was not, as Mark had suggested, kidding her along. He had loved her, but had that love survived the humiliation she had put upon him in the police court?

It was then she had a faint hint of what caused the fits of desperate unhappiness to which she was subjected.

Mark was no fool. The symptoms his little talk had revealed could admit of only one diagnosis. After she had left the table he sat, his hands thrust in his pockets, on his face an expression of blank amazement.

She liked Bradley; she wasn't in love with him, of course – but – where would this lead? Her faith in him was shattered. Any attempt at its renewal was futile. A coalition between Bradley and her would have tremendous consequences. He could not see her turning King's evidence; he could not imagine her standing in the box and testifying against him; but the real damaging evidence is not given in court, but in a little room at Scotland Yard.

Ann knew more about his "work" than she realised. She might not know what she carried by night in that car of hers, but she knew to whom it was carried. Every thread of the confederation was in her hands. He had never thought of marriage; it had now become a part of his settled policy. If Bradley loved her, he would kill two birds with one stone – silence a most damaging witness, and hurt the man he hated. Marriage had no permanence in Mark's eyes, and was not a serious matter that required any very long consideration.

Certain happenings had been reported to him which rather disturbed him. The police activity in the country might have ceased, but in the metropolitan area a systematic and ruthless search was in progress. As the waters of a flood send the rats scurrying to high ground, so did this comb-out which Scotland Yard had organised bring scores of darkly working men and women into the open. The car thieves and receivers felt the immediate effects. One night, in response to a telephone invitation urgently made, Mark met by appointment a notorious receiver of stolen machines, who in the past had been very useful to him.

"They're working in the dock district," said the man. "They've cleared up Bergson's yard and uncrated three cars that were being put on board an Indian boat next week. They pulled Bergson, and got his son, and I've had the office that they've promised to make it light for him if he'll put up a squeak about your sniff stuff."

"Did they mention me?" asked Mark quickly.

"They didn't mention any names, but they meant you," said the man. "Did you ever use any of the Bergson people to put your stuff around?"

Mark considered.

"No," he said.

"The point is this," insisted his companion: "the boys think it's your 'coke' trade that's stirring up the Yard, and they're a bit sore about it. I've sent all my machines up to Birmingham – what about your yard?"

Mark rented three garages in London, though "garage" was a courtesy term which described no more than untidy yards and converted stables in which he used to store certain articles which it was very desirable should be kept out of sight, and which were certainly too dangerous to have in his flat.

"There are practically no cars there," he said uneasily; "two at the most. Both of those are in other names."

Though he did not say so, one of those names was Ann Perryman.

"I'm telling you to look out," warned his friend. "And another thing, has old Sedeman got anything on you? He's out of stir today, and he's talking big. The old boy was a pal of Yoseph's; he used to live there when he wasn't sponging on the Home. What does he know?"

"Nothing," said Mark angrily.

The sight of a third person in the Kensington square which was their rendezvous was sufficient to send him melting into the darkness.

Mark went back to his flat, a very thoughtful man. For a long time he sat smoking before the fire, and then he remembered the little case which had arrived in the afternoon and, taking it from the safe, looked at the glittering thing on its blue velvet bed. He rang the bell for the man who acted as butler and valet. Ledson came, not in the best frame of mind, for he had been kept beyond his usual hour. He slept out, as did all Mark's servants.

"Go across the landing, Ledson, and ask Miss Perryman if she'll kindly come in for a minute."

Ledson groaned inwardly, for this might mean another hour. Usually when Ann came in to supper Mark kept him in attendance.

"I heard the front door of her flat slam a little time ago, sir. I don't think she's in," he said.

Mark turned with a snarl.

"Go and find out — don't argue!"

He had one hold on his servants — he paid them well. Ledson was a family man, and swallowed the humiliation.

He opened the door to find Tiser standing on the mat. He was mopping his face as though he had been running, but that signified very little.

"Is Mr McGill in?" he asked in a whisper. "Tell me, Ledson, my good fellow, is he in a good mood, eh?"

"I don't know, sir. Shall I tell him — "

"No, I'll see him."

He sidled into the room and for a little while Mark was unaware of his presence.

"What the devil do you want?" he asked unpromisingly.

Tiser was agitated, but that meant nothing. It was his normal condition. He came shuffling across the room, rubbing one hand over the other, and his voice was low and confidential.

"My dear fellow, what do you think they've done? They raided the Home tonight."

Mark frowned.

"Bradley?"

"Oh, that man!" wailed Tiser. "No, it wasn't Bradley. One of his satellites, my dear Mark. They took poor Benny and Walky and little Lew Marks – oh, half a dozen of the nicest boys! And they were doing nothing, my dear Mark. I swear to you that it's the most iniquitous case of persecution that has ever been brought to my notice! These poor fellows were sitting round drinking beer – "

"They didn't find any stuff there, did they?" asked Mark quickly. "I told you not to let any of them have so much as a sniff on the premises."

Tiser was pained.

"My dear fellow! You know I don't allow the stuff in the Home! You don't trust me, Mark. I slave and I think and I worry from morning till night; my life is a complete and absolute misery. I give you my best service – "

"Shut up!" growled Mark. "What was the raid about?"

The arrival of Ann coincided with the question.

"Hallo, my lovely!" said Mark cheerfully. "Here's your *bête noir* – bear with him; he's brought all his fears and troubles."

Tiser smiled ingratiatingly. He knew that in her presence he would at least be spared some of the inevitable abuse which came his way.

"Good evening, Miss Ann. How lovely you're looking!" he breathed. "I can't help it – I simply had to say it!"

She addressed Mark.

"Do you want to see me, Mark? Shall I come back later?"

He shook his head.

"No, no; Tiser isn't staying. He's come to tell me that his place has been raided tonight and some of the people at the Home have been arrested."

Her eyes were fixed on his. If she had shown any emotion at all he would have been relieved.

"Why?" she asked.

Mr Tiser supplied the answer.

"It's over something that happened a week or so ago. It appears that a gang of men set upon Bradley – very wrong of them, of course – "

"Attacked him?" she asked quickly. She had to check herself adding "He did not tell me."

"So they say," said Mr Tiser; "but you can't believe the police." He shook his head sadly. "It seems this was the second attack – somebody slashed him with a razor."

Her face puckered in a grimace of disgust.

"How beastly!" she said.

Mr Tiser was taken aback.

"Yes. Unfortunately – er – fortunately, they didn't get his face. It was altogether dreadful – "

"Did you know anything about this?" Mark's face was white with anger.

"Not me, Mark. I swear to you I knew nothing about it. Some of the lads resented the nine months that those poor boys got."

"Did you know anything about it, you sneaking little rat? Was it one of your little schemes, you poor, brainless soak?"

A look from Ann silenced him.

"You know who did it?" she said, addressing Tiser.

He could only smile feebly and say something about "common talk."

"Was he hurt?"

"Does it matter very much?" interrupted Mark impatiently. "I wish they'd cut his damned throat! That would have justified the attack. To go for him and not to get him – ach!"

For a moment in his anger he threw caution to the winds.

"You're an imbecile, Tiser; you can think with only one half your brain, and you don't use that right. If you'd lit 'em up and sent 'em out with gats – there would have been no Mr Bradley."

" 'Lit them up'?" repeated Ann slowly, and Mark took hold of himself and laughed.

"For God's sake, Ann, take a joke, can't you?"

"Lit them up with what?" she asked.

"A drink, of course," said Mark. "Take one, Tiser; I don't want you fainting on my carpet!"

Mr Tiser accepted the invitation eagerly and came back with a tumbler half filled with neat whisky.

"I wonder that man hasn't been laughed out of the force," he said. Suddenly, thrusting his hand into his inside pocket, he took out a case and opened it. He waited until he had swallowed the drink, and then he showed her what the case contained – a thick wad of press-cuttings. "I always keep these by me – I'll have them framed one day." He looked at one and chuckled stupidly.

" 'Remarkable Scene in Court. Famous Detective and Woman Prisoner,' " he read; "and here's another: 'Prison Love. Woman's Remarkable Charge against Police Chief' – "

So far he got when Ann snatched the cuttings from his hand. Her face was white, her eyes were blazing with fury.

"If you want amusing, find something else to play with," she breathed, and even Mark was astounded by her vehemence.

"What's the matter with you, Ann?" he demanded. It took her some seconds to control her voice.

"Does it occur to you that I'm being made to look as big a fool as Bradley?" she demanded. "Do you think I want this" – she failed to find an appropriate name for Tiser – "to carry these cuttings about to show his friends, and chortle with his filthy associates over my humiliation?"

"You didn't seem to mind that a week ago," grumbled Mark. "I really don't know what's happening to you, Ann. You jump down people's throats at the least provocation."

Mr Tiser was all apologies.

"You're the last person in the world I should think of offending, Miss Perryman. It was merely as an historical record that I kept them."

"It was just as funny when it happened," insisted Mark. "You bought up all the papers and gloated over them."

Ann shrugged.

"They bore me now. Who has been arrested?" she asked.

"They are unimportant people," Tiser hastened to assure her. "Bradley said he recognised them, which was an obvious lie. In the first place, they had the collars of their coats turned up when they made the attack – "

He met Mark's malignant eye again.

"One would think, to hear you talk, you knew all about it," he said deliberately, and changed the subject. "Ann, I've got a little present for you." He walked to the mantelpiece and took down a flat case. "We made a bit of money out of the last consignment."

She shook her head.

"I wish you wouldn't," she said.

"Why not?" asked Mark.

It took her some time to collect her thoughts into words that would give the least offence.

"I'm going to tell you, Mark. I'm not sorry Mr Tiser is here, because he knows just as much about your business as you do. I've been with you over a year; I have made twenty journeys to various parts of the country in the month before I was arrested, and I've never taken more than two pounds of stuff on any journey."

"Well?" said Mark, when she paused.

"That's forty pounds," she nodded. "Six hundred and forty ounces. You told me that we made a profit of three shillings an ounce on smuggled saccharine – that is less than a hundred pounds profit in a month – less my expenses, which were nearly a hundred pounds."

"That's not a bad profit, my dear Miss Perryman," Tiser hastened to assure her. "Plenty of firms would be only too pleased to make a hundred pounds a month."

"Besides, you haven't distributed all the stuff, my dear," said Mark with a genial smile. "You're only one of many."

He offered the little case to her.

"Bradley said I was ungracious," she said. "I hope I'm not. May I see what is in the case?"

She opened the case, looked and admired.

"How lovely!" she said. "Octagonal diamonds – and how queer!"

"They're not unusual," said Mark. "A little jeweller I know made this piece for me."

She heard Tiser murmur something ecstatic.

"Octagonal diamonds!" repeated Ann slowly. "I was trying to remember. There was a raid in Bond Street nearly two months ago – octagonal diamonds – that's right! A man named Smith shot a shop assistant."

She saw the colour leave Mark's face.

"Don't be a fool. There are thousands of diamonds that shape. You don't think I'd give you the same setting – ?"

She thrust the case back into his hand. Her eyes were wide with some horrible memory, and he wondered what it was that had so moved her.

"We were waiting in the passage at the police court when they went to bring Smith," she said in a low voice. "They herded us in our cells and locked us in so that we should not look upon the face of a murderer. It was awful!"

"Have you gone crazy?" growled Mark, and slammed the bracelet into the case viciously. "What's the matter with you? Tiser!" He nodded significantly towards the door. "I want to see you later."

Tiser had to make an elaborate pretence that his departure was natural. His damp hand caught Ann's and wrung it.

"I must look after those poor fellows at the police station. The police would starve them to death if they could. I'll say good night, Miss Perryman."

Mark waited until the door closed on the man. "Now, Ann, sit down and be good. There's something wrong; what is it?"

She laid down her bag on the table and walked across to the fireplace.

"I don't know," she said in a dispirited tone.

In such a mood Mark, prince of opportunists, might press home an important and a vital point.

"You're perfectly right about our profits," he said easily. "They're not as big as they should be. In fact, I thought of cutting down expenses."

She nodded at the fire.

"I'm probably your biggest expense," she said, without turning her head.

"You are." He smiled. "I reckon your flat costs a thousand a year." She turned at this.

"I've always wanted to go somewhere cheaper, Mark," and he laughed loudly, and Mark very seldom laughed.

"I'm not going to turn you out into the cold, old girl. That isn't the idea at all."

Now he avoided her eyes and looked down at the carpet, studying the pattern.

"I've two rooms here which I never use," he said.

"In this flat?" she asked quickly, and, when he nodded: "Do you suggest that I should use those two rooms?"

"There's nothing wrong about it – " he began, but she smiled and shook her head.

"That wouldn't be cheaper – for me," she said.

"But it does seem absurd, doesn't it?" said Mark genially. "You alone in that big flat on the other side of the landing, and I alone in this!"

Apparently it did not seem so silly to her.

"It is more expensive, I admit – shall I be frank and ungrateful?" He waited.

"I should like to live somewhere else," she said.

"Away from me?"

She nodded.

"You think you're getting talked about?" he bantered her, and he heard the beginning of a laugh.

"That doesn't worry me," she said. "Tiser just reminded me that I was talked about in prison."

He came over to her and dropped his hand on her shoulder.

"What's the matter with you, Ann?" he asked, and when she shook her head: "You think people are under the impression that you're living with me – as Bradley thinks?"

She looked up quickly enough at this.

"Does he?" she asked.

"Of course he does. He said as much in the court."

She smiled sceptically, unbelievingly.

"He didn't. He said: 'If you haven't gone already.' He was mad with me then – he'd have said anything. But he doesn't think so. If I thought he did – "

He shook her gently by the shoulders, but to his annoyance found her disengaging herself.

"You'd be tickled to death, eh? You'd like to hurt that swine, and so would I. You couldn't do anything to hurt him more than" – a pause – "changing your flat."

"That might hurt me most," she said quietly, and he did not immediately pursue the subject.

"He's a queer devil, Bradley. Ronnie used to talk about him by the hour. They were almost friends – "

What was happening to him lately? He asked himself with a curse. The look of startled surprise in her eyes warned him that he had gone too far to retreat.

"Well, they weren't exactly friends – " he began.

"You told me that Ronnie hated him and that he hated Ronnie." It was an accusation.

"And that was true," he said loudly, but she was not convinced.

"It's hard to believe that he killed Ronnie – it grows harder every day. I don't know why, but it does. That is what *he* said – that he was a friend of Ronnie," she said softly.

Mark McGill shifted uncomfortably.

"There was a sort of friendship?" she suggested. "You know, Mark, you've rather staggered me!"

"There's nothing to be staggered about," he snapped.

He came here to the dead end of explanations, found himself in a *cul de sac*, from which he could not escape except by retracing his steps. She was standing by the fire, staring down at it, biting her nether lip.

"There isn't the ghost of a chance that Mr Bradley's story is true, is there?" she asked slowly. "No, not about Ronnie. I mean, that the stuff I have been taking around the country and collecting from aeroplanes is – dope?"

She believed that it was. That was the startling discovery he made. All this elaborate fabric of deception which he had built up to screen himself had collapsed – when? In the past week? In the court? From something she had learned?

He tried to laugh her fears away.

"Good God! You're not believing Bradley, are you? The man is a liar. The average policeman is a bigger liar than the average criminal. Dope! What a ghastly charge to make!"

She shook her head.

"I've never believed it; I've trusted you implicitly – the thought that I was carrying on Ronnie's work went to my head a little and I didn't think a great deal about it. I suppose I'm a fool."

If she would only look at him he could act; but she did not look at him: he had to depend entirely upon his voice, and the voice of man is his great betrayer.

"Water constantly dripping wears away stone, eh? Bradley's nearly wearing away your faith in us! Ann, you're beginning to believe him."

She shook her head.

"I can't forget that man Smith. They left the grating in my cell door open, and I saw him as he passed – like a wild animal."

"He was sentenced to death yesterday," said Mark callously, and when he heard her exclamation of horror: "Well, my dear, if people do these things they've got to suffer for them! He'll meet Mr Steen."

"Mark!" she said in horror, and Mark grinned.

"I'm glad Tiser wasn't there when we met the hangman. He'd have thrown ten million fits. I'll bet he would have dropped dead in his tracks!"

"Your nerves must be like iron," she said.

"I've got none!" said Mark cheerfully. "Now, what about this flat? I think you'll be happy enough here," he said. "You needn't see any more of me than you want. I'd get a new lot of servants."

"Why?" she asked quickly.

"Well – it would be a little less embarrassing." Mark himself was slightly embarrassed when he saw her quiet smile.

"I see," she said.

And then something came over him – some urge, some wild desire, born in a second, and in a second satisfied. She was standing close to him; his hands had but to reach out to touch her. In an instant she was in his arms, and he was kissing the white face upturned to his. She did not fight; she stood stiffly erect, and something in her passivity chilled him and he let her go.

She walked over to the table where she had put her bag and opened it; took out something.

"You see this, Mark?"

He saw now – a little Browning pistol.

"Why are you carrying a gun?" he asked breathlessly, but she did not answer the question.

"The next time you do that – I will kill you."

Her voice was iron steady; there was not so much as a tremor in it. He was shocked.

"I'm not raving at you or having hysterics," she said. "I'm just telling you."

Mark was breathing heavily; found it more difficult to articulate than she.

"You're making a fuss about nothing," he said at last.

There was a knock at the door.

"It's a big thing for me," said Ann, as she walked from the room.

There was an elderly and patriarchal figure in the hall, and for a moment, at the sight of him, she forgot her anger.

"Good evening, my charming young lady," said Mr Sedeman in the lordly way. "Well, here am I, out again from durance! You had the good fortune – "

She laughed.

"You make me feel like a fellow-sufferer, Mr Sedeman. I was so sorry when I heard."

Mr Sedeman had been the guest of his country for three weeks, and was not ashamed to admit it.

"You know the police, my dear – they'll stop at nothing to bring a good man down. I am thinking of writing a book about it," he added gravely.

Mark came into the hall at that moment, and, though Mr Sedeman was by no means a welcome visitor, he was glad of his presence if it brought Ann to a new frame of mind. For old Mr Sedeman amused her. She had a soft spot in her heart for that venerable sinner, and required no invitation to return with him. She saw Mark's relief and smiled to herself, though Mark would go a long way before he wiped out the memory of that lapse of his.

"Have you sent your butler away?" asked Sedeman innocently. "You used to have rather an hospitable fellow – "

Mark pointed.

"There's a drink over there. Where are you staying?"

"I have abandoned the Home and changed my lodgings," said Mr Sedeman with a shrug. "My landlady's husband was rather offensive. I like her, but there was nothing wrong."

The audacity of this ancient philanderer took Ann's breath away for a moment.

"You're hopeless," she said, not without awe.

"Never without hope," said he, and held the glass to the light.

Evidently Sedeman wished to see his host alone. When she suggested this, Mr Sedeman, who had no finesse when business was on hand, admitted as much. At the door she turned.

"You heard, Mark, what Mr Sedeman said about living in the same house as an engaging female?"

She did not wait for his reply.

"Well, what do you want?" said Mark in his unfriendliest tone when they were left alone.

"A little help," said Mr Sedeman. "I have a very heavy bill to meet on Monday – my doctor – a veterinary surgeon."

Mark looked at him through narrowed eyelids.

"How long do you think this is going on?" he asked.

"For ever, I trust," said Mr Sedeman piously.

Mark's glance was murderous, but his visitor remained unwithered.

"Do you think I'm the sort of man who'll pay blackmail for ever? I don't believe you saw a thing at Lady's Stairs."

"I never said I did," said Mr Sedeman, "but I was in the house. You did not know that till I told you. I was a sort of boy messenger for dear old Li. There was, I believe, an interesting epistle which he wished me to deliver to Scotland Yard. Shall I put it vulgarly? It was a squeak. I was waiting downstairs – "

"Li Yoseph went out," said Mark deliberately.

"I heard him go out," said the calm Mr Sedeman. "It was a noisy exit!"

McGill went to the door to make sure that Ann had properly closed it.

"Does it occur to you that if I settled with Li Yoseph, I shouldn't think twice about settling with you?" he asked.

Mr Sedeman murmured something about "respect for one's elders."

"There's another thing," Mark went on. "I know that you're only guessing. But suppose you've guessed right, and something did happen, and Tiser put up a squeak – do you realise that you would be in this – up to your neck?"

The old man looked round uneasily.

"Mr Tiser would do nothing so dishonourable," he said. "I cannot imagine that he would ever bite the hand that feeds us."

Mark smiled.

"That's put the matter in another light, hasn't it?" Until he had poured out a drink Mr Sedeman did not reply.

"I saw nothing – I merely surmised. I brought an interesting theory to you, and you were kind enough to say that you'd be good to me. I can't help people being good to me. I seem to attract benevolence. Only this morning a lady stopped me and asked me to accept two shillings. I don't know whether she had any ulterior motive. She looked respectable."

Mark took a note from his pocket, fingered it to be sure that it was not two, and pushed it across the table.

"I'm giving you a tenner, and I want you to keep yourself reasonably sober and reasonably scarce. If you want a cheap thrill" – he took a small gold box out of his pocket – "have you ever tried this stuff?"

Mr Sedeman peered short-sightedly down at the little gold box and its crystalline contents.

"Are you trying to lead me astray?" he asked reproachfully.

"You'll get more fun out of a sniff of this than out of a bottle of whisky," suggested Mark.

Sedeman took the box from his hand and carried it towards the fireplace. Then, before Mark could realise what was happening, the old man had thrown the contents into the fire.

"You damned old fool, give me that!" cried Mark savagely, and gripped Sedeman by the arm, but the old man shook him off, and the arm that came round flung his assailant back against the table.

Mark could only stare at this amazing display of strength.

"I'll break your neck for that!" he breathed.

"The man who could break my neck could break records," said Sedeman, and Mark remembered, a little late, that this old man, whose age must be well over seventy, had been famous for forty years for the strength of his arm. "Try any of that rough stuff with me, my boy," he warned, "and I'll give you a punch in the jaw that'll make you think you've been hit by a steam-roller. I may be old, but I'm vigorous."

Mark forced a laugh.

"You've got a bit of brawn – Methuselah!"

"Methuselah is a compliment," said Sedeman, "if it's taken in the right way. I know I've wasted about five pounds' worth of dope, but it's dirty stuff, my boy. It's murder and suicide and lunatic asylums. If you ever want to tempt me, offer me the good brown wine of Scotland."

He turned his head quickly at the sound of hurrying footsteps. It was Tiser, breathless, white, beyond speech till Mark thrust him down into a chair.

"Get out," he said. "Take your money and clear."

The old man pocketed the note that was offered him, and was not unthankful for the diversion which led his benefactor to forget that he had already received a tenner. But he was loath to go.

"You can say anything you like before me."

Mark rang the bell, and, to Ledson:

"Show Mr Sedeman out."

The old man dropped his head on one side like a bird.

"Did you say 'show' or 'throw'? Oh, very well."

He strutted forth at his leisure. When the door had slammed:

"What's the trouble?"

Tiser recovered his voice now.

"One of those fellows has told the police everything."

"Which fellows?" asked Mark quickly.

"It isn't one of the men who tried to do Bradley," sobbed Tiser; "it's the driver."

Mark frowned down at him.

"Who is he? What could he have squeaked about?"

When Tiser mentioned his name, he remembered. An out-of-work lorry-driver, recently released from prison, whom he had employed to carry out urgent work.

"All the flyers are looking for the stuff," said the tremulous Tiser, "but the fellow who squeaked can't tell them where it's kept. He only knows it's in a garage in London. Bradley's crowd are combing the garages now. And, Mark, we've got the biggest parcel we've ever held – "

Mark stopped him with a gesture.

"They've been combing garages for this last week," he said.

But the situation was dangerous. If the police knew what they were after, if they had the slightest hint, ruin, imprisonment...anything might happen. If anybody scared him it was Tiser. The pitiable cowardice of the man made him capable of the basest treachery.

"We'll have to get the stuff away," he said.

"A hell of a chance there is of getting it away!" snapped Tiser fretfully. "There's a police tender on all the main roads out of London.

They're holding up cars at Savernake and Staines – that's how I got to hear of the squeak. I guessed something was wrong, Mark, and I put through a couple of inquiries."

"All the squads are out?" asked Mark.

"Every one of them – Bradley's on the job."

Mark strode up and down the big room, his hands behind him, his chin on his breast.

"It must be got out of London," he insisted, but Tiser made a gesture of despair.

"Whoever takes it will be pinched: there's nothing more certain than that," he said.

"Pinched or not, it must go. It will be easy to trace my connection with the garage – and there are a dozen guns there, too."

The two men looked at each other for a while, and Tiser read his partner's thoughts.

"We can't risk Ann – can we?" he asked.

Mark pursed his lips.

"Why not? It had better be found in her car than in my garage."

Some sense of the treachery that the man contemplated penetrated even the hide of Tiser.

"But – you – good God, Mark, you couldn't do that! They'd catch her. You know what Bradley is. If he got her again… You can't do that!"

"Why not?" asked Mark coolly. "Bradley's fond of her. He hid her up once: why shouldn't he hide her up again? If they find the stuff where it is they've got me on a felony charge. The worst they could do to her is to give her six months."

"But, my dear Mark," wailed the other, "you couldn't let that dear young lady go to prison!"

Mark regarded him balefully.

"Well, you take it – you can drive a car." And, as Tiser shrank back, his face contorted with terror at the suggestion: "You'd only get six months."

Tiser was silent. He made no reply, nor did Mark expect one. He rang the bell for Ledson.

"Can I phone to the Home?" asked Tiser. "I've got a man there collecting information – I want to know just where they are."

Mark shook his head.

"Not this phone," he said firmly. "There's a booth in Regent Street – go there; I'll go with you."

Ledson came in at that moment.

"Get me my coat and hat: I'm going out for five minutes."

When the man had retired:

"What a damned coward you are, Tiser! There's a drink over there."

But the shaking man had already found his way to the decanter. Mark heard the clatter of the bottle against the glass.

Ledson returned with his coat and hat.

"Ask Miss Perryman if she'll kindly come over in a few minutes; it's rather important," he said.

He had to drag Tiser away from the sideboard. Minutes counted now. Mark sensed the urgency of the situation. The stuff had to be got out of London, and there was only one person he could trust to do it – Ann. There was no need to call her: she telephoned through almost as the door slammed on Mark, and Ledson gave her the message.

He was tidying up the room when he heard a knock at the door, and went out instantly to open it. The man he expected was standing on the mat.

"Come in, Mr Bradley," said Ledson nervously. He followed the detective into the sitting-room. "Mr McGill will be back very soon. I thought you weren't coming till later."

"Where has he gone?"

"He's gone to telephone, sir. I think I'd better clear out – I can always say you sent me."

Bradley nodded. Left alone, he strolled about the room, but made no attempt to examine the papers on Mark's desk or to conduct anything in the nature of a search.

He was looking at the photographs on the mantelpiece and wondering whether McGill had relations, when he heard a key turn in the lock and the front door close. He turned about, expecting to

135

see Mark, but it was Ann who stood in the doorway, surveying him with a look of blank surprise.

"Good evening," said Bradley gravely.

"Why…good evening, Mr Bradley," she stammered. Her voice and manner betrayed embarrassment.

Ledson, who had not left the flat, came in at that moment.

"It's all right, Ledson: I let myself in with a key," she said hastily. "Mr McGill lent it me this morning." Her voice rose with the last sentence, and she laid a small flat key ostentatiously on the table. "Remind him that I left it."

Ledson looked from one to the other.

"Nothing I can do for you, miss?"

She shook her head, and, when he had gone:

"I don't usually carry the keys of other people's flats."

There was a certain defiance in her tone, as though she were inviting him to challenge the statement.

"I am sure you don't," he smiled. There followed an awkward pause.

"Won't you sit down?" He pulled up a chair.

Again a pause.

"I've often wondered what I should say to you – when I had an opportunity of saying anything. I did not have that the other night, did I? I am terribly ashamed of myself."

He knew to which incident she referred.

"I don't think you were quite normal that day."

She shrugged.

"Well…no. I'm glad you think that. It is very – generous of you. I am so pleased you didn't get into trouble through my stupidity."

She picked up the key from the table and played with it, and he knew that she was deliberately calling his attention to her entrance.

"It is curious that I should have let myself into this flat tonight – Mr McGill lent me the key because I wanted to come in when he was out, you know…to find things…sometimes I leave things behind. I'm rather careless…not that I'm often here."

She was a trifle incoherent. Bradley was secretly amused.

"A key is very convenient," he said.

"Yes, but I don't often – I don't think I've borrowed it more than once." She laughed nervously. "I don't know why I'm talking about it, but I'm sure you're not the kind of man who would think things about people – uncharitable things."

Bradley thought a lot of uncharitable things about people, but not about her. He told her so, and she was childishly pleased.

"Really?" she asked eagerly.

"Nothing like the uncharitable things that you think about me," he said severely.

She shook her head.

"I don't know. I wish I could do some penance for my past stupidity – for striking you, for saying the things I said in court."

"I'll give you a penance," he answered quickly. "I want you to promise me that in no circumstances will you go out of the house this night."

"But I don't live here, you know." She was insistent upon this. "My flat is on the other side of the landing – I don't really live here. This is Mr McGill's flat – I use it quite a lot, but – "

"Very well; promise me that you won't leave this building tonight," said Bradley.

"I don't intend leaving it – "

"You might not intend leaving it now," he interrupted; "but I want you to promise me that nothing will induce you to leave this building tonight – nothing!"

She smiled at his vehemence.

"Suppose there's a fire?"

"Don't be silly," he said, almost testily, and they laughed together.

"Don't tell me I'm silly: it infuriates me. All right, I promise."

"Word of honour?" said Bradley.

"Word of honour," said Ann solemnly.

Their hands gripped on the bond. His relief was so evident that she was a little alarmed, and asked him why. His answer that it was a miserable night seemed rather futile.

"I mean for driving a car."

Ann looked at him steadily.

"You thought I might be getting into mischief tonight? You're quite a guardian angel! But how could I? You've been very careful to take my licence away!"

"Even unlicensed drivers have taken a car out," he said good-humouredly.

There was another lacuna in the conversation. Then she said suddenly, as though she were voicing a thought:

"Did you – no, I won't ask you that."

"Go on," he encouraged.

"Did you – look after Ronnie as you're looking after me?"

"I tried to," said Bradley quietly; "but you don't believe that?"

Ann sighed heavily.

"I do," she said, and at that moment they heard the sound of the door opening and Mark's voice in the hall.

He came in, his face as black as thunder.

"Well, Bradley, what do you want?"

Bradley looked past him, saw Tiser hanging his hat in the hall, and waited till the other man came in.

"I want a little talk."

"Friendly?" asked Mark, with a scowl.

"More or less," said the other coolly. Mark looked at the girl.

"All right, my dear, I'll see you in about five minutes," he said, but Bradley interposed.

"Miss Perryman can hear all that I've got to say – it is about Li Yoseph."

Mark was obviously relieved.

"Oh, only that! I saw some of your flyers about tonight…don't tell me you've found Li Yoseph? You know my view: he got away to Holland – there was a Dutch ship going down on the tide that night. He had pals on board all of them."

A little smile flickered at the corner of Bradley's mouth.

"That's your theory, is it? Well, we gave up dragging nearly a month ago."

"A month ago?" repeated Mark. "A year after his disappearance? You're a patient crowd."

"Immensely," said Bradley. "Patience is our favourite game."

"Mine is – " began Mark.

"Beggar your neighbour," said Bradley instantly. "You rather liked Li Yoseph, didn't you, Miss Perryman?"

She nodded.

"Yes. I only saw him for a few minutes, but there was something rather pathetic about him – something rather sweet. His imaginary children... I almost saw them."

"Fearfully unnerving, my dear young friend," quavered Tiser's voice.

He almost ducked behind McGill when the detective's head was turned in his direction.

"Hallo, Tiser, you're here, I see! He unnerved you, did he?"

"What do you want to know about the old man?" asked Mark gruffly.

The presence of the detective infuriated him. That he should have been alone with Ann, even for a few minutes, set his suspicious mind working.

"Do you know anything about his present place of residence?" asked Bradley.

"Li Yoseph? I've told you, no. You're devilishly mysterious, Inspector."

"We thrive on mysteries," said Bradley coolly. He met the girl's eyes. "You weren't afraid of him, were you? Of course you weren't." He smiled again, picked up his hat and walked to the door.

"Good night, Miss Perryman – it is a miserable night."

She knew what he meant.

"Good night, McGill – I don't suppose I shall meet you on the Great West Road?"

For a long time after he had gone nobody spoke.

"What is he driving at?" asked Mark at last.

"That man's inhuman, Mark," twittered Tiser. "There's something behind all this – there is, I'm sure! Miserable night – Great West Road; do you think he knows?"

Mark rang the bell for Ledson.

"I shan't want you again tonight," he said, and the man was out of the room in a second.

He saw Ann moving towards the door and stopped her.

"Don't go, my dear. I hope you're not very tired?"

"Why?" she asked.

Mark looked at Tiser and then at her.

"I wanted your help tonight," he said.

There was another who would have liked to disappear.

"Can I slip away, my dear Mark?" pleaded Tiser. "I am feeling none too well."

"Stay here," snapped Mark. "I want you to take Ann to the garage."

She looked up at this.

"To the garage? Tonight?"

"To the place in the Edgware Road," said Mark easily. "I had your car taken round there after that affair. I thought it might be useful in case of an accident – and the accident has happened."

She came back and sat down on the chair which Bradley had vacated.

"I know you'll help me, my dear; I'm really in a tight place. There are ten kilos of stuff here – and a dozen automatics. You'll find the box just behind the petrol tins."

Her mouth opened in amazement.

"Automatics – pistols?"

"Yes; I got them from Belgium for sale," said Mark irritably. "There's a big profit on them. I want all this junk taken to Bristol tonight. I've got a man there who'll put them in a safe place."

"You've done it before, my dear," pleaded Tiser. "It's only a little thing…"

"Bradley's not on the job either," Mark went on. "Don't take the Bath Road: go by Uxbridge and branch off – "

"I can't," said Ann.

His eyes narrowed.

"What? You can't? You mean you won't?"

"I can't leave this building tonight."

"Why not?" asked Mark.

She shrugged her shoulders.

"I just can't, that's all. Besides, I haven't a driving licence. You seem to have overlooked that little point."

"Nobody's going to know that," said Mark. "I want you to do this to oblige me."

Ann shook her head.

"To oblige nobody."

Mark McGill walked up to her, dropped his hand on her shoulder and looked her straight in the eyes.

"What is the matter?"

"I'm not going out tonight," she said, slowly and deliberately.

"But don't you realise," wailed Tiser, "that poor, dear Mark and you and everybody may be in terrible danger if you don't do this?"

"I'm not leaving this building tonight," repeated Ann. "I'll go tomorrow if you wish."

"Tomorrow will be too late," said Mark. "Now do be reasonable, Ann. You know I wouldn't insist if there were not a very good reason. And you know that I wouldn't send you out if there were any risk to you."

"I'm not worrying about the risk," said Ann quietly; "I don't want to go, that's all."

Tiser made a whimpering noise, but the other silenced him with an oath.

"Leave her alone. All right, Ann, have your own way. Don't go, my dear." He took up a cigar and lit it. "What did Bradley have to talk about?"

The subject was definitely changed.

"Nothing very much," said Ann.

"I really wonder you can talk to the man at all," said Tiser, mopping his wet face.

"What did he say?" asked Mark.

Ann shrugged indifferently.

"How d'you do, and all that sort of thing."

"Was he here when you came in?"

She nodded.

"Didn't Ledson tell you he was here?"

"No," said Ann. "I let myself in with the key." A slow smile dawned on Mark's face.

"Oh ho! That was rather a smack in the eye for him."

She considered this.

"I don't think it was," she said.

She had walked across to the big piano and stood deep in thought, her fingers touching the notes.

"He isn't the kind of man who would think – nastily."

Again Mark smiled.

"Indeed?"

She sat down at the piano and ran her fingers softly over the keys; played a bar of "Lohengrin" and stopped.

"I suppose he deals with so many rotten people that it is difficult to feel nicely about anybody," she said. "It is curious he should talk about Li Yoseph – I've been thinking a lot about him today."

Mark stood regarding her, a heavy frown on his face.

"I've never seen you in this mood, Ann." And then, irritably: "Stop twiddling on that piano – play something; you haven't played for weeks."

She started guiltily.

"I don't feel like playing," she said, and then: "Oh, very well...do you remember how that magistrate said 'Very well'?"

She played with the soft pedal down. Mark beckoned Tiser to him.

"There's something wrong with Ann," he said under his breath.

"I don't understand it," shivered Tiser. "My nerves are all on edge."

Ann called out from the piano. "Turn off some of those lights – I can't play Chopin in this blaze."

Mark went over to the switch and turned out all the lights but the standard lamp near the piano and the two candle-lights in the wall above the fireplace; and, as each light went out, Tiser screwed up his face into a grimace of utter misery.

"Gives me the creeps; she's damnably temperamental, that girl, Mark."

But McGill was not listening to him.

"Why is that fellow interested in Li Yoseph?" he asked.

Tiser looked round and lowered his voice.

"Do you think he knows he's alive?"

"Alive? You damned fool!" said Mark contemptuously. "I shot him at six paces. I could see the mark where the bullet hit his spine – alive! He couldn't have escaped; it was absolutely impossible. He's in that mud-hole under the house."

The music changed; the tune was now eerily familiar. She was playing the "Chanson d'Adieu." Tiser gripped his arm.

"Mark! Do you hear what she's playing? Stop her, Mark, for God's sake! It's the tune he used to play on his fiddle!"

"Shut up, you fool!" growled Mark. "It would take more than a tune to make me shake."

Suddenly Ann's music stopped with a crash and she looked up.

"What is it? Did you hear anything?" she asked.

"I heard nothing. You probably heard Tiser speaking."

She shook her head.

"It was the sound of a violin," she said.

"Imagination," said Mark.

Even as he spoke, he heard the faint notes of a fiddle floating through the room. It was the tune that old Li played, taken up from the air that Ann had been strumming on the piano.

"Listen!"

It came from the next room – from Mark's bedroom. "Somebody's playing the fool," said McGill, took one step, and then he saw the door of his bedroom slowly open, and there shuffled into the light...

"Li Yoseph!" he gasped.

A little greyer, a little more bent, his hair a little more unkempt; the old fur hat greasier and more battered. His fiddle was under his arm; he held the bow in his blue-veined hand.

Ann had risen from the piano and was standing watching, not in fear, but intensely absorbed in this apparition. She heard a scream from Tiser and saw him fall flat upon the floor, his face hidden in his arms.

"Take him away! Take him away!... You're dead...six paces!"

"Li Yoseph!" breathed Mark again.

The old man showed his uneven teeth in a grin. "Ah, der goot Mark! Und der goot Tiser! Komm in, my leedle ones!" He waved into the room his invisible little children. "See der goot friendts of Li Yoseph...you see, little Heinrich und Hans? It is der goot Mark."

"Where – where have you come from?" asked Mark huskily.

"From all der places dat I know." The visitor chuckled. "You kommen soon to Lady's Stairs, eh, Mark? Und you, young lady, who is Ronnie's sister – you komm and see Li Yoseph? Soon you will komm?"

Ann nodded.

"I tell you. When the police give me my house I will send for you."

No further word he spoke to Mark or to the writhing coward on the floor. He shuffled across the room, and Mark did not challenge him. The big man watched him, petrified with amazement, and soon after heard the front door slam.

The sound of it seemed to awaken him from his daze. He flew down the passage, flung open the door and ran down the stairs; but Li Yoseph was not in sight. As he came back to his sitting-room he heard the telephone bell sound shrilly, and went to the instrument.

"Is that you, McGill?" It was Bradley's voice. "I am Inspector Bradley. I'm speaking from Scotland Yard. I understand Li Yoseph is in London – I think I ought to warn you."

"Why warn me?" asked Mark furiously.

"If you don't know, nobody knows," was the cryptic reply, and he heard the click of the receiver as it was hung up.

17

Up and down the drab streets which crowd around Lady's Stairs the rumour ran swiftly. Li Yoseph had returned. Nobody was really surprised. Li Yoseph, with his ghost children, had something of immortality in him. And he was wide – there wasn't a wider man than old Li Yoseph in the world. Hadn't he carried on his business under the very nose of the police, and diddled every busy who tried to shop him? The Meadows and the dingy thoroughfares about settled down to the discussion of one problem: would Li Yoseph be pinched or would he not?

Everybody knew now why the police had stopped their dragging. How like the old boy to give them so much trouble, and wait till the very last minute before he showed himself!

Nobody had seen him, but the untidy Mrs Shiffan, who "did" for him, and her shiftless husband had gone importantly to Lady's Stairs and let themselves in. The keys had come to them the night before, with a scribbled note telling them to make the house tidy.

Mrs Shiffan was a whining young woman, not without her personal attractions. Her husband, whom she met between bouts of imprisonment, became a person of importance, but even after his return from Lady's Stairs he could give no information about Li Yoseph, except that it was to a very untidy house he was returning.

"The police has been everywhere," he said despairingly; "pulled up the boards, pulled down the ceilings – old Li ought to get a thousand pounds out of 'em."

The policeman on the beat could supply no information either, but gave the impression that he could. One morning the neighbour-

145

hood saw Bradley arrive and pass into the house. He came out and drove away; but still there were no signs of Li. The rumour spread that he was under detention, but there was no substantial basis for the rumour. It was believed that old Li had many quiet pitches in London whither he could retire in the event of trouble, and it was accepted as a most likely possibility that in one of these he had spent the last year.

Ann Perryman was more interested than perturbed by the reappearance of the old man, but she could not fail to notice the effect it had on Mark McGill and his friend. Mark became sullen, uncommunicative, bad-tempered; he spent a lot of time behind the locked door of his bedroom. Once, when she came in to see him, she found the grate choked with the black ashes of paper.

Tiser conveyed the impression of a normal condition of drunkenness. He was never wholly sober, never objectionably inebriated; only he grew a little more incoherent than usual, and some instinct in him drew him nearer to the girl. It was as though he recognised in her the elements and possibilities of safety.

There was no patent reason why Mark should be disgruntled. The imminent danger which threatened him had passed. By a fluke he had succeeded in inducing one of the inmates of Tiser's home to carry a dangerous cargo to Bristol – only just in time, as it proved, for half an hour after the car had disappeared came the police, who made a very careful search of the garage.

Mark's nerves, he boasted, were like iron; yet he had been to some extent shaken by the persistence of Bradley, and now that Li Yoseph had returned he recognised how serious was the situation. From the night Li Yoseph had appeared, only to vanish instantly, he had not seen him again. He had called at Lady's Stairs, only to find Mr and Mrs Shiffan engaged in preparation for the wanderer's return. The old man remained apparently more elusive than he had ever been.

"Once bitten, twice shy, my dear Mark," said Tiser tremulously. "You don't expect this fellow will give you another chance to – "

His trembling hand strayed to his lips.

"Li Yoseph is working with Bradley," said Mark harshly. "If you think he isn't, you've got a shock coming. He has told Bradley everything that happened."

"Then why, if you will excuse the question, doesn't Bradley arrest you for the attempted murder?"

Mark shook his head, and his lips pursed in a smile.

"Because he wants me for Ronnie: that's as clear as daylight. The evidence of old Yoseph isn't sufficient to get a conviction. He's waiting for another squeaker."

His keen eyes were on his companion, and he saw a strange look come in his face.

"They wouldn't accept your evidence, Tiser," he said with a sneer. "Get that idea out of your mind!"

"I swear to you – " began Tiser, but Mark McGill cut him short.

"That's the only satisfaction I have – that you can't possibly round on me," he said. "If there's any swinging to do, there will be two of us going to the scaffold – to meet Mr Steen."

Tiser shivered.

"I wish you wouldn't talk like that," he whined. "Scaffold! What does Ann say about it?"

Mark was silent, Ann had said singularly little, but her attitude was eloquent.

"You don't think she's – weakening?" asked Tiser anxiously. And then, after a moment: "I had an idea – "

"The first I've heard about it," snapped Mark. "You're talking of Ann, aren't you – and Bradley?"

Tiser nodded.

"You don't think she's in love with him?" he scoffed.

To his amazement, Tiser nodded.

Tiser he despised for his cowardice, for all the sneaking quantities in his make-up, for his sliminess, his hypocrisy – but he respected the man's judgment. He had an uncanny knack of discovery which was almost divination.

"You think Ann's fond of him?" he asked in amazement.

Tiser nodded.

"And that he knows?"

Tiser nodded again.

He went to the door and peered out. The servant was nowhere in sight, and he came tiptoeing back to his companion. That was a favourite and dramatic gesture of his, but this time Mark was neither amused nor was he wrathful.

"Does it occur to you, my dear fellow," he said breathlessly, "that Ann may be a very great – asset?"

McGill turned sharply at this and stared down with his cold, snake eyes into the face of the other.

"An asset? Of course she's an asset, and will be more of one when she gets her licence back."

Tiser pulled up a chair to the table, and, sitting down, signalled his chief to a vacant chair.

"Let us think of it for a moment, my dear fellow," he went on, with a beaming smile which did not quite fit in either with his face or voice.

The gesture was so imperious that for the moment Mark was startled into obedience. It was not till he sat down that he realised that for the first time he was acting under the instructions of Tiser, and he was both bewildered and annoyed.

"What is your big idea?" he asked angrily.

Tiser looked past him; it was very difficult to get this sleek man to meet your eye.

"Bradley perjured himself to save our dear Ann," he said, in his mincing, genteel way. "He couldn't exactly hide up a crime more serious."

Mark looked at him from under his lowered eyelids.

"I don't quite see what you're driving at."

Mr Tiser smiled – it was a pained but humble smile.

"Does it occur to you that we might give our friend Bradley a very complete occupation? God forbid that I should hurt Ann, or place her in a position of – er – shall I say peril? But suppose – just imagine this, my dear Mark – suppose he held Ann Perryman on another charge...a more serious charge. Suppose, against his will, he had to give evidence against – a murderess?"

Mark came to his feet instantly.

"What are you driving at?" he asked harshly. "Ann Perryman isn't a murderess – "

At that moment he understood how much more quickly Mr Tiser's brain worked.

"Ann is an encumbrance," Tiser went on. "I have an idea she hasn't been very kind to you, my poor friend. And there is a break coming – "

"How do you know that?" demanded Mark quickly.

Tiser smiled.

"There are so many facts that come to me," he said. "Also she may be a source of danger. Would it not be possible to – " He spread out his hands and shrugged his shoulders, and did not complete the sentence.

Mark stared at him in bewilderment.

"You want to fix Bradley – yes? And you expect me to settle the girl?"

Again Tiser nodded.

"Imagine," he went on slowly, "that this girl was held on a capital charge – discredit from the outset – with Bradley as her chief prosecutor, breaking his heart over her. I don't think he could hide up that, my dear Mark."

Mark McGill did not take his eyes from his companion.

"Have you fixed the murder?" he asked sarcastically.

Tiser smiled very broadly.

"That is the easiest task," he said with a sly smile.

Mark McGill thought quickly, and at last:

"I think I can give you a better solution," he said slowly, "and a more important victim than you can suggest."

Mark went into his bedroom and made his hand a little picturesque. Then he crossed the landing and knocked at Ann's door. She opened it herself, and at the sight of him the reserve that had grown up between them was broken down.

149

"What on earth has happened to your hand?" she asked.

His hand was heavily bandaged; he carried it in a black silk sling.

"It is nothing. I was starting up my car and the handle kicked back," he said; "but it's rather a nuisance. You wouldn't like to act as secretary for me? There are one or two important letters I wish to write."

She hesitated for a moment; her natural sympathies urged her to help him, her natural suspicion held her back.

"I can't use a typewriter."

"It doesn't matter," he said. "I only want a note or two written. I'm in rather a fix."

"Of course I'll help you, Mark," she said, and followed him back to his flat – it was the first time she had been there since the night of Bradley's visit.

The first letter he dictated, slowly, was to a man in Paris, asking him to postpone a visit which he had apparently contemplated. The next letter…

"I want a note to go to Tiser," he said. "I dare not telephone because our friend Bradley has probably a man listening-in at the exchange. Start it 'My dear friend'."

Ann carried out his instructions.

"Say this," dictated Mark: " 'I have something of the greatest importance to tell you. Can you meet me in the park opposite Queen's Gate at eleven o'clock tonight? Come alone.' You needn't sign it: he'll know who it's from."

She handed him the letter, and he read it with no evidence of the exultation which filled his heart. Bradley would recognise the writing.

18

It was no unusual thing for Ann Perryman to act as secretary to Mark. He hated letter-writing, and the peculiar nature of his business prohibited the employment of an ordinary stenographer. During the weeks of her inaction she was glad to find some employment. Mark had given her a great deal of correspondence dealing with the more innocuous of his importations. It was perfectly true that he had begun his career as a smuggler of dutiable articles, and had made a very handsome profit therefrom. The new and more sinister traffic arose out of this, and Mark had pursued his nefarious course with such success, and had enjoyed so much immunity, that he had grown just a little careless.

This he was the first to recognise. He had no illusions; he knew that the police were infinitely patient, and that they were literally weaving the net about him. There was no apparent evidence that they were actively engaged in trapping him, and yet he knew that at that moment he was to all intents and purposes a prisoner. He had sent his passport to be renewed at the Foreign Office, and had received a curt note, telling him that owing to "certain irregularities" there would be a delay in reissuing the document. This in itself was no great hardship, for Mark had two or three passports in different names; but he knew all too well that an attempt on his part to leave England on one of these might lead to irretrievable disaster.

Ann had ceased to be an asset: she was becoming an increasing danger, and he must get rid of her. Tiser, villain as he was, would have been horrified if he could have read the black mind of his friend and partner.

And yet, such was the peculiar mentality of Mark McGill, that he felt no hatred of the woman whose life he would soon jeopardise. There was nothing of malignity in his plan, conceived so cold-bloodedly. She was just the cause which would produce a certain effect. His passion, suddenly inflamed, had as suddenly grown cold again. In this spirit of indifference Mark McGill lived – and would probably die.

He folded the letter carefully and placed it in an envelope. This he addressed with great care to Chief Inspector Bradley of Scotland Yard. A cab took him to the West End, and at Charing Cross Post Office he dropped the letter into the box with a little satisfied smile.

Half an hour after Ann had written the letter, and whilst she was changing her dress in preparation for a walk, her telephone bell rang, and she was a little disconcerted to hear the voice of Tiser. That sleek man had only once before called her on the telephone. His voice was normally agitated, and his first sentence was so incomprehensible that she asked him to repeat it.

"…to Bristol. Will you tell our dear friend that I lost the first train, but I am leaving at midday. I tried to get him on the phone. You know what Mark is, my dear young lady – so terribly autocratic."

"Did he know you were going to Bristol?" she asked after a pause.

"My dear little friend, of course he knows," said Tiser's voice irritably. "I promised to leave by the ten o'clock – "

"Are you coming back tonight?" she interrupted.

"Tomorrow night – I was most anxious to return tonight, but Mark…well, you know what Mark is! Is there any news, my young friend? I am depressed – my nerves are in rags! Don't you think it's possible you could speak to dear Mr Bradley and persuade him that there is no harm in the Home? The police pursue these poor, unfortunate fellows with a malignity which is beyond understanding. That man Sedeman, too, is giving us a great deal of trouble. I am not sure that he isn't engaged in" – he lowered his voice – "police work. You will tell Mark?"

Before she could reply he had hung up the telephone. Ann sat down at her writing-table, her hands clasped before her, a frown on her pretty face. Mark knew that this man was going out of London, knew that he would not be back that night. Why, then, had he written this note? And why had he addressed him as "My dear friend"? She knew from what Tiser said that relations were strained between them, and Mark was not the kind of man who would indulge in empty compliments.

Now that she came to think of it, Mark never wrote to Tiser; and if he wrote at all, why should he make an appointment in the park? The police knew that Tiser was in the habit of calling at the flat; there was no secret about the association of the two men.

She thought for a long time and then made a decision. Mark was out, his servant told her: he had left a quarter of an hour before. She went into the sitting-room. On the writing-table were envelopes and note-paper, and in the waste-paper basket a torn envelope. She took this out, saw the word "Cheif" – Mark always made the mistake of putting the "e" before the "i" in the word "Chief."

She stared at the envelope, puzzled; and then the truth dawned on her and she gasped. That was the envelope he had begun to write to Chief Inspector Bradley – and he was sending the letter she had written. She tried hard to remember every sentence, but she had paid such little attention to the note that she could only recall the purport. It was a letter written in her own hand and had been addressed to Bradley – Bradley would know her writing and would come to that rendezvous in the belief that she had something to communicate to him. Why did Mark wish to bring him there? She went cold at the thought.

When she got back to her own flat the telephone was ringing furiously. It was Tiser again, and his voice was shrill with anxiety.

"Is that you, my dear Miss Perryman? I am not going to Bristol – my memory is simply terrible. I have only just remembered that Mark said he was sending me a letter today – rather an important one."

A faint smile curled her lips.

"When did you remember this?" she asked. "He hasn't by any chance – " She stopped herself in time.

"Only a few moments ago," said the voice. "It is quite unnecessary to give my message to Mark. I am sending another – um – gentleman."

She was still smiling a little hardly when she hung up the receiver. Mark must have called up the Home to find out if Tiser had gone, and learned from him that he had been in communication with her. Hence Tiser's agitation.

Her own peril did not occur to her. That such a letter, found in the possession of a killed or wounded Bradley, must be deadly evidence against her, she did not even think about. She saw only the danger to Bradley, and with infinite trouble got herself connected with Scotland Yard.

Bradley was out; she spoke to his clerk.

"When he comes in, will you ask him to call me up?" she said, and gave her name.

She thought the clerk's tone sounded a little surprised.

"All right, miss, I'll see to that," he said, and she settled down to wait for Bradley's call.

The afternoon came before she realised she had eaten nothing since breakfast time, and she prepared herself a little lunch. She had already dismissed her one servant, and was undertaking the housework herself. She had employed the last day or two in a search for a flat. Obviously she must break instantly with Mark McGill and his gang.

She had a little money; Mark had paid her well, but she had not saved. She could go back to her teaching; and her first act after the night Li Yoseph appeared was to write to the old school at Auteuil and ask for a position. An answer had come, saying that the principal was away in the south of France – she must wait until she could discover whether that avenue of escape was open.

Four o'clock came, and still no message from Bradley. At six o'clock she rang up Scotland Yard, but could not get in touch with the man she had spoken with that morning. Bradley apparently had been in, "to collect his letters." She asked for information as to his present whereabouts, but that either could not or would not be given. The man who spoke to her, however, said that Bradley had only been in for a few minutes, and obviously her message had not been delivered to him.

With the passing of the hours her fears grew. At half-past ten o'clock she put on her coat and went out. On the doorstep she met Mark McGill coming in.

"Hallo!" he said in surprise. "Where are you going?"

"For a little walk," she said.

"I'll come with you," he suggested.

She shook her head.

"I don't think I want you, Mark," she said.

Her apparent cheerfulness deceived him — the fact that she was going out at all at that hour was all to the good.

"Don't get into mischief," he said good-humouredly. She reached Queen's Gate at a quarter to eleven, and as she came to the park gates she heard the clang of an ambulance bell, and her heart turned sick.

She saw the figure of a man — it was a park-keeper — coming slowly and suspiciously towards her.

"Has there — has there been an accident?" she asked faintly.

"Yes, miss; a man was knocked down near Marble Arch. I don't think he's badly hurt."

She nodded, too breathless for speech, and with a word of thanks hurried past him, crossed the road and walked a little distance.

There was only one pedestrian in sight. He passed, looking sideways at her, and was on the point of speaking when she turned abruptly away. A vacant-faced youth, who could be dealt with if he became offensive. He stopped, hesitated for a moment, then resumed his walk.

From what point would Bradley appear, and where would the danger come from? Danger there was — she was sure of this.

A policeman loomed out of the darkness. She was almost hysterically grateful to see him, and did not even resent his curt inquiry.

"Now, young lady, you oughtn't to be in the park at this time of night."

"I'm expecting – a friend," she said huskily.

She could feel his keen eyes scrutinising her, and could guess just what his thoughts were.

"I advise you to go home, miss."

And then she had an inspiration.

"I'm waiting to see Detective Inspector Bradley of Scotland Yard," she said breathlessly, and could see the man was impressed.

"Oh, are you, miss? Well, that's a different matter."

"I wish you'd stay till he comes," she went on. "I – I want to warn him about something. I'm afraid there's going to be an attack made upon him."

The man bent his head a little towards her.

"I've seen you – aren't you the young lady who was charged a few weeks ago? I was down in that court, giving evidence. Miss Perryman, isn't it?"

"Yes," she said.

He looked from her to the gate, and seemed undecided.

"Does Mr Bradley know you're coming?"

"I – I think so," she answered.

At that moment she saw a figure come swinging through the gate, and half crossed the road to meet him.

"Do you want to see me?" said Bradley quickly. "What is the trouble? I only had your letter at half-past ten tonight when I came back. I telephoned to you, but you were out."

Then he saw the policeman.

"What does he want?" he asked.

She explained, a little incoherently, why she had come, and then:

"I asked him to stay. I didn't know if you might need help."

"You didn't send the letter to me, of course?"

She shook her head.

"McGill did that?"

The question alarmed her. Until then she had not realised that she might be doing Mark irreparable injury, and that was the last thing she wished to do.

"I only know I wrote it. And then it struck me that you might think I had written to you – "

"Which I did," he said with a little smile.

He looked up and down the deserted roadway.

"Constable, go up there. Stand ready to offer any assistance that's required. You know me?"

"Yes, I know you, Mr Bradley."

"Good!" said Bradley, and laughed. "I don't know what use you're going to be to me... Yes, I do – search the ground at the back of me, and see if there's anybody lying on the grass."

The constable disappeared.

"Now, Ann Perryman, what am I going to do with you?"

"Do you think there's any danger?" she asked in a horrified whisper.

He nodded.

"I think so. McGill knew, of course, that I should recognise your handwriting, and he knew a little more – just how I feel about you, Ann."

She was silent at this.

"Do you want me to go away?" she asked. "Couldn't I find another policeman for you?"

At that moment a church bell struck eleven.

"It's too late, I'm afraid," said Bradley. He put his hand in his hip pocket and took out something that glistened in the light. Looking to the left, he saw the dim lights of a car moving along the centre of the road, coming towards the gate, and he guessed that here was the danger. He called sharply to the officer, and turning to the girl, he gripped her arm and half pushed her over the low rail separating the park from the pathway.

"Lie down – flat on your face," he commanded.

"But – " she began.

"Don't argue; do as I tell you."

In another instant she found herself lying on the grass, her face wet with dew. From where she lay she could see the car. It was moving a little more quickly now. Suddenly it swerved towards the place where Bradley was standing. And then – She could not tell whether three or four shots were fired. She heard the whistle and whine of bullets which seemed to pass close to her and thudded into the ground behind. Then she heard a police whistle blow, and the car passed out of her line of vision.

It was Bradley shooting now. She heard the staccato "pang!" of his automatic, and the sound of running feet.

"Get up and go home!" shouted Bradley's voice.

When she got to her knees he had disappeared.

Police whistles were shrilling in every direction. Crossing the road, she ran against the park-keeper, and from him had a brief account of what had happened.

"The car passed out of the gate like a streak…was nearly run down by an omnibus…went down Exhibition Road at full pelt. Did you see the shooting?"

She shook her head.

"Where is Mr Bradley? Is that the man who was chasing them? He got on a taxi, and he's following them."

At that moment the big policeman came up, very out of breath, and more distressed than any policeman she had ever seen.

"Somebody shot at him from the car. Were you there, miss?"

She told him she was lying on the ground.

The policeman was stolidly aware of one duty.

"I'm afraid I'll have to take your name and address," he said, and seemed more comfortable when he had inscribed these in his little paper-covered notebook.

He seemed, however, in some doubt as to whether he should let her go, but eventually she persuaded him, and she went back to her flat, dreading to meet Mark's eye. Mark apparently was wholly incurious. She gained her own flat without meeting him, and sat for the greater part of an hour trying to put the chaos of her mind in order.

The door bell rang and her heart sank. It was Mark. She would have to tell him…

It was Bradley. She nearly wept with relief at the sight of him.

"It was an old dodge – they've tried it on before," he said as soon as he was in her room. "Except that the car was armour-plated – we found it abandoned in Pimlico. The interior was lined with sheet-iron – these birds took no risk."

He looked at her oddly for a moment.

"As I'm not killed – you will not be arrested," he said.

She stared at him open-mouthed.

"I arrested? Why?" she asked.

"Don't you realise that if I had been killed or badly hurt, and my colleagues had come to investigate the matter, the first thing they would have looked for would have been some explanation as to my presence near Queen's Gate at that fatal hour, and they would have found your letter, and would have had no difficulty in identifying you, because I had very foolishly written in pencil the word 'Ann' where your signature should have been?"

He saw the bewilderment and horror that came into her eyes.

"But that was unintentional," she blurted. "He could never have meant that – I mean, to incriminate me."

He made no immediate reply.

"You don't dream he would have done such a thing?" she asked.

"I'm going to find out," he said. "I gather that you aren't anxious to appear in this matter, and I'll keep your name out of it as far as I can."

He rang at Mark's flat, and she listened behind her own closed door with a beating heart and heard Mark's servant explain that his master had been out since ten o'clock. He said something else, and then she heard the door close and Bradley's knuckles tap gently on the panel of her door. She opened it to him.

"McGill was at the Craley Restaurant. He came in to tell his servant he was going, and must have followed you out. And at the Craley Restaurant he was, I'll swear, at the time of the shooting. He is a great establisher of alibis."

"You didn't find the men who were in the car?"

He shook his head.

"No. The car was stolen at Highbury last week. Its sheet-iron fittings could have been bought anywhere." And then, abruptly: "Good night, Ann."

Her hand went into his and he held it for a moment.

"What are we going to do with you, Ann?" he said.

She shook her head.

"I don't know. I'm going to get back to Paris if I can." And then, as a thought occurred to her: "Have you seen Li Yoseph?"

He nodded.

"Yes; he's going down to Lady's Stairs tomorrow. You'll find him a good friend if you're in any kind of trouble."

She was startled to hear this, and looked at him in amazement.

"Li Yoseph a good friend? I thought he was – "

"He's had twelve months to recover from his evil habits," he said with a smile. "I only want to tell you that you can trust him. You're not frightened of him?"

"You asked me that before," she smiled.

And then, in the most natural way in the world, he bent forward and she felt his lips for an instant against her cheek.

"Good night, Ann," he said, and patted her gently on the arm.

She stood where he had left her, motionless, her breath coming a little quicker, trying to analyse her own emotions. Of one thing she was certain: she did not resent that kiss.

Bradley was a good prophet. There was evidence enough at the restaurant to which Mark had gone that he had been there when the crime was attempted. He had only left a quarter of an hour before Bradley arrived. At eleven o'clock he had called the proprietor's attention to the fact that the restaurant clock was five minutes slow, and he had not left the place for nearly an hour after that. All this Bradley had expected. He might go back to Mark McGill's flat and ask him a few inconvenient questions, but he was prepared to accept this outrage as one of the items which might be included in the sum of McGill's iniquities.

He knew that Tiser had left for Bristol that morning on the twelve o'clock train. The man had been shadowed and his arrival in Bristol reported. Whilst he was out of town the culmination of Bradley's plan was deferred. He banked upon Tiser, who alone could give him the information he required.

At two o'clock in the morning he arrived at Scotland Yard, dead tired, and began to write his report.

The Squads were very busy that night; news came of them at odd intervals and from strange places. A raid had been made on the respectable Mr Laring. Enough stuff had been found in an outhouse to justify his arrest, and at that moment this comfort-loving man was trying to woo sleep on a hard plank bed.

That night Bradley slept on a sofa in his office: a disconcerting decision of his to the two men who had gained admission to his lodgings and were waiting in the dark room for his appearance. Mark McGill invariably had two strings to his bow, and the second was by far the more deadly.

19

In the morning:

"Come over," said Mark's voice on the telephone.

Ann hung up the receiver, and finished her dressing at leisure. The morning mail had brought a letter from Paris, inviting her to take up her old position, and her relief was for some reason tempered with a sense of unhappiness. This, then, was the end of her grand work for Ronnie! She was going back to the dreary round of a finishing school, and carrying with her a little heartache that was quite different from that which Ronnie's death had brought.

She was wholly indifferent to Mark McGill's pleasure or displeasure. He had never seen her so completely mistress of herself as when she came into his sitting-room.

"You took your time, my dear," he said with some acerbity. And then, without waiting for her rejoinder: "Bradley seems to have been in the wars last night, judging by the morning papers. Somebody shot at him in Hyde Park. That doesn't seem to surprise you," he added sharply.

Ann Perryman smiled.

"I also read the newspapers, Mark," she said.

Mark rubbed his big, unshaven chin.

"Naturally Bradley thinks I'm at the back of it. I'm an obsession to that man."

"Have they caught the people who shot at him?" she asked innocently.

Mark's crooked smile was his answer.

"Personally, I don't believe anything of the sort happened," he said. "Bradley is keen on publicity. That is his weakness – one of 'em. You're another."

She met the challenge of his eyes unflinchingly.

"Have you seen him lately?"

She nodded.

"Yes, I saw him late last night."

She knew that he was aware of this. Probably the hall porter, who suffered from insomnia and was in the habit of perambulating the streets after midnight, was his informant.

"What did he want?" he asked. "He surely didn't suspect you of trying to send him out?"

"Why should he?"

Mark shrugged.

"You didn't volunteer the statement that you'd seen him last night," he said. "You told me you'd read it in the newspapers. Ann, you're not going back on your old friends, are you?"

She shook her head.

"If you mean, am I going to betray you – no. Could I do any more than tell the story I told in the police court? He knows I'm a smuggler – of saccharine."

He looked at her keenly.

"Why did you pause before 'saccharine'?" he asked. "You're not believing that yarn about dope, are you?"

She did not answer.

"Suppose it was dope?" he went on. "After all, people are entitled to what they want. Would you squeak, then?"

"Would I go to the police and tell them?" she asked. "No, I don't think I would."

Mark laughed, took her by the arm in the friendliest way and shook her gently.

"What an old sceptic you're becoming, Ann! You don't think I regret your friendship with Bradley?"

"It's hardly a friendship, is it?"

"Whatever it is," he shrugged, "I don't care two hoots. If you could only persuade him that I've gone entirely out of business – saccharine or whatever it was – and that I'm not that master criminal which sensational novelists write about, you'd be doing me a good turn, Ann. I'm tired of all this business; I've made enough money to live on, and I'm out of the game for good. There's a big bonus for you, my dear."

"I don't want a bonus, big or little," she answered quietly. "I'm going back to Paris."

"To the school?" He was evidently surprised.

She nodded. And then she heard his sigh of relief.

"Well, that's that," he said. "I think perhaps you're wise. We'll talk about the money later."

"Did Mr Tiser get his letter?"

The unexpectedness of the question took him aback.

"I – I suppose so. Why?"

He tried to meet her steady gaze, but failed.

"Because I rang him up at the Home this morning. The man in charge said that he went to Bristol yesterday morning. You must have had a long wait."

She saw his brows meet.

"I don't quite understand you – "

"In the park, opposite Queen's Gate, at eleven o'clock last night," she said deliberately. "That was where you wished Mr Tiser to meet you, wasn't it?"

He was silent.

"And that was exactly the place and time somebody shot at Mr Bradley," she went on. "One would almost imagine that by some mistake he had received the letter I wrote, and went there to meet me."

He forced a smile.

"Then he'd be disappointed, wouldn't he?"

She shook her head slowly, and saw his mouth open in amazement.

"You were there?" incredulously.

"I was there," she said. "What would have happened if he – if he had been killed, and my letter had been found in his pocket?"

He roared with laughter, but it was an artificial laugh. It was a trick of Mark's to laugh like that when he had to gain time and wanted to think.

"What stupid idea have you got in your head now?" he said. "Tiser had your letter. He called me up last night and told me he couldn't keep the appointment."

"From Bristol?" she asked quietly.

"Of course not! You don't imagine that Tiser tells those fellows in the Home all his business, do you? He didn't leave London last night; as a matter of fact, I saw him at the restaurant where I was having supper – only for a few minutes, but I managed to pass on the information I had."

He was surveying her thoughtfully. Those cold eyes of his had some of the qualities of the snake.

"So you went to meet Mr Bradley and warned him, did you? That is perilously near being a squeak, my dear. Are you passionately in love with him?"

He was being faintly sarcastic rather than sneering; was a little amused too, she thought. Mark had a peculiar gift of detachment, and could stand on one side and view dispassionately not only the rest of the world, but himself.

"You won't answer that? Don't make a mistake, Ann: this fellow is playing up to you as he would play up to a servant girl if he wanted to find her lover. Don't – er – be very confident about him. You remember what you said to him in the police court? He lives on broken lives and broken hearts. I should not like to see you food for him. That would be too bad."

And then abruptly he changed the subject.

"I suppose you've not seen or heard of Li Yoseph in your wanderings? He was not in Hyde Park by any chance?"

She shook her head.

"I have not seen him since he was here."

"And nobody else. The old devil's lying low. I haven't heard his violin either."

As she was going out he called her back.

"You're not forgetting Ronnie, are you, Ann? No matter what I am or what I've done, whether I trade in dope or that sweet stuff, it doesn't alter the fact that Bradley killed your brother."

"What *were* you trading in?" she challenged, and an enigmatic smile was his answer.

"Saccharine," he said calmly. "But would it matter, so far as Ronnie's death was concerned?"

It mattered a great deal: she had never realised this before. Bradley checking the activities of men smuggling innocuous commodities must be judged in a different light from Bradley fighting this beastly traffic.

"I don't know." She spoke with some difficulty, almost frightened by the judgment she was giving.

"If I were a police officer, and I knew people were distributing that awful stuff, I don't think I should hesitate at − killing the man who carried it. It's a horrible thing to say, Mark, but that is how I feel. When you realise what it means to the people who − who take it, how it destroys in them all decent feeling, all hope − almost everything that is human, death seems quite a small penalty."

He opened his eyes wide in astonishment.

"Would you say this of Ronnie?"

"Of anybody," she said quietly. Again he laughed.

"You ought to join Tiser and speak at one of his open-air meetings," he said. "God! Ann, you're marvellous! I never dreamt you had such a moral stance! Yes?"

It was the servant with a telegram. He took it from the man and tore it open carelessly as he was speaking to her.

"Would you be surprised to learn that Ronnie developed these qualms? They didn't last very long: Ronnie was rather keen on money. He owed me the greater part of a thousand pounds when he died: I've never told you that, but it is unimportant. He was rather a ready borrower."

He glanced down at the telegram in his hand, and as he read she saw him frown.

"That's awkward," he said.

She checked the indignation which rose at his slighting references to her brother. To quarrel with Mark was profitless.

He tapped the telegram with his forefinger.

"A month or so ago this would have been good news. But now, with my little Mercury under a ban, very suspicious, and on the most friendly terms with the Flying Squad, my asset is a liability."

His tone was flippant, but she saw that he was perturbed.

"Has some – saccharine arrived?" she asked, with a faint smile.

He nodded, and passed the telegram to her. It was dated from Birmingham, and ran:

L. 75 K.K. Believed seen. Bunk inquiries.

The message was unsigned. She only knew that "bunk" was a word that was used by Mark's couriers to denote hangar. She could guess the purport of the remainder of the message.

Mark's face was dark and gloomy.

"I told the fools to send no more. This must be Luteur's parcel."

He looked at the girl and his lips curled in a grim smile.

"I suppose if I suggested you should collect this little lot, you'd ring up Bradley and have me pinched?"

"Saccharine?" she asked.

"I'll swear it."

He was so earnest that she was deceived. For a moment she hesitated.

"I couldn't collect it, however much I wanted to," she said, and he took her up quickly.

"If by 'collected' you mean brought here, that's the last thing in the world I want. But it is necessary that somebody should find the packet and dump it into the nearest pond. If the aeroplane has been seen, they will search the common, which means that they've only to find the pilot to get to it."

"Where is it?" she asked curiously.

" 'L' is Ashdown Forest, I believe."

He went to his desk and took out a flat package that had the appearance of being a blotting pad; indeed, there was blotting paper neatly attached to the top of it. Beneath this, from a pocket he drew a dozen thin sheets of transparent tracing paper. These were ruled into tiny squares, and at the top and sides of the sheet was an indicator number or letter. From a shelf he took a large, flat book, each page of which was nearly as big as the writing-table on which it was laid. He turned the leaves and smoothed the page flat.

"Yes, it is Ashdown Forest," he said.

He laid two sheets of tracing paper carefully over the map.

"Here's the place it was dropped." He pointed to a square. "Naturally, he can only make a rough guess, unless he was flying very low, as I suppose he was, but we ought to find it within a radius of fifty yards. It is not so far from a road, and should be easily found – it is on the south side of a pond. These pilots invariably take water as their guide."

He marked a circle on the map.

"The pond will be handy to dump the stuff. What do you say, Ann?"

She did not answer immediately. It was no novel errand – she had a dozen commons near London for these packages. Sometimes it was neither convenient nor easy to meet the plane, and the parcels had to be collected.

Mark McGill could not guess what was passing through her mind. His impression was that she was weakening – he could not believe that she contemplated his betrayal to Bradley. Knowing Ann as he did, that was unthinkable.

But in Ann's mind was another consideration. She had a chance here of settling for all time her doubts. Since she had lost faith in Mark she had had no opportunity of verifying the truth of his claims.

"How can I go? They would see me driving the car and I should probably be arrested," she said.

He was not prepared for this surrender, and for the moment was at a loss for a reply.

"That can be managed," he said at last. "I'll phone one of the hire companies to pick you up somewhere. You can be Miss Smith, Jones or Robinson; tell the driver to take you to Ashdown Forest, leave the car for a little walk – or, better still, tell him to pick you up an hour later. You haven't to bring the stuff back, so there's no danger."

She nodded slowly.

"You'll do it? What a brick you are!"

He gripped Ann's hand in both of his, and he was so relieved and delighted that for a second she felt ashamed of herself.

Mark McGill was something of a draughtsman. In a quarter of an hour he had pencilled a map of the locality.

"Go through East Grinstead and take this fork road…"

She went to her room and made preparations for the journey. When she returned to Mark she found that he had already ordered the car; it was to pick her up in half an hour at the Kensington end of Ladbroke Grove.

"You can take a taxi there, my dear – give the driver a flyer before you start, and tell him to make for East Grinstead." He eyed her thoughtfully. "I won't ask you whether you'll keep this little adventure a secret, because I trust you, Ann. I know that however much you like Bradley, you wouldn't willingly get me into trouble."

"It is saccharine?"

"I swear it – or you can take my word of honour. I don't know which is the least valuable."

She had an idea that Bradley was watching the house, but there was no sign of a detective shadowing her as she made her way to Bond Street. Here she took a taxi, and ten minutes later dismissed it at the rendezvous. The car did not arrive for another ten minutes, a big, handsome limousine, and after paying the man and giving him instructions she made herself comfortable in the roomy interior.

Like all expert drivers, she hated being driven at a fast speed, and she was fortunate in her driver, for the car made a smooth but leisurely passage. Clear of Grinstead, she examined the map. It could have been read by a child. She was able to direct the driver where to turn, and presently reached the place at which she had decided beforehand to begin her search.

The sky had been overcast when she left the house, and she had gone back for her mackintosh. She was glad of this now, for rain was falling steadily. It was a circumstance, however, which made her explanation to the driver sound feeble.

"I want you to come back and pick me up in half an hour's time," she said. "A friend of mine was here recently and lost something. I am going to look for it."

"Couldn't I help you, miss?" said the chauffeur, half rising to his feet.

"No, no," said Ann hastily; "I'd rather search myself."

He was reluctant to leave her on the deserted heath, the more so since they were in an unfrequented part. Eventually, and in desperation, she compromised by telling him to drive five hundred yards up the uneven road and wait for her.

Her first objective was the pond. She had passed it before the car stopped, and now she went back and skirted its margin. It was a sheet of water of respectable size, and, she imagined, rather deep, for there was a notice board prohibiting bathing. There was a little forest of blackberry bushes and a tangle of undergrowth which made an ideal place for concealment.

She traversed the ground systematically, probing into every bush with the walking-stick she had brought. Half an hour's search revealed nothing. She was worried lest the chauffeur, from a misguided desire to help, should return. Possibly the police had already combed the place and the parcel had been found. The possibility that she might herself be under observation, and be associated with the package, filled her with momentary panic.

She was on the point of giving up the search when she saw a broken branch of a little tree. It had been snapped off and the broken bough lay on the ground at her feet. The fracture had been recent, and she began a more careful search of the undergrowth. And then she found the package. Its brown paper cover was soaked through, and one of the cords which tied it had been broken. It was almost in the shape of a ball, and she knew that the contents had been most carefully wrapped with corrugated paper. She took from her pocket the knife that she had brought with her, cut the string and removed the packing. In the centre was a square tin, the lid of which was sealed with adhesive tape. This she ripped open, removing the lid, and shook out a dozen familiar packages.

She opened one of these. It contained a white, crystalline powder, and quickly she transferred about a spoonful into the box she had brought for the purpose. When she had done this she gathered the remaining packages and the tin, and, going back to the pond, threw them as far as she could into the centre. The tin was still floating on the surface when she heard the chauffeur's voice. Fortunately she was invisible, and she hurried back to the road.

"I was rather worried about you, miss. I just saw an old tramp watching you."

"Where is he?" she asked quickly.

She looked round; there was no human being in sight. Her heart was racing as she came back to the car, the little box containing the "saccharine" clasped in her hand.

"Did you find what you wanted?"

"Yes," she said breathlessly.

Before she got into the car she heard the chauffeur's exclamation and looked back. It might have been a tramp who was making his slow way in the opposite direction, or a labouring man. Even from this distance she saw he was roughly dressed.

"I didn't see the motorist, did you, miss?"

"Motorist?" she asked.

"I heard the car but I didn't see it. It sounded to me like a – " He named with uncomplimentary intonation a popular make of machine.

She took a quick survey of the common: she could see no motorcar. The tramp, or whatever he was, had already vanished.

"I think we'll go home," she said. "Drop me in Cavendish Square."

Several times she looked back in the course of her journey, expecting to find the mysterious car on her trail, but until they were entering the outskirts of London, cars were few and far between, and most of those they passed, for she had given the chauffeur orders to hurry.

When she reached her flat her first act was to hide the little box. After she had done this she went across to Mark's room and found him stretched on the settee, reading. He got up quickly at the sight of her.

"Did you find it?"

She nodded.

"And dump it? Splendid!"

She noticed that he wore an old suit of rough tweed, which was curious, because Mark was rather a dandy in his way.

"You came back by the longest route," he said coolly, as he resumed his prone position on the settee. "And you took the devil of a time to get the stuff. I thought you were never going to find it."

"How do you know?" she asked in surprise.

"Because I was watching you," he said coolly. "No, I didn't actually see you find it, but I knew that you had. I don't think it matters very much about the tin floating."

"Did you follow me?" she asked, half indignant, half amused.

"Naturally," was the calm reply. "I can't afford to take risks."

"Why didn't you look for it yourself?" she demanded.

"I repeat, I can't afford to take risks," he said; "and it would have been a very grave risk for me to have been found in possession of that stuff, even for a few minutes."

"You'd rather I took all the risks that were going?"

"To you there is no risk, my lovely," he said airily. "You have a guardian angel at Scotland Yard – I have a pursuing devil."

He twisted his head round and looked at her, the smile still on his face.

"Thank you, Ann. Bradley's man lost you, curiously enough, between Bond Street and Bayswater. I saw him sitting in his two-seater, looking very crestfallen. He picked you up on the way back, and I presume he has now gone to the hire company to make a few inquiries."

She was startled.

"Did you see him?"

He nodded.

"I know all these fellows by sight. They aren't particularly beautiful to look at, but they're useful to know. Bradley will be on the phone to you in a few minutes, asking you where you've been. He'll do it rather nicely, because he's fond of you."

She had not been back in her flat ten minutes before the telephone bell rang and she heard Bradley's voice.

"Have you been out this afternoon?"

"Yes," she replied; and then, maliciously: "I'm afraid your detective missed me."

There was a little pause.

"You didn't see him?"

"Yes, I did," she answered untruthfully. "You don't want me to tell you where I've been – I went to Ashdown Forest."

Another little silence.

"I'll only ask you one question, Ann: did you bring anything back from Ashdown Forest?"

"I brought nothing back for Mark," she answered. This time he was so long silent that she thought she had been cut off, and called him by name.

"Yes, I'm here. You found it, did you? We've been looking for it all the morning. I hope you dumped it?" And then, before she could answer: "Can I see you tonight?"

This was an unexpected request.

"Where?" she asked.

"At your flat? Will you be at home at nine?" And, when she did not reply: "You're not worried about what McGill thinks, are you? You can tell him if you wish."

"I'll see you at nine," she said hurriedly, and put up the receiver.

Ann had a very useful collection of books, including the "Encyclopaedia Britannica," and she had already studied the properties of the drug which she believed the parcel contained. There was a long and exhaustive article on the subject, and particulars of the tests which could be applied to discover its character. She went over the article again, making a few notes, and later went out into the street just before the shops closed and bought test tubes and the necessary chemicals to conduct her experiments. She had none of the delicate instruments that were requisite, and she could make a rough examination of the properties, but no more. The chemical names of these products appalled her. Saccharine was the imide of ortho-sulpho-benzoic acid – it was also a very sweet substance. She tasted the contents of the box with a finger lightly powdered with its crystalline contents, and it was not sweet. Moreover, where it had touched, her tongue grew numb and had no feeling.

There was no need for her test tubes or her crude little experiments. This was cocaine – and she had known it all the time, had been convinced when Bradley had told her.

With practically no knowledge of chemistry, her further experiments confused rather than helped her. At last she washed the test tubes clean and threw the contents and the box into the fire. She had all the proof she needed.

While she awaited the coming of Bradley she wrote a long letter to Paris, and resolved to ask Bradley's aid to enable her to leave by the morning train.

20

What Bradley called sardonically "The Home for Lost Souls" had ceased to function. Tiser came back from Bristol and found the hall porter brooding before a small coke fire.

"They've gone, Mr Tiser," he said, talking over his shoulder.

"Gone? Who?"

The porter jerked his thumb in the direction of the common-room, and slowly it dawned upon Tiser that his ostensible occupation was gone.

"All of them?" he asked incredulously. "There were three men coming today: didn't they turn up?"

The porter shook his head.

"No; some of the boys met them when they came out this morning, and they didn't turn up. The only man that's come is old Sedeman."

Mr Tiser made a wry face.

"Where is he?"

"Having some food," said the porter despondently. "I asked him to pay for it, and he threatened to give me a punch on the nose. I thought you didn't want trouble, so I let him have it."

A week before, the news would have caused Mr Tiser considerable unhappiness; but he had recognised the inevitability of some such thing happening. The habitual criminal is a shy bird, and the constant raids which had been made on the Home, the almost daily appearance of detective officers pursuing their inquiries, had made this sanctuary a most disturbing habitation.

The Home, as such, was doomed. It had cost Mark a lot of money, and, now that it served no useful purpose, he had placed the property in the hands of an agent, with instructions to sell.

Tiser was not sorry at the prospect of leaving a spot where inquisitive people were sure of finding him.

He went into the common-room and found Sedeman nodding over the remainder of his meal. Mr Sedeman looked at him with a fiery eye.

"We have no room for you, Sedeman," said Tiser, and his voice was distinctly unfriendly.

The old man glowered at him.

"Do you imagine that I would sleep in this home of iniquity, my good man?" he demanded truculently. "It is, I admit, a little more healthy since your disreputable friends have retired. But even so, a man of my social connections could not afford to be found on these premises, even if he were in an advanced stage of intoxication – which, thank God, I am not!"

He had, however, made considerable advance towards that stage, and Tiser, who knew him, very wisely temporised.

"We're always glad to see you, my dear friend," he said. "Have you seen Mark?"

"I have not seen Mark," said Sedeman loudly. "I have reformed."

He beckoned the hall porter, who stood in the doorway.

"Get me a drink, Arthur," he said, and Tiser nodded his agreement.

Later, when the man reported that Sedeman had gone, he gave definite instructions for his exclusion.

"Tell him the Home is closed," he said.

He settled himself down, with a large glass of whisky, to work out the day's transactions. His trip to Bristol had been a profitable one. Fortunately, the syndicate (he always referred to Mark and himself in those terms) had cached a large quantity of the stuff before the real trouble commenced, and although it had been difficult to recover, he had at last succeeded in making a profitable distribution. He was so engaged when he heard the door bell clang, and a few seconds after Mark strode into the room and closed both doors behind him.

"Is anybody in the house?"

"Sedeman was, but he's gone," said Tiser.

Mark pursed his thick underlip.

"Bradley's stool pigeon – keep him out of here," he said.

His companion pushed the rough draft of his report towards him, but Mark did not so much as glance at it.

"We may have very bad trouble before the morning," he said. "I sent Ann out to get some stuff that had been dropped in Ashdown Wood."

"Not to bring it to the flat?" gasped Tiser, in horror.

"Don't interrupt me," snarled the other. "No, she had orders to dump it, and she did – all except an ounce or two."

"All except an ounce or two?" repeated Tiser. "What do you mean, my dear Mark?"

"She brought a little back in a box. That puzzles me. I was watching her all the time – I'm not trusting Ann: she's too matey with Bradley. But I don't think she'd put up a squeak. I took a car down just behind her, and was watching her when she found the parcel. As I say, she dumped most of it; she brought back enough to make trouble. That worried me, but tonight I made a little discovery. She had a date with Bradley; he was calling at her flat."

"How do you know?" asked Tiser.

Mark was strangely tractable. As a rule he was an autocrat who resented even the least offensive of questions. But now he took a letter from his pocket and cast it on the table.

"A note from Bradley," he explained. "I met a messenger boy coming up the stairs and took it from him."

The note was short and formal.

DEAR ANN

I am afraid I can't come to you tonight; I have rather an important call. May I see you tomorrow?

Tiser leaned back in his chair, pale and trembling.

"What does it mean?" he quavered.

Mark McGill's lips curled in contempt.

"Will you throw a fit if I tell you? She's either got the coke for Bradley, which means big trouble, or else she brought it back to satisfy herself that it is cocaine she's been carrying. Whichever way it is, she's dangerous. Somebody's got to go to Paris tomorrow morning and send a wire from Boulogne to Bradley, wishing him goodbye in Ann's name."

Tiser raised his eyes slowly from the blotting pad.

"What's going to happen to Ann?" he asked in the high-pitched voice which betrayed his perturbation.

"The Home's empty, you say – that ought to be easy – "

The telephone bell rang and Tiser leapt in terror.

"See who it is," commanded Mark.

His quaking companion lifted the hook. "Who – " he began, and then he heard the voice.

"Is dat der goot Tiser? Is Mark mit you? To Mark I would speak."

Tiser covered the mouthpiece with a shaking hand.

"It's Li!" he whispered hoarsely. "He wants to talk to you, Mark…"

Mark snatched the instrument from him.

"Well, Li, what do you want?" he asked sharply. "Where are you speaking from?"

He heard a low chuckle.

"Not from Lady's Stairs, eh? The telephonie we have not – it is too grand for Lady's Stairs. Soon I shall see you, Mark."

"Where are you?" asked Mark again.

"Come to Lady's Stairs, Mark – not tomorrow, but der next day, and bring mit you de young lady, eh – Ronnie's sister. The poor boy…"

Mark heard him muttering injunctions to his invisible children, and smiled.

"Lady's Stairs? Right, I'll be there."

"And der goot Tiser, you will breeng him? I think you will come, Mark, eh? My lost memory she return very well."

There was no mistaking the threat in that sentence, and Mark had to swallow something before he replied.

"Friday, at what time?"

The old man did not reply, and the listener heard the click as the receiver was hung up.

"What did he want, Mark? He isn't going to give us any trouble, is he?"

Mark looked down at the moist face of his cowardly companion and would have found a savage pleasure in striking it.

"He's getting his memory back, that's all. Who'll believe that crazy old devil?"

He reached out his hand and drew the telephone towards him. Tiser heard him give a familiar number. Presently:

"Is that you, Ann? It's Mark speaking. I'm at the Home. Bradley's here: he wants to see you about that stuff you brought back from Ashdown."

Ann gasped.

"Stuff – ?"

"You know, Ann. He says you brought back a small box full of coke…yes, cocaine; don't be a fool, you know what coke is."

His tone was purposely impatient. His very brusqueness convinced her that he was speaking the truth, that Bradley was there, and that there was an inquiry in progress.

"I'll come down immediately."

"Take a taxi," he said, and hung up.

Tiser was staring at him.

"Why are you bringing her here?" he asked tremulously, but Mark McGill ignored the question.

He lit a cigarette and blew the smoke to the ceiling.

"Do you remember the trouble we got in about four or five years ago, over men getting tight and kicking up hell late at night?" he asked.

Tiser nodded slowly.

"What did we do with them?" asked Mark.

The other fetched a long, shaky sigh.

"My dear Mark, you know what we did. It was your suggestion, I think. We put them in Number Six. But we haven't used it for years."

Mark nodded.

"We put 'em in Six so that they could yell their heads off and nobody would hear – a splendid idea of mine, eh?" He barked the inquiry. "Is it empty now?"

"Yes, Mark…but you wouldn't…this is the first place they'd look for her."

"Why?" asked the other. "If Bradley gets a wire in the morning saying that Ann has left, he'll not worry. I'll see that her boxes are cleared out."

Tiser was swaying to and fro in his chair like a man in pain, clasping and unclasping his hands.

"Don't do it, my dear fellow, don't do it! That poor young lady –"

"You're not thinking about your poor self, are you?" asked Mark coldly. "Have you ever thought what the last twenty-four hours in a condemned cell are like – what time you go to bed and what time you wake up – what you think of when you open your eyes? If they will accept old Li's evidence, we'll swing, you and I, Tiser. They can only hang us once if we killed every man, woman and child in London."

"You're not going to kill her?" Tiser almost shrieked the words. "Mark, I'll not stand it – "

Mark's big hand closed over Tiser's mouth and he was forced down into his chair.

"Sit quiet, or I'll save Mr Steen a job!" he hissed. "What are you afraid of, you – Thing!"

It was a long time before Tiser had approached composure. There was a tap on the outer door; Mark pulled it open. It was Ann.

"Who let you in?" he asked quickly.

"The door was open."

Mark brushed past her. The hall porter was gone. He had anticipated his dismissal, and had retired with a number of valuable articles which were never missed. Mark slammed the door closed, and went back to the girl, who was just inside the room.

"Where is Mr Bradley?" she asked.

"He's gone out; he'll be back in a minute. It was he who left the door open," he said. "Sit down, Ann. What's this yarn about your bringing coke back to London?"

For a while she sat, her eyes on the floor, then suddenly she looked up.

"Yes, I brought a little cocaine to London. I wanted to be sure. Mark, you have lied to me all this time – it was that awful stuff I was carrying. Mr Bradley was right."

"Mr Bradley was right, was he?" he mocked her. "Isn't he always right? A paladin amongst policemen! You've got me into very serious trouble, Ann, and you've got to get me out. Bradley has found a stock of the stuff here, and wants you to identify the packages you've carried."

She stared at him.

"How can I do that? I seldom saw them," she said.

She took no notice of Tiser, sitting huddled up in his chair, his face ashen, his long, bony fingers twining and untwining one about the other.

"If you can identify them you're at liberty to do so," said Mark. "There are fifty or so."

He opened the door and beckoned her to follow him, and she went without hesitation up the stairs in his wake. At the head of the stairs was a heavy door, and this he thrust open. It was quite dark, but he touched a switch on the outside wall and a ceiling light illuminated a room barely furnished, with an untidy looking bed, a cracked water jug and a chair.

"There it is." He pointed behind the door, and incautiously she went in.

His foot kicked out and the door closed. For a second she stood staring at him uncomprehendingly; and then she made a dart toward the door, but he caught her in his arms and held her.

"You're wasting your breath if you scream," he said. "This room was specially prepared to prevent the genteel people of Hammersmith being disturbed. We've had a few cases of delirium tremens in this room."

She saw now that the walls were covered with satin, tightly stitched and padded; that there was no window – only a small ventilator near the ceiling; and, as she realised her danger, he saw her face go white.

"Your Flying Squad will have to fly to catch this pigeon," he said humorously. "Ann, you've been a naughty girl."

"Let me out, please."

"You're going to stay here for a day or two – in fact, till I'm well out of the country. If you give me any trouble, you'll be out of the country and out of the world long before I have reached Southampton."

He said this pleasantly, but she recognised the deadliness of his threat.

Ann Perryman was not easily frightened, but she was frightened now. She knew that Bradley was not in the house, and had never been there; that the story of his discovery was an invention.

"Mark, you're being very melodramatic," she said, steadying her voice. "You know why I brought the cocaine back to London – I wanted to be absolutely sure that I was not carrying saccharine, and that was the only way I could be certain."

"You didn't send it to the analyst, by any chance?" he asked sarcastically.

"It wasn't necessary. I had only to touch it with my tongue to know that it was not saccharine, but this horrible drug. If I had been trying to betray you to the police, shouldn't I have brought the whole package back to London – why should I have destroyed the evidence by throwing it into the pond?"

Mark thought for a moment. He had a logical mind.

"That's a sound argument, Ann, my dear, but I'm going to keep you here for a day or two in case of accidents. I'll see that you have everything you require in the shape of food."

"Why not let me go to Paris?" In spite of her self-control her voice shook a little. "I should be out of the way then, Mark. You would have no fear that I should see Mr Bradley — "

"You can go to Paris in a couple of days," said Mark. "In the meantime you'll stay here — and be thankful that when you go to sleep tonight you're pretty sure to wake up in the morning."

He opened the door, and for a moment his back was toward her. Before he knew what was happening she had gripped him by the arm and swung him round. For a second he was off his balance, and before he could recover himself she had jerked open the door and run out. Before she could reach the head of the stairs, one arm was round her, the other hand was over her face.

"What's the game?"

Mark looked round and beheld a strange sight. In the light of an overhead lamp Sedeman was standing. He was clad simply in his trousers and a discoloured shirt; his white beard floated sideways in the draught from an open window, giving his face a curiously grotesque twist. The bald head shone like a well-waxed dome, and in his hand he gripped the heavy ash walking-stick without which he never moved.

"What's the game, Mark?"

Mark shot one baleful glare at him and dragged the girl nearer to the door of the padded room; but, with an agility surprising in one of his years, Sedeman leaped forward and barred the way.

"Let go that young lady or I'll beat the head off you!"

Mark had already had one proof of this old man's extraordinary strength, and his grip on the girl relaxed. She stood, leaning against the wall, breathless, half fainting.

"And keep your hand from your pocket, will you!" roared Sedeman, but at that instant Mark's automatic covered him.

"Get out of the way!" he growled.

A broad smile creased the old man's face.

"You're going on like the hero of one of those pernicious penny dreadfuls," he said. "My dear Mark, I shall not get out of the way, and you will not shoot! And why? Because there isn't a rozzer within five hundred yards who wouldn't hear your gun. Put it down."

He spoke mildly enough, but his hand shot out in a vicious lunge. Mark felt as if his wrist had been broken, and heard the clatter of the pistol as it fell down the stairs.

"Now, young lady, are you going or staying?"

"I'm going," said Ann in a low voice.

"You're not fit to go out like this," said Mark. He had recovered his equanimity with remarkable rapidity. "Come and sit down in Tiser's room. I promise you to have no more of those little jokes. Better have Sedeman down – I suppose he wants a cheap drink."

He turned to the girl.

"Ann, I'm terribly sorry! I'm desperate – you know that. I wouldn't have done that unless I was scared of what is going to happen. I shouldn't have hurt you – I swear I shouldn't."

Her legs were trembling under her as she went down the stairs. Even if she had been willing, she could not have walked out of the house and into the street without attracting attention, and that was what she least desired. She followed old Sedeman into Tiser's frowsy sitting-room, and they found the lank-haired man sitting as she had left him, his face tense and drawn, his long fingers twining one about the other.

Sedeman was in an hilarious mood, and chortled at the consternation Tiser displayed at the sight of him.

"There's no beds like the beds at the Home, Tiser, my boy," he said as he poured out some whisky into a glass. "Try a little of this, young lady."

Ann shook her head.

"What a blessing I was here – what a blessing! The noble Marcus was going against his better nature – naughty, naughty!" He shook his head sadly, but Ann noticed that he still retained a hold of his thick walking-stick.

There was no chance of a private talk with the girl: Mark realised that what he had to say must be said before the old man.

"Are you going to forgive me, Ann?"

"I suppose so." She had grown suddenly tired and listless; all her vitality had gone from her: she was incapable of harbouring enmity, incapable even of fear. "I think I'll go home now."

"Off you pop," said Sedeman cheerfully. "I'll watch you to the end of the street. There are plenty of taxis."

He was as good as his word, pushed back the obsequious Tiser, who would have accompanied her to the main street, and stood in his bare feet on the cold pavement until she had disappeared from view. Then he returned to where he had left the brooding Mark.

"I've saved you from a lot of trouble, my valiant pal," he said jovially. "You don't think I did? I'm telling you! Bradley's got a date with me at eleven o'clock – here!"

21

Mark listened to the old man, apparently unmoved. Nobody who could see his impassive face could dream of the murderous hate in his heart.

"Is he climbing the rain-pipe to see you?" he asked.

Old Sedeman smiled loftily.

"When I say a date, I mean that, like Romeo, he will stand beneath my casement and I shall converse with him."

Mark shut the door.

"Sit down, Sedeman," he said mildly. "I'd like to get the hang of this mystery. What can you tell Bradley?"

"That I am well and likely to pass a good night," said Sedeman gravely. "The man worries about me – it is a novel experience, my dear Mark. The thought that there is someone thinking about you." He shook his head ecstatically, and seemed at a loss for words.

"In other words, Bradley is paying you to watch me – is that the strength of it?" asked Mark. "Well, let me tell you that you're going to have a soft job."

He turned the subject abruptly.

"Have you seen Li Yoseph?"

Sedeman shook his head.

"I have heard rumours. It is an amazing thing – the dead return to life."

"He was never dead," said Mark loudly. "He was – "

"Mark!"

He looked round. Tiser was standing near the window, his face puckered in a grimace of fear.

"What's the matter with you, you damned fool?" demanded Mark savagely.

"Listen!"

There was a silence. For a moment Mark heard nothing, and then the wail of a violin came faintly to him. He bent his head.

"Do you hear that?"

McGill strode past him and pulled aside the curtains. He could see nothing but the faint glow of a distant street lamp. The window was fastened with a screw and a patent catch.

"Open these," he said impatiently.

"Mark, for God's sake don't do anything stupid…couldn't we send somebody to bring him in?"

"Whom have we got to send? Anyway, I want to see – open the window."

Tiser unscrewed the bolt and pushed back the catch with a hand that trembled so much that at last Mark pushed him aside and completed the work himself. He drew up the sash and leaned out. The sound of the violin came more clearly now. Peering along the street, he saw a figure standing on the kerb midway between two street lamps.

At that moment the music ceased and he heard an authoritative voice. A policeman had come from the shadows and had crossed the road towards the musician.

"Put out the lights," said Mark, and Tiser obeyed.

They were too far off for him to hear the colloquy, but presently Mark saw them walking slowly towards where he was. And then he heard Li Yoseph's voice:

"My goot friend, I make music for my leedle ones."

"Your leedle ones?"

The policeman peered down at the bent figure.

"You're a foreigner, are you? Well, you can't play at this time of night – get a move on."

Mark watched the shuffling old man and the slowly pacing officer of the law until they vanished in the night.

"If it hadn't been for the copper I'd have had a talk to that old swine."

"Li Yoseph!" Sedeman's face was a picture of amazement.

"You saw him, did you? Well, is he alive or dead?"

"Excuse me," said Mr Sedeman, "my nerves are upset."

He half filled a tumbler with whisky and added a minute quantity of soda-water. It was not easy to upset Mr Sedeman's nerves; but he was a great opportunist, and Tiser saw his whisky vanish with a sense of pain.

"Well, well, well," said Sedeman, smacking his lips. "Old Li Yoseph!"

Something in his tone made Mark look at him sharply.

"Was it such a surprise to you?" he asked.

"I said so," said Mr Sedeman in his loftiest manner.

McGill walked over to where the old man sat and scowled down at him.

"You knew he was alive. Where is he staying? Now, Sedeman" – in a more friendly tone – "there's no sense in our working at cross purposes. What is the game? Bradley's sent him here, hasn't he?"

At that moment there came a rat-tat on the outer door.

"There's Bradley: you'd better ask him," said Sedeman.

Tiser went out with some reluctance to open the door. It was Bradley, and he was alone. He came into the little room and greeted Mark with his inscrutable smile.

"You've been having a little music, they tell me? Li Yoseph is a very considerate old gentleman, but I never knew he'd carry his friendliness so far as to entertain you."

"He has not been here," said Mark.

Bradley's eyebrows rose.

"I thought he might be another inmate of your interesting institute – you're rather short on reformed characters just now."

He ignored Sedeman, and the old gentleman made no attempt to meet his eyes, but sat staring stonily in front of him. Without invitation, Bradley pulled a chair up to the table and took from his pocket a small pill-box. Mark's eyes only left this to return again instantly. But the detective made no attempt to remove the lid.

"You used to have an automatic, didn't you, McGill? Rather an unusual size, and not of the ordinary Browning type?"

He did not answer, and Bradley repeated the question; then it was that Mark smiled slowly.

"What's the idea? Has the old boy been suggesting I shot him?" he asked, and Tiser's blood ran cold at the daring of the question.

"Not exactly," said Bradley slowly. "But suppose I said that, searching the floor of Lady's Stairs – the floor of the room from which Li Yoseph – disappeared – I found two bullets embedded? Quite recently," he added carelessly.

Mark waited.

"Suppose," the other went on, "that I suggest those bullets were fired from a pistol which was at that time in your possession, and, for all I know, may still be your property – what then?"

"What's the idea?" asked Mark again coolly. "That I've done a little target practice in Li Yoseph's house? It is certainly a place where one could loose off a gun without doing very much damage to anybody, but I don't recollect that I was ever drunk at Li Yoseph's – or that I was ever in possession of a gun," he added quickly.

Bradley lifted the lid of the box, and Mark's eyes focussed on the little white object. Presently the lid was lifted, and McGill saw something lying on cotton wool in the interior – two cone-shaped pieces of nickel, the head of one of which was bent over until it almost formed a note of interrogation.

"Ever seen these before?" Bradley shook the contents of the box into his palm. "Don't touch them – just look."

"I don't remember," said Mark.

"Well, take them in your hand. Do they represent the calibre of your automatic?"

But McGill made no attempt to touch them.

"I haven't an automatic," he said. "I never carry one – I think I have explained that fact to your flying gentlemen once or twice, but you're sceptical."

"That is my business – scepticism is half my stock in trade, patience is the other half – and I've told you that before," smiled Bradley, as he dropped the two bullets back into the box and fixed the lid. "Where do you carry your gun as a rule? Oh, I forgot, you don't carry one."

His hand shot out and pressed against Mark's hip pocket. It was empty.

Not a muscle of Mark McGill's face moved. That cruel little smile of his still twisted his lips; his slumbrous eyes were unfathomable.

"Satisfied?" he asked.

Bradley put the pill-box in his pocket.

"Almost," he said.

"You got them out of the floor, did you?" Mark was amused. "Really, my opinion of the police is going up a point or two."

"If I said 'them,' I made a mistake. I found one of them at Lady's Stairs. The other – I dug out of a tree in Hyde Park. Our experts say they were both fired from the same type of pistol, but not necessarily the same pistol. I could have told them that, because your alibi was complete the other night. I knew before I sent for you that it was fool-proof."

He took up the box again and, opening it, selected the one with the bent top.

"I found that at Lady's Stairs. I've been looking for it for twelve months."

Again McGill's lips twitched.

"Did Li Yoseph help you to find it?" he asked flippantly.

"Li Yoseph helped me find it," nodded Bradley.

He took out of his pocket a slip of paper and laid it on the table.

"I'm going to make a search of this house. There's the warrant," he said in a more businesslike tone. "I have an idea – I may be wrong – that I shall find the duplicate of both those pistols somewhere in this place. If you don't mind, we'll start here."

Only for a second did Mark McGill look ugly, and Bradley, interpreting the look, laughed.

"I'm not alone, McGill. My cohort is surrounding the house; I'll bring a few in if you don't mind."

The search was as conscientious and as systematic as anything that the terrified Tiser had seen. He sat on the edge of a chair, quaking and suffering an agony of mind that even Bradley could not have realised. Room by room the house was searched. Under a floor-board was found a quantity of old silver, the presence of which only the probabilities could explain, for the room had been in the occupation of an old lodger of the Home – one of the men who had disappeared with violent suddenness following an attack upon Bradley.

"I can't hold you responsible for that, and I shan't," said Bradley, when the articles were brought in and put on the table. "No dope, Simmonds?"

"None, sir."

"Nor guns?" asked Mark innocently.

"I found this in the padded room upstairs," said Simmonds, and Mark gasped as he saw a handbag, which he recognised instantly.

Bradley took it in his hand and turned it over, and his eyes rose to McGill's.

"Whose is this?" and, when Mark did not answer, he opened the clasp.

The first thing he saw was a card. He looked up sharply.

"What was Miss Perryman doing here?"

"She often comes," said Mark indifferently. "We're very good friends – you may not think so. Much better friends than you imagine. I suppose that's not the sort of thing one says to another man, but you're a policeman, and I always like to tell the police the truth."

"You're very good friends, are you?" Bradley's voice was cold and even; he was not easily rattled.

He closed the clasp with a snap.

"Exactly how good friends are you?"

Mark smiled cryptically.

"You're a man of the world – " he began, but Bradley's soft laughter interrupted him.

"You're degenerating, McGill. A year ago you would have said that and I might have believed you – you've even lost the art of lying!

When I see Li Yoseph tonight I shall have to tell him it will be worth his coming back to Lady's Stairs to hear."

Bradley had been gone a quarter of an hour before Mark McGill spoke. Sedeman had slipped out of the room while the interview was still in progress, and when Tiser was sent upstairs to find him his room was empty.

Mark walked up and down the room like a caged lion, his hands in his pockets, his chin on his breast. The old man was back at Lady's Stairs — and yet none of his satellites had reported his return.

Suddenly he stopped in his walk and jerked out his watch.

"Put on your coat," he said brusquely.

"You don't want me to go out tonight, Mark, do you?" asked the tremulous Tiser.

"You're coming with me — to Lady's Stairs. I want to have a talk with Mr Li Yoseph."

22

Ann Perryman reached home with her last reserves of strength exhausted. She had no sooner locked and bolted her door than she dropped into a chair. She thought she was going to faint, but after ten minutes' rest that feeling of collapse wore off.

She knew Mark McGill for what he was, and for the first time she allowed her mind to dwell upon the part she had played in his iniquitous trade. It was a horrifying thought, and she went cold as it came to her that she personally might be responsible for a score of unknown crimes – unknown to her.

She heard a knock at the front door and started up. If it was Mark she would not admit him: she would take no risks and would leave her flat in the morning.

She went into the corridor as the knock was repeated.

"Who's there?" she asked, and to her relief she heard the voice of the hall porter.

She drew the bolts and unfastened the door.

"Your taximan, miss. He wants to know if you want him again."

She had forgotten all about the taximan who had brought her, and went back hurriedly to find her bag. It was only then she discovered its loss. She had some money, however, in her bedroom, and gave it to the waiting attendant.

"Could I have a minute's conversation with you, miss?"

"Now?" she asked in surprise. "Certainly – come back."

When the cab had been discharged she brought the porter into her sitting-room.

"I've got something on my mind, miss, that I'd like to talk about," said the man uneasily. "To tell you the truth, I'm in a bit of trouble, over a certain affair that I can't exactly explain."

She smiled faintly.

"That's very mysterious, Ritchie."

She liked the man, an elderly pensioner who had been in charge of the building, as he had told her, for over twenty years.

"Miss Findon came down yesterday from Scotland," he said. "She's on her way to Paris, and she called in to see if everything was all right."

"She's Sir Arthur Findon's daughter, the lady who plays the violin, isn't she?" asked Ann.

"Yes, miss. She's a very impetuous young lady, and I can't say that I'm very fond of her, but that's neither here nor there. She found somebody had been to her violin case and borrowed a bow – as a matter of fact, they'd left it out. She didn't come to me, but went to the secretary, and as I've got the key of the flat it made things rather awkward, especially as I'd said I'd say nothing to anybody. Of course, if Sir Arthur were down here it could easily be explained. As it is, if I keep my mouth shut I get into trouble, and if I talk I get into trouble."

She remembered the violin-playing and knew exactly who it was who had borrowed the bow and forgotten to return it.

"Do you know Mr Li Yoseph?" she asked, and he was taken aback by this direct question.

"I don't know anybody by name," he said, "but I have seen an old gentleman come in, and I thought he had permission, and the police told me I wasn't to interfere with him – "

He stopped suddenly as though he realised he had said too much.

"Which police – Mr Bradley? You know Mr Bradley?"

He nodded.

"Yes, miss, I knew Mr Bradley very well. And I knew your brother very well."

She stared at him. For some reason she had never associated this building with Ronnie, had never thought of him as a visitor to Mark's flat.

"You knew Ronnie – my brother?" she said.

"Very well, miss," said Ritchie. "He used to sleep in Mr McGill's flat when he was – " He hesitated for a word; she could guess what it was, and relieved him from his embarrassment.

"I don't know what I can do for you, Ritchie, except to speak to Mr McGill – "

"Don't speak to him, miss," said the man quickly. "No, if you want to do me a turn you might explain to Mr Bradley what has happened. I know he's a friend of yours. Naturally, I don't want to lose a good job, and at the same time I don't want to say why I let the old man into Sir Arthur's flat – I might get into worse trouble."

In spite of her anxiety she laughed.

"Yes, I will speak to Mr Bradley if I see him," she said, "and I'm terribly sorry you've got into hot water. Mr Bradley knew my brother?"

Here came the second shock of the evening.

"Yes, miss, Mr Bradley and Mr Perryman were very good friends. When I say they were very good friends I mean that Mr Bradley was friendly. They often went out in the evenings together, and I know how upset Mr Bradley was when your brother got into trouble. He did his best to save young Perryman."

Ritchie left her something to think about. But if she had been shocked, she was not altogether surprised by the news he had given her. More and more satisfied was she that the story of Bradley's animosity against Ronnie had been manufactured to stimulate her antagonism towards the man whom Mark hated. Ronnie must have met with an accident – fallen out of the boat in his desire to escape the officers of the law.

And then she remembered the verdict of the coroner's jury – wilful murder against some person or persons unknown. She had not brought herself to read the details, but Ronnie's death had been impartially and thoroughly investigated. There had been medical evidence, she supposed, which had left no doubt in the minds either of the coroner or his jury that murder had been committed.

But she had already ruled out Bradley as the slayer, and could not bring herself to find a substitute. Mark? It was unthinkable; and yet she had had evidence of his ruthlessness, his cold-blooded audacity. Old Li Yoseph knew. She remembered now that interview in the dark room at Lady's Stairs – his hesitation when Mark had insisted upon his telling the story, and his almost monosyllabic replies.

She was turning this over in her mind when she heard a soft knock at the door of her flat. It was Mark's signal. She turned the switch softly and put out the light, then crept noiselessly into the hall, felt for the safety catch on the lock and pressed it up. So far as she knew, Mark had no key to the flat, but she could afford to take no risks. Her apprehensions were instantly justified, for a key rattled into the lock and she heard the click as it attempted to turn. The safety catch held, however, and presently the key was withdrawn, and soon after that she heard the door of Mark's flat close, and slipped in the two bolts for further protection.

Who killed Ronnie Perryman? The porter's words had stirred this dormant problem to life. It had become in an instant the most absorbing of all questions, dominating her own sense of peril. She must know. Perhaps it was the realisation that ran in and out the woof and web of her thoughts that Bradley was becoming something more to her than a friend, which made this issue so vital.

Presently she heard the low thud of a door. Mark was going out. Again he signalled at her own door, and again she remained silent, comforted by the knowledge of the bolts she had shot.

The knock was not repeated and, extinguishing the light, she went to the window which overlooked the square; after a while she saw him emerge, cross the square in the direction of Regent Street and disappear.

She tried to bring her mind to the thoughts of bed and sleep, but she was very wide awake. The torture of curiosity was acute. She had an irresistible desire to know the truth about Ronnie, and only one man could tell her – Li Yoseph!

It was past midnight when the mad idea came to her. She rejected it at first because of its very craziness; but the thought grew and grew until, when she had put on her coat and pulled down a small, close-fitting hat upon her head, it seemed that she was about to do the most natural thing in the world, in the most normal circumstances.

She crossed the square in the same direction that Mark had gone, and it was characteristic of her attitude of mind that she was wholly indifferent as to whether she met him or not.

Regent Street was deserted save for a few cars hurrying homeward, and an occasional pedestrian. She had to walk half its length before she found a cab. The driver listened to her directions and pulled a long face.

"I should lose money on the job," he said. "I couldn't possibly get a pick-up there."

She explained that she wanted him to wait for her, and he was more agreeable.

Apparently he knew the district.

"That's a pretty rough spot, young lady, for you to go alone, unless you're visiting friends," he said. "Lady's Stairs – lord, yes, I know the house! An old Jew used to live there."

He also had lived in the neighbourhood until a few months before.

"But the house is empty, miss. I was over there last week and somebody told me the old gentleman hadn't come back."

Ann hesitated. Should she take this mad journey? She settled the question by opening the door of the cab and stepping in.

As the taxi drove down Regent Street she saw two men standing on the edge of the pavement, and one of them signalled the cab to stop, thinking seemingly that it was for hire. As she flashed past she saw that it was Mark McGill, and with him a man who was a stranger to her. She breathed a sigh of relief. Mark, at any rate, was accounted for; he was probably driving to one of the clubs of which he was a member. He was a born gambler, and remarkably lucky at cards – so fortunate, indeed, that the management of two of these clubs had asked him to refrain from attendance.

Except for her momentary qualm, she felt no uneasiness, even when the car was threading the narrow streets which served as an approach to Lady's Stairs. She stopped the cab before the house and got out. No light showed in any of the gaunt and grimy windows. There came to her ears the lapping of the tide against moored barges, and she shivered slightly.

"I told you the place was empty. I don't suppose you'll find anybody there unless it's the copper on duty."

A thought struck her as she crossed the pavement, and she turned back.

"If I can get in, will you take your cab into that side street" – she pointed – "and wait for me there?"

She opened her bag and, taking out a Treasury note, gave it to the man.

"I don't suppose for one moment that anybody is in," she said.

She felt for the bell, which she remembered was in one of the architraves, and in doing so pressed the door. Instantly it swung back. It almost seemed as though Li Yoseph were expecting her. For a moment she stood undecidedly on the doorstep, then walked into the dark little passage.

Upstairs there was a faint glimmer of light, sufficient to guide her, and she ascended with her heart throbbing painfully. Half-way up she discovered where the light came from: the door into Li Yoseph's room was open; suspended from the ceiling on its flex was an unshaded electric globe which burnt dimly. There was no sign of Li Yoseph, or indeed of any human being.

She stood in the doorway, surveying the room.

"Is anybody there?" she asked nervously.

Only the echo of her words came back to her.

The place was in some disorder, but much cleaner than Ann had expected. She did not know until afterwards that Mr and Mrs Shiffan had pursued their leisurely labours for days to remove a mass of debris and cartloads of dust.

Li's iron bedstead lay bare and gaunt; the bedding had been long since removed. The windows that looked out on to the creek were fairly clean, and through them she saw the riding lights of steamers tied up to an opposite wharf.

"Is anybody here?"

Her voice was louder, but there was no reply.

She did not know what lay behind the two doors which opened from the room, and she needed all her self-control to screw up courage to investigate. She was taking a step in the direction of the door when the one light of the room went out and she was left in complete darkness.

She shrank back towards the landing, and as she did so she heard the sound of wood sliding against wood, and in the centre of the floor there appeared a faintly outlined square of space. In another second a man's head came into view. Higher and higher it rose; and then she saw, in the light of the lamp he carried, the face of the intruder.

It was the dead Jew!

Should she speak to him? Before she could make up her mind she heard a second voice whisper, and the lamp was extinguished. Somebody else was coming up – not one, not two men, but three. She heard the swish of their soft footsteps on the floor, and then there was another muttered colloquy, and she saw the square of light vanish and heard the thud of the trap as it closed.

She waited for a few seconds, trying to overhear what was being said, and then the whispers retreated, a door latched loudly, and as suddenly as it had gone off the light came on again. The room was empty.

She stood motionless in the doorway, waiting for something to happen. The first sound she heard was from the stairs below; it was the tramp of a heavy foot, and the intruder must have seen her, for she heard her name spoken in a tone of amazement.

"Ann!" And then sharply: "What are you doing here?"

It was Mark, and he was alone.

He pushed her gently into the room, and, catching her by the shoulders, turned her round so that she faced him, as his dark, suspicious eyes peered into hers.

"Who brought you here?"

"A cab," she said, with an assumption of indifference she did not feel.

"Why did you come? Did Bradley send for you?"

She opened her eyes wider at this.

"Mr Bradley? No. I came to see Li Yoseph."

"What about?" he asked sharply. "You're not going to tell me that curiosity brought you here?"

"I'm going to tell you just what I want to tell you, Mark," she said quietly. "I am not accountable to you for my actions."

He thought for a moment, his forehead puckered in an ugly frown.

"Have you seen Li Yoseph?" he asked.

It was on the tip of her tongue to tell him what she had seen, but something impelled her to equivocation.

"No, I have not seen him," she said. Fortunately he was not looking at her at that moment, for Ann was a bad liar.

He crossed the room to the door at which she had been waiting when Li Yoseph had appeared, and throwing it open, passed through. He was absent for five minutes, then came back, dusting his hands.

"There's nobody there," he said.

Suddenly he lifted his head.

"What's that?"

Ann had heard it too – the sound of low, chuckling laughter, which seemed to come from the room above them.

23

Ann looked at the man at her side.

"Who was that?" she asked in a low voice.

"It sounds like Li," he said with a frown. "He's as crazy as a coot."

They waited, but no other sound came; and then, for some reason, Ann felt terribly afraid. She had a feeling that she was being watched by unseen eyes.

"Don't go," he said as she turned towards the door. "I'll take you back – "

"I'll go back alone: I have a cab."

"Oh, it was yours, was it?" he said. "I saw it in a side street and thought it was a flyer."

He followed her down the stairs into the street, and stared at the unexpected sight which met his eyes. Three police cars were parked on the opposite kerb, one behind the other. Except for the three drivers who sat motionless at the wheel, there was no sign of the Squad.

"What are they doing here? I didn't see them when I came in," said Mark, and for once his voice betrayed his perturbation. "You haven't seen your friend Bradley by any chance, have you?"

She did not answer this, but crossed the road quickly to the side street where her cab was waiting, the driver slumbering over his steering wheel.

By this time Mark had recovered something of his old buoyancy.

"You wouldn't like to give me a lift, I suppose? Well, it isn't necessary. Why did you come, Ann?" he asked in a different tone. "Did Bradley suggest you should see the old man?"

"No," she answered shortly as she stepped into the cab and slammed the door behind her.

She was so tired that she dozed all the way back to town, and was half asleep when the cab drew up at her flat. She saw the figure of a man half a dozen yards from where the cab had stopped, and as she was paying the cabman he came rapidly towards her and she recognised his gait. It was Tiser.

"Have you seen Mark, Miss Ann?" he asked, his voice trembling. "I have been waiting for him."

"He's at Lady's Stairs," she said.

"Lady's Stairs!" he repeated shrilly. "And you have been there? Oh, my dear Miss Ann, how hazardous, how foolish!"

She would have passed him, but he stood in her way.

"Don't go yet, Miss Ann," he said. "I have something to say to you, something rather important, about − um − the awkward situation in which we all find ourselves."

She was puzzled by his attitude, by his rambling speech. Her first impression was that he had been drinking; but by now she had come to understand him, and recognised the symptoms. He was sober enough.

"I'd rather discuss this in the morning, Mr Tiser − " she began.

And then, to her amazement, he turned abruptly from her and fled into the darkness. She heard the whirr of car wheels, saw two bright lights come flying round the circle of the gardens, and a car pulled up at the kerb with a jerk. It was one of the police tenders she had seen, and she recognised the man who sprang out before he spoke.

"Why on earth are you waiting in the street? Haven't you a key?" asked Bradley.

His presence brought to her a ridiculous sense of comfort and safety, and her laugh was almost hysterical.

"Yes − only Mr Tiser wanted to talk to me."

"Tiser, eh? I thought he was waiting in McGill's flat," said Bradley. "What did he say?"

She shook her head.

"Nothing of importance," she said.

"You've been to Lady's Stairs, haven't you?" And then, with a chuckle: "I won't be mysterious – I know you have. I'd rather you didn't go there, Ann, until I ask you to pay a visit – and then I'll be there to see that nothing happens to you. Can I come up to your flat?"

Oddly enough, she saw nothing unusual in his request, though it must have been nearly three o'clock.

"What did Tiser talk about?" He seemed strangely interested in the movements of Mr Tiser.

It was impossible to tell him, because she herself had not the slightest idea why the man had intercepted her.

"That's queer," he said when she had told him all there was to tell. "It almost seems as though – "

He did not finish his sentence. He took the key from her hand, opened the outer door and preceded her up the stairs. It was he who unlocked the door of her flat and walked in ahead of her.

He opened the door of the dining-room, put in his hand and switched on the light, and stood for a moment, watching with grim enjoyment the discomfiture of Mark McGill, who was sitting at the table, waiting to enjoy a similar experience when Ann saw his face.

"Did you have any trouble getting in?" asked Bradley. His voice was silky in its politeness.

"I had my key," said McGill coolly.

Bradley nodded.

"I gather you arrived about a minute ahead of Miss Perryman, and sent Tiser down to the street to meet and engage her in conversation whilst you settled yourself in her flat."

Ann was staring at the intruder, speechless with amazement. She remembered now that as they were approaching Westminster Bridge a big car had passed the cab, and in her sleepy way she thought it had familiar lines.

"There are two things I could do," said Bradley slowly. "If I followed my primitive instincts, I would open that window and throw you out. I could arrest you now on one of the two minor charges that

203

I can bring against you. But I prefer to get you on the major charge."

"Which is?" asked Mark, almost pleasantly.

Bradley smiled.

"I don't think I need explain what that is," he said. "You went down to see Li Yoseph – well, you shall see him one night this week, and you shall hear him make an accusation. I am banking very heavily upon how you receive Li Yoseph's charge."

Mark was amused.

"Will you put him in the witness-box, and will you call his ghost to corroborate his evidence?" he demanded. "You can't scare me, Bradley, and you can't bluff me. And as to my being here, Miss Perryman knows why I came. She gave me the key."

Ann's resentment toward the man flamed to anger.

"How dare you say that – " she began, but Bradley stopped her with a glance.

"He's not trying to rattle you, but to rattle me," he said, "and I'm the most difficult man in the world to throw off his balance."

He jerked his head to the door.

"Get out, McGill."

For a moment Mark McGill looked ugly, and then, with a shrug, he walked out of the flat, and they heard his door slam violently.

"I've never asked you, Ann, but have you any friends or relations in London?"

She shook her head.

"Then you must go to an hotel – I think you'll be safe enough tonight, but you must leave this flat in the morning. Have you any money?"

She smiled at this.

"I have my ill-gotten gains," she said ruefully. "I suppose I really ought not to take a penny away from this place. I think I'll go to Paris tomorrow."

"I'd rather you didn't leave London yet awhile," he said quickly. "I want to catch McGill, but my real reason comes into the realm of personal vanity. I want to convince you that Ronnie – "

She interrupted him with a gesture.

"If you want me to stay until you clear yourself of that stupid charge, I shall leave this minute," she said.

"You mean that? You haven't even the edge of a suspicion?"

"Not even the edge. What quaint terms you use!" she said with a laugh.

He considered this for a long time before he spoke.

"Do you remember when we first met, in old Li Yoseph's house – how you said that you would never be happy until you had brought your brother's murderer to the scaffold?"

She shivered.

"I don't think I feel like that any more – it was a rhetorical phrase then. I'm beginning to understand the horror of it now."

There followed a long period during which neither spoke. He seemed loath to leave her; she was as reluctant to see him go.

"The trade of the law isn't a nice trade, is it? You remember we had that out in the police court? Would it worry you terribly if you were" – he found a difficulty in finishing the question – "if you were married to a detective?" And when she did not answer he continued: "Whatever happens, I am leaving the police force at the end of this year. I have been offered the management of a large coffee plantation in Brazil – you did not know I was an authority upon coffee?"

She shook her head.

"That would be more comfortable than being the wife of a policeman, wouldn't it?"

Ann did not meet his eyes.

"Yes, I suppose it would be." And then: "Are you thinking of getting married, Mr Bradley?"

She forced herself to meet his eyes.

"I am thinking of wanting to get married," he said. "The only question is whether the girl I want to marry would have a fit if I suggested – " He ended lamely.

"I think it is time you went home, Mr Bradley," she said as she opened the door for him. "Half-past three in the morning is not the best hour to discuss matrimony, is it?"

Still he lingered.

"Are you keen on coffee?"

She did not answer until he was safely outside the door of the flat.

"I shall drink nothing else in the future," she said as she closed the door upon him.

24

When, the next morning, her maid came in to tell her that Mark was waiting outside and wished to see her, she was surprisingly unfluttered. There had come to her a new strength and confidence. She told the girl to admit him, and gave him an almost buoyant "Good morning." When he began to apologise to her for his conduct of last night she cut him short.

"That must be the end of our friendship, Mark," she said quietly. "It really ended quite a long time ago – when I discovered just what you had made me do for you."

He was amused at this, made no attempt to protest the innocent character of the smuggled drugs, but rather emphasised the nature of his illicit dealings.

"There's a pile of money in it and little competition," he said coolly. "I was getting it organised when Bradley took charge of the dope squad. It will take me years to recover, for in the meantime there's a new agent in the market."

She looked at him in shocked wonder.

"Doesn't it ever keep you awake – the thought of what you're doing?" she asked. "All the lives you are ruining, the young people you are degrading, these terrible crimes that are being committed – there was a case today in Manchester – "

"Don't be silly." He smiled. "Really, Ann, you're becoming a sentimentalist! You can't even live without hurting somebody. The day you go your flat will be snapped up by a family that has a smaller one; their flat in turn will be taken by another growing family – if you look right down the line you'd find that your living in this flat kept somebody pigging it in the slums. There isn't a stitch of clothing you wear that hasn't hurt somebody to make – that doesn't keep you awake, does it?"

The argument was so fallacious that she did not attempt to contest it.

"No," he said, shaking his head, "the only thing that keeps me awake is, who's got my trade? I could have sold my connection for a hundred thousand, and as soon as I got under the eye of the police I expected at any rate a fair offer for it; but my agents are being snapped up by the Great Unknown, which means that somebody will be getting rich quick on my brains and my industry."

He seemed absorbed in this problem, so absorbed that she had the impression that he had come to discuss this and nothing else.

"The distribution is going to kill 'em. You were terribly useful to me, Ann: I don't know what I should have done without you."

She shuddered at the compliment. Then it was that he revealed the object of his visit.

"I don't know how long you'll be in the country, but before you go it is pretty certain that you'll be approached by these people for information. There are some agents that nobody knows anything about, only you and I – I've trusted you as I've never trusted a soul in my life. If any inquiry is put to you, I want you to tell me who it is who approaches you."

"I shall be in England for a very short time," she said, and he nodded.

"They know that as well as I," he said. "That's why I've come over this morning and taken the chance of a snubbing. You haven't told Bradley?" he asked quickly.

She shook her head.

"Somehow I didn't think you would. But you might tell somebody else. I don't know that I wouldn't rather you told Bradley. The worst thing that can happen to them is that they get pinched, and I don't care two hoots if they spend the rest of their lives in Dartmoor, but I don't want anybody to profit by my organisation."

He was a staggering man. It might have been imagined that he was a business man discussing a purely commercial problem. He was neither ashamed nor foolishly proud of his evil work. If there was pride at all, it was in the consciousness of the business acumen which had organised a network of agencies through the length and breadth of the land.

He changed the subject abruptly, asked about her plans, and made no reference whatever either to the scene in the Home or his presence in her room when she had returned from Lady's Stairs; nor did he mention Li Yoseph until he was on the point of departure.

"I know exactly what I've got to look for from old Li," he said. "He sold himself to the police before – before he disappeared. He's hand-in-glove with them now, and if Bradley could get independent testimony I should be behind bars. But he can't."

"You think Mr Yoseph has betrayed you?" she asked.

"Betrayed me!" scoffed Mark. "Of course he hasn't! There are five hundred people in this country who would betray me, but none of them has corroborative evidence."

She went out that afternoon, and in the course of her travels saw Sedeman at a distance. He was slightly intoxicated, unsteady on his feet. Mr Sedeman was singing raucously at the top of his voice, and was followed slowly by a policeman who was shepherding him to the next beat.

Ann was shopping half-heartedly in preparation for her journey to Paris. It was strange to her how little enthusiasm there was and how little sincerity in her purchases. Mostly when she entered a store she did not quite know what she required. For if her mind said Paris her heart said Brazil, and most of her purchases perhaps passed the test of utility for the latter destination.

She was in an Oxford Street store when she became aware of Tiser's presence. She had imagined she had seen him before. He was always soberly attired, but today his sobriety approached sombreness. He caught her eye with an ingratiating smile, and his white hands began running over one another with extraordinary rapidity. When Mr Tiser was agitated his hands were invariably busy. He was normally nervous, she noticed, for he threw a quick glance back over his shoulder as though expecting to find himself under a malignant observation. She brought her attention back quickly to the articles she had been examining, and expected him to melt away in the crowd which thronged the great departmental store. A few seconds later, to her surprise, she found him at her elbow.

"Good afternoon, Miss Ann. I do hope I have not arrived at an inconvenient moment, but would you do me the great honour of taking tea with me...there is a refreshment department on the fourth floor."

Her first inclination was to decline; but Ann hated to hurt the feelings of even the meanest of her fellows. Subconsciously she may have welcomed his advent, as representing another source of information.

"I will go upstairs and reserve a table," he said eagerly when she nodded. "I am sure I can rely upon you, my dear Miss Ann, not to disappoint me."

Tiser had a trick of vanishing. His movements were so stealthy and rapid that the careless eye did not follow him. He disappeared now almost before she could turn her head; it was some time before she went up in the elevator to the restaurant floor, and she found him sitting at a table in a corner near a window overlooking Oxford Street. He rose with such rapidity that he nearly upset the table, and was incoherent in his thanks.

"First of all, my dear young lady," he began when she was seated, "I was not responsible for what happened last night. I was horrified when Mark – "

"Don't let us discuss that, Mr Tiser," she said.

"Exactly, exactly," he said hastily. "It was very unpleasant. It was unmannerly...disgraceful! But Mark is like that – a bully, my dear Miss Ann."

"Have you seen Li Yoseph?" she asked.

If it was possible his face went a little paler.

"No, I have not seen that dear old gentleman. What a character! He might have stepped out of one of Mr Dickens's books!"

It was on the tip of her tongue to tell Tiser that he himself was not without resemblance to a certain slimy character in "David Copperfield," but she refrained.

"His ghosts, for example," Tiser went on. "There is something almost pathetic in that, don't you think? Not that I imagine for one moment he sees ghosts – you don't believe in such things, do you, dear Miss Ann?"

He shot a swift sidelong glance at her. There was anxiety in his eyes. What made her say it she could not tell, but before she could think she had asked:

"He sees Ronnie's ghost, doesn't he?"

She was shocked at her own irreverence. The effect upon Mr Tiser was pitiable: his jaw dropped, and his face was contorted with fear.

"Don't say that! For God's sake don't speak about that!" he said shrilly. "I can't bear it – really I can't! It is indecent – horrible."

"Do you believe in these things?"

She asked the question more to soothe him than to solicit his confidence.

"No, I don't! It's absurd – unscientific. I took a degree, you know, Miss Ann…natural science. Such things are absurd. But I am a nervous man, and cannot bear even to discuss…ghosts!"

But Ann had hardened her heart. She could say things now that a few weeks ago would have been unthinkable.

"Li Yoseph saw him killed, didn't he?"

Tiser made no gesture of assent or denial; he stared at her, blinking quickly; his mouth opened in something that looked to be a smile but was no more than a horrifying grimace. She repeated the question.

"I don't know – do for goodness' sake let us discuss something else."

He pulled out a large white handkerchief and mopped his face.

"Some day you must come to tea with me at my little house – no, no, not the Home. I have a *pied-à-terre* off the Bayswater Road."

He stopped suddenly, his mouth wide open.

"Whatever made me say that?" he asked in a fearful whisper. "You will not tell Mark, my dear Miss Ann? I don't know why I said it, I

211

don't know why I told you. It only shows my confidence in you." He made this quick recovery. "I should like to show it to you. I have three thousand pounds' worth of furniture there…one has saved a little money. But you will not tell Mark?"

She shook her head.

"I am unlikely to discuss anything with Mr McGill," she said.

He sighed heavily and smiled.

"Mark is peculiar, but, I fear, finished. It is so foolish to get yourself talked about by the police, and I am afraid he has made an enemy of dear Mr Bradley – what a genius that man is! He is much too good for the police force. He ought to be – "

He was stuck for a simile. Ann thought she could have supplied the missing words.

"Yes, Mark is finished." Mr Tiser became almost cheerful at the thought. "He has had a long innings, and now, if he's wise, he will fade away out of sight and be no more seen, as the good Book says. Vanity is his downfall. What a pity it is, my dear Miss Ann, that so many men, otherwise intelligent, peculiarly fitted for their occupation, should sink their careers upon the same rock!" He shook his head despondently.

"In what direction has his vanity taken him?" asked Ann. She would have been amused in other circumstances by the blatant hypocrisy of the man.

Tiser shrugged his thin shoulders.

"His vanity has many aspects," he said. "For example, he imagines that he and he alone built up his organisation, and that he and he alone can work it. It is true there are a number of his agents who are at present unknown to anybody but himself." He smiled cunningly. "But not to you, eh, my dear Miss Ann? I am sure not. The Cardiff agent, for example – what a mysterious individual! You used to go to him, didn't you?"

Ann did not reply, and Mr Tiser shook his head waggishly.

"What a discreet soul you are, Miss Ann! I suppose you'll go to Paris and you'll be starting all over again? It will be a terrible handicap for you. And I'm quite sure Mark hasn't been at all generous to you – confess it!"

"I haven't given him an opportunity of being generous," she answered.

Mr Tiser smiled.

"Naturally! One couldn't accept favours from that kind of man. But I'm not that kind of man. I said to myself this morning: 'Tiser, you must do the right thing by that young lady. Go to your bank and draw five hundred pounds' – which I did." He tapped his waistcoat and she heard the crispness of notes. "Five hundred pounds," he repeated. "It would give you a start – "

"You want the name of the Cardiff agent, and that is the price you will pay?" she asked bluntly.

"Exactly. What a business woman you are!"

Her lips curled; he thought she was flattered.

"You're the Great Unknown, then?"

"Eh?" said Mr Tiser apprehensively.

"You're the man that Mark's talking about, who has stolen his nasty business?"

His face began twitching.

"Mark said what?" he stammered. "…Nasty business… saccharine…"

"Cocaine," said Ann. "Mark knows there's somebody who is using his organisation – "

"It isn't me," protested the man fearfully. "I beg of you, my dear Miss Ann, if he should inquire of you, to say that it isn't me. I was merely testing you – ha ha!" His laugh was dismal and most unconvincing. "Loyalty to Mark is the keystone of my life, dear Miss Ann."

She poured out a cup of tea. Had she not been in need of it she might have declined his invitation: she realised that now.

Ann did not speak for a moment, and then:

"Who killed my brother?"

She raised her eyes with the question, and Tiser shrank back in his chair; for a few seconds he was unable to articulate.

"Bradley," he said hollowly. "Mark told you…"

"Who killed him? Was it you?"

He nearly jumped out of his chair.

"Me?" he squeaked. "Good God! I wouldn't raise my hand to my worst enemy! I don't know who killed him. It may have been an accident."

"Then why do you say Bradley killed him?" she went on remorselessly. "Wasn't it Mark?"

He stared at her, fascinated.

"Was it Mark?" she repeated.

"My dear Miss Bradley – I mean Miss Ann – why do you ask such questions? They're stupid, aren't they? I can't understand you – really I can't. I don't know anything about it."

At that moment a terrifying thought struck him.

"You're working with Mr Bradley – I'm sure you are, Miss Ann. Such an admirable man! I don't know that there's another in the world I admire so much."

She cut short his eulogies.

"I'm working for nobody, not even for you, Mr Tiser," she said. "You'll have to put that five hundred pounds back in the bank – or possibly you might like to make reparation to some of the poor souls you and Mark have ruined."

She drank the remainder of her tea, put down her cup, and, rising, without a word, left him. It was too fine a gesture, she discovered to her consternation, for when she had made a small purchase on the ground floor she remembered she had left her bag in the restaurant. The situation was something of an anti-climax, but Ann had a sense of humour and her only embarrassment was the possibility of Tiser renewing his offer. She was relieved to see him coming out of the broad doorway as she went back, to meet half-way a waitress carrying the bag.

That was twice she had lost it in the past few days. Bradley had restored it once. She slipped the handle over her arm and went out into the street. Mr Tiser saw her passing slowly eastward, and beckoned to the man who, unknown to the girl, had been Tiser's shadow all that day.

He was a singularly ill-favoured man, and even his patently new collar and his ready-to-wear overcoat did not give him any semblance of respectability.

"There's the woman: keep her in sight," he said. "There are half a dozen busies patrolling the street – tell the first one you meet."

The man slipped away in pursuit of Ann, and Mr Tiser, waiting till he was out of sight, called a cab and went home.

Ann did not dream that she was being followed. She pursued her leisurely way, stopping to look in store windows. There was one that fascinated her – a tropical outfitter's, the windows filled with topees and the equipment of hot climates. So standing, a well-dressed, military-looking man bumped against her. He apologised instantly, raised his hat and walked on. Ann forgot this incident for a little time, and then:

"Excuse me, miss."

The voice was gruff and authoritative, and she knew instinctively it was a detective.

"Have you seen this man before?" He pointed to him of the clean collar.

Ann shook her head in astonishment.

"No, I have never seen him before."

"Have you ever offered to sell him anything?"

"Sell him anything?" repeated Ann in bewilderment. "Why, of course not! I have nothing to sell."

"Did you offer him two packets of cocaine from your bag?"

"Certainly not," said Ann indignantly. "I have nothing in my – "

She looked down. Her bag was wide open and empty. Fortunately, her money was in a secure little pocket at the side. It was then that she remembered the military-looking man.

"I've been robbed," she said. "Somebody pushed against me..."

She told the story, and the detective sensed the truth of it, yet suggested gently that she should walk with him to the police station.

Her accuser would have melted away, but the police officer was prepared for this.

"You walk in front, my son," he said, and reluctantly the man obeyed.

On arrival at the police station Ann heard the amazing story. The man with the clean collar had complained that she had offered him two packets of cocaine, and swore that he had seen a dozen other packets in her bag. He had complained to the first detective he saw, with the result that Ann had been stopped.

It was an unfortunate day for the accuser, for at the police station there was a detective with a larger knowledge of the underworld, who recognised him instantly and greeted him as a friend.

"I'm extremely sorry, Miss Perryman," said the man who had arrested her, "but the police have evidently been hoaxed by this man. Will you describe the fellow who knocked against you?"

She described the military-looking gentleman faithfully, and he grinned.

"I know him," he said emphatically.

As she was leaving the police station the man who had charged her would have followed, but an unfriendly hand detained him.

"You're inside," said the officer with a happy smile.

"What's the charge?" demanded the indignant man, and learned that it was the very comprehensive "loitering with intent" that he would have to answer in the morning.

The detective who had taken her to the station accompanied Ann down the street. She thought his manner was very respectful, and when he said, later, that he had worked with Bradley, she gathered, somewhat uncomfortably, that she was not altogether unknown in police circles.

"I can't understand that man charging you," he said. "He must have been absolutely certain you had coke in your possession."

"But that is absurd – " she began.

"Not so absurd as you think, Miss Perryman. I'm wondering whether he dropped in a few packets in order to get a charge against you. You didn't leave your bag anywhere – "

Ann remembered with a gasp.

"Yes, I left it in the tea-room."

"Were you with anybody?"

She hesitated.

"Nobody that matters," she said.

It was Tiser, of course. There was something feline in the spite of this man, and her first impression was that he was aiming at Bradley through her.

When she got home Mark's door was open, and apparently he had watched her coming along the street from the window.

"Come in for a moment, Ann, if you will."

His tone was urgent rather than peremptory.

"You needn't be afraid: the house is full of servants, male and female."

He shut the door behind her and followed her into the sitting-room, which had already begun to have an unfamiliar appearance. Mark McGill shut the door.

"Why did they pinch you?" he asked.

She told him exactly the facts.

"You went to tea and left your bag behind? Who was with you?"

Should she tell him? There seemed no great harm, though she resolved not to betray Tiser's duplicity.

"Mr Tiser," she said. "I can't imagine he would do anything so beastly."

Mark pursed his lips as though he were going to whistle.

"Tiser, eh? Thought he was going to get back on me, did he?"

"I don't think – " she began.

"Of course it was he!" His eyes narrowed. "It will be curious if I swing for Tiser – and yet I think I'd get a kick out of it."

"Why should he do it?"

"Why should he do it?" he sneered. "Because he's a rat, and he knew that if you were pinched I'd be brought into it. Tiser is the Great Unknown: I discovered that this afternoon whilst you were out. Did he try to buy my Cardiff man?"

Ann sighed.

217

"I don't know what he tried to buy. I'm so heartily sick of this beastly business – I shall be so glad to be away."

"Are you still going to Paris?" He eyed her keenly.

"I think so."

"Not sure, eh? Your position in London will be rather awkward, won't it, Ann? After all, you've got a certain reputation at police headquarters, and it isn't going to do Bradley any good – when you're married to him."

She did not reply.

"Perhaps he's coming out of the police?"

"They all do sooner or later, don't they?" she answered coolly.

His laugh was harsh; he was evidently unamused.

"That will be the queerest development of all – marrying a copper, I mean. You might have done better than that, Ann."

"I might have married a trafficker in dope," she said deliberately.

"Hardly!" he said, with the greatest sang-froid. "I'm married already – I don't know where she is or whether I could divorce her. I hardly think I could. Shocked?"

She shook her head.

"Nothing shocks me, Mark – nothing about you."

He patted her gently on the shoulder and she shrank under his touch.

"Don't be a fool: I'm not going to murder you. If I strangle anybody this night, it will be – you know. That's all, Ann."

He opened the door for her, and as she was going out he said:

"Do you know what Tiser's afraid of?"

"You?" she suggested.

He shook his head.

"Steen." He chuckled for a long time, and seemed tickled by the thought that was in his mind. "He's afraid of being hanged! And it's a perfectly painless death – and terribly picturesque. I shan't mind it a bit."

Her eyes came slowly up to his, and she searched their inscrutable depths.

"Whom have you killed, Mark?"

She thought she saw him wince. Evidently there were raw places where he could be hurt.

"I've killed four people," he said. "I'm only sorry about one. Now off you go." He almost pushed her out of the room, and, contrary to his general custom, did not accompany her to the front door.

When she got into her own flat the phone bell was ringing, and she heard Bradley's voice.

"They pulled you in, did they? You're getting almost a bad character, Ann. I'm terribly sorry."

"Oh, my dear, it was nothing – " she began, and felt herself go scarlet.

"Say that again – no, I won't ask you. Ann, keep in touch with me: I may want you at any moment. You're not afraid of Li Yoseph or his ghosts?"

"You know I'm not: you asked me that before."

A little pause.

"I went down the other night, you know – you never asked me why."

"I guessed that," he said. "Were you frightened when the light went out?"

She did not ask him how he knew that the light went out. His knowledge of all that happened at Lady's Stairs was uncanny.

It was curious what little things worried her. The cloud on her mind at the moment was the probability that she would have to prosecute the pickpocket who had stolen a few articles from her bag which were of no great value. This became a certainty in the afternoon, when a detective called to say that the man had been arrested, and that in his possession was a small gold cigarette case which she sometimes carried and which bore her initials. And here again the ubiquitous Mr Bradley intervened to save her discomfort.

"The inspector has seen Mr Bradley, and he says that all that is necessary for you to do is to identify the articles. We want him on other charges."

That unpleasant business was soon over. She was able to identify the debonair prisoner, who seemed in no wise abashed by his humiliating position.

Mark had bought a new car. She saw him with the demonstrator trying it out in Cavendish Place, and as she passed he waved to her with the greatest unconcern. She thought he might make this an excuse to call, but she did not see him again that night, though she heard from him just before she went to bed, when he phoned her.

"I believe Tiser's got a house of his own. Have you any idea where it is?"

"Isn't he at the Home?" she fenced with the question.

"No, he's not at the Home. Everything of his has been cleared out. The fox has gone to earth."

"Why do you want to see him?"

She heard him laugh.

"Is it unnatural that I should desire the companionship of a loyal and faithful comrade?" he asked sarcastically, and hung up before she could answer.

Events were moving rapidly to a crisis. She had a sensation that she was being carried along at breakneck speed to some terrific climax. There was no solid foundation for this illusion. Apparently nothing unusual was happening.

The following morning as she was sitting at the window she saw Mark walk across the road, wearing a top hat and morning coat that showed his powerful frame to the best advantage. He might have been going to a wedding; he was, in point of fact, interviewing the Controller of Passports, and Mark was a shrewd believer in the psychology of appearance. She ought to have guessed that it was some such audacious enterprise on which he had set forth so gaily attired.

That afternoon she saw something which filled her with horror and self-loathing. She was in Regent Street, and saw, without noticing, a dingy touring car moving slowly towards Oxford Street. The pace slackened; there was at that moment a very clear road space ahead, and the reason for its slowness did not seem apparent. Then suddenly she heard a crash and a startled cry, and saw a man running in the direction of the car, pursued by a policeman. As he leaped on to the running-board of the car, which was now accelerating its pace, he turned, and she heard the stinging explosion of an automatic. Another shot followed; the policeman staggered and went on to his knees. In a second the car was flying up the street and had turned round a corner.

She was one of the first to reach the policeman, who was apparently unhurt, though there was a jagged gash in his helmet. Almost before he could clear himself of the crowd, she saw another car flying in the same direction that the touring machine had taken. It was loaded with men, and at the sound of its peculiar siren the police held up traffic. That, too, vanished round the corner, seeming to take the angle on two wheels. She heard somebody say "Flying Squad," and wondered from what blue it had fallen.

And then she heard a man say something which made her shiver.

"Did you see the fellow that did the shooting? He had a face as white as a sheet. If he wasn't a dope, I'm not a doctor."

She turned sick with horror. Perhaps she had brought that beastly powder to the reach of this half-mad criminal. If the policeman had died, his life would have been on her soul.

She hurried home, physically nauseated by the thought, by the knowledge of all that had happened in that year of madness.

When she got to Cavendish Square she saw a crowd surrounding some huge object. She did not attempt to look, but hurried up to her room. From her window she had a clear view: it was the grey car, lying on its side, and, locked to its bonnet, a smaller car. Even at this distance she could see the stains of blood on the roadway.

Ritchie came up, full of information.

"They got two of the men – they weren't hurt. The others went to the hospital... Oh, yes, the gentleman in the small car was killed. It was a head-on collision, but these fellows don't mind what they do. They say the driver was half crazy with dope..."

She did not want to hear any more, but waved the astonished man from the door and slammed it in his face.

There was no end to it, then, this ghastly business of Mark's. It began with those little packets she used to collect, and distributed with such lightness of heart, rejoicing, like the fool she was, in the fact that she was baffling the police; and ended – in the death of innocent people, in dingy police courts, in dark condemned cells where men waited the inevitable and dreadful hour.

The evening brought a visitor – Mr Sedeman, rather better dressed than usual, his white top hat a thing of restored beauty. Nobody knew at what age Mr Sedeman began his petty criminal career. He had seen the interior of almost every prison in England, and was almost welcomed by a dozen prison staffs as a light relief to their gloomy labours. He was perfectly sober, and in his more loquacious mood.

The curious thing about Mr Sedeman was that the more sober he was, the more boastful he became. He loved to talk of his imaginary friends in good society, of this foreign duke and that continental nobleman, and retail with a flourish his experience in the homes of the mighty. There must have been a substratum of truth in most of these stories, for he was an educated man, spoke French and German with great fluency, and had a working knowledge of Spanish and Italian. He had told her twice that he had a degree at one of the oldest of the universities, and probably this was the truth.

"Sit down, Mr Sedeman. I thought I saw you yesterday – "

"Inebriated, I fear." Mr Sedeman shook his hoary head. "Wines are not what they were in my young days – or possibly the labels are a little different. I was inveigled unfortunately into drinking with royalty at a bar in Long Acre. Whether the man is royalty or not I have the gravest doubts. He claims to be the real King of Abyssinia and was trying to raise the price of two postage stamps to write to the Prime Minister of that interesting country. He was at any rate black, and I have since discovered that he sells tips on racecourses, which hardly tallies with his description of his early life at court."

He sighed heavily.

"I've come to see you to ask you to dissuade our very excellent friend, Mr Bradley, who is both a policeman and a gentleman, from a misguided scheme to place me in an institution. I have been dodging institutions all my life" – he coughed – "with the exception of one in the region of Pentonville – and I am satisfied that I am temperamentally unsuited. In the first place, I am not old, unless you would call forty-nine old?" His pale eyes challenged her, but Ann kept a straight face. "In the second place, I am a lover of the great open spaces about which one sees so much at the cinema. In the third place, a lady friend of mine has offered to give me a good Christian home, if the police will be patient – she comes out of Holloway Prison next week. In the meantime, my dear Miss Perryman – which bears such a resemblance to Sedeman that I think we may possibly be related – no? Well, as I was saying, in spite of my misfortunes and the worries incidental to my nomad life, if I may use that expression before a lady, I am still interested in the downtrodden poor, and I have a great scheme, if I can raise sufficient money, to build a row of cottages somewhere in the region of Esher, which is a good pitch. I've raised, or I've had the promise of, some three thousand seven hundred pounds, and kind friends are contributing just what they can spare to this deserving cause."

He said this very pointedly. Ann opened her bag and took out a pound note.

"Thank you," said Mr Sedeman gravely. "You will receive a receipt from the treasurer in due course. The police are not very considerate, I am sorry to say. I have made three journeys to Lady's Stairs, involving very heavy expenditure in the shape of tram fares and refreshment, but up to now my bill of expenses has been ignored."

"Do you go often to Lady's Stairs?"

He nodded gravely.

"Have you met Mrs Shiffan? She is the cicerone of the place – a comely wench, married to a husband of no great moral quality. She herself" – the reprobate looked out of the window, smiled, and smacked his lips.

"Really, Mr Sedeman!"

"I admire beauty in the abstract," the old man hastened to assure her, "as one admires a painting of Leonardo da Vinci, or a statuette of Benvenuto, or an Italian sunset."

And then, abruptly:

"I have a message for you." He dived his hand inside his long ulster and brought out an official-looking envelope. She knew by the writing that it was from Bradley.

The message was short.

Please do not leave your house today, however urgent may seem the reason. Check any information you get by calling up Treasury 5000 Extension 49.

"From a mutual friend," said Mr Sedeman complacently.

As he was leaving the room:

"I beg of you not to mention to Mr Bradley this little Home of mine — I do not think he is greatly in sympathy with it, and as my actions have been so misunderstood in the past, it is quite possible that he may put the foulest construction upon my philanthropy."

Ann laughed, in spite of her anxiety.

"You mean my philanthropy," she said.

"Exactly," said Mr Sedeman.

There was, she discovered, need for a warning. At seven o'clock that evening she was having her dinner when a district messenger brought a note, written on notepaper headed "Scotland Yard," and asking her to take the car she would find at the door. She was in her bedroom, changing, when she remembered Bradley's letter and called up the number he had given her.

"No, miss, we've not sent for anybody. Just pretend you're going, and we'll be round in three minutes."

As she looked out of the window a closed car came to the kerb. She went back to the messenger boy and gave him a message.

"Ask the driver to wait: I'll be down in a few minutes," she said.

Evidently whoever was in the car was taking no risks. When she went back to the front of the house to watch for the arrival of the police tender, she saw the machine moving off.

It was Bradley himself who came, with his squad.

"Why on earth do they want to get hold of me? I should be more of a nuisance than a use to them."

Bradley shook his head.

"You are a pretty good bargaining point," he said. "By the way, Mark would know nothing about that incident this afternoon – that was Tiser's own little joke. He's as spiteful as a jealous woman. I'm sending a woman to keep you company tonight – do you mind? She is a member of the women's police force, and very efficient. I hate giving you police protection, but this is the most unostentatious method I can think of."

Truth to tell, Ann was heartily glad to see the plainly dressed and raw-boned lady who came to spend the evening with her, though, as she subsequently discovered, her snores were so terrific that Ann seemed to be waking up every few minutes.

Nothing happened that night. There was no word from Mark or from Tiser. Tiser had spent a very unhappy evening, and had no thought for anybody but himself. His house was a small one, in a tiny square leading from the Bayswater Road. He lived entirely alone, employing two daily servants, who left at six. Any food that was required after that hour Mr Tiser cooked for himself; and he was engaged in frying a rasher of bacon and an egg when the bell in the kitchen rang shrilly. The last person he expected or wished to see was the menacing figure that stood on the doorstep.

"Come in, my dear Mark," he said faintly. "I was sending you a note round tonight, asking you to come along and see my new quarters."

"I've saved you the price of a post card," said Mark. "Anybody in the house?"

Tiser grinned crookedly.

"Only a couple of men and a woman servant." He called up the stairs. "I am not to be disturbed. Mr Mark McGill is here."

When he turned, Mark was smiling.

"Crude, rather, isn't it?" he said. "Even if I hadn't seen your servants go, I should have known you were alone. You needn't worry, I'm not going to 'bump' you."

There followed, in the small, half-furnished room which Tiser used as a study, an interview which was not as unpleasant as Tiser had every right to anticipate. He could endure the cold-blooded insults which were levelled at him, but what he had expected was something more drastic, and Mark, who knew his thoughts and saw the relief which was obvious in the face of his companion, explained why the more violent argument had not been pointed.

"You're lucky, Tiser," he said, in that staccato tone which invariably accompanied his fits of cold fury. "If I had had longer notice, and the matter was not urgent, I should have called on you – a little later, when I hadn't a busy treading on my heels."

"You were followed?" stammered Tiser.

Mark nodded.

"I can trust you up to this point, Tiser, that if I swing, you swing. You're too much in this business to turn King's evidence. Bradley is as anxious to hang you as to hang me, and if that happens I'm going to petition the Home Office that the executions be on different days! I refuse to have my last moments harrowed by a screaming little sewer-rat like you!" Then, abruptly: "We are going to Li Yoseph's tomorrow to have this matter out with him."

"Where is he?"

"He's back at Lady's Stairs. He's been there for a couple of days."

He took from his pocket a dirty scrap of paper and laid it on the table before him. Scrawled in pencil was an ill-written message.

Come tomorrow to Lady's Stairs. I will show you something, good Mark, at eleven by the clock. Li.

"Come to my house tomorrow morning," said Mark as he folded the note. "We'll go down together – "

"I won't, I won't!" Tiser almost screamed the words. "I'll not go in that place again, Mark! It's a trick of Bradley's – "

"A trick of Bradley's!" repeated Mark contemptuously. "Don't you think I know all his tricks backwards? You're coming, if I have to drag you there. What have you to be afraid of? You don't suppose any jury would convict on the evidence of that mad old fool? You don't imagine that we shouldn't be inside now if Li Yoseph's statement was enough? He's squeaked as much as he can squeak. And Bradley's too clever to put us on trial on the evidence of Li Yoseph. You've got nothing to be scared of – neither have I."

He saw a look come into the man's face and laughed aloud.

"That's a good thought of yours, Tiser: how often have you had it? You think Bradley would accept King's evidence from you? You're crazy! He could have had it any time for the asking, but you're too deeply involved in Ronnie Perryman's death. You were an accessory – "

"I tried to save him – you know I tried to save him, Mark!" whimpered Tiser. "I begged of you not to shoot, didn't I, Mark? You've always been fair to me, Mark – you wouldn't let them hang me for something you did? What good would that do you? I tried to save Ronnie. I told you – "

"You told me nothing," said Mark roughly, "except that it would be a good thing if we put him out of the way. He never met you without insulting you, and you hated him. I never hated him. It was necessary he should go out, and in a way I was sorry to see him go. But you got a kick out of it. It was you who caught him by the arm when I hit him."

Tiser sat huddled up in the chair, his long white hands twining and intertwining, his twitching face puckered into an expression that was hardly human. He was paralysed with fear. This man had too vivid an imagination. The matter-of-fact way in which Mark McGill had protested they should not be hanged together had shocked him to a point of dementia.

"I'll tell you something, Tiser. You won't be able to leave this house. I told you I had a man following me – there's another busy watching this place. The police aren't fools: they know exactly what you have been doing and how long you've been here. They could pick you up just when they wanted you."

He took a pair of gloves from his pocket, pulled one on and buttoned it with the greatest care.

"Tomorrow morning at ten o'clock you'll report at my flat," he said. "There can only be one excuse for your absence, and that is that you're dead; and if you try any funny business with me, that excuse will be a real one."

He went out, leaving a gibbering wreck of a man to fill the long night with wild and impossible schemes to escape the net that was closing around him.

25

Lady's Stairs had gained a new importance. Old Li Yoseph was back. Mrs Shiffan had seen him late at night – a slinking, bowed figure moving from room to room, muttering to himself and talking to his invisible children. She had spoken to him, but had received no answer. Her husband had made a bolder attempt to get friendly with the returned owner of the house. He had met the old man on the stairs, but the attempt at light and airy conversation had been ruthlessly defeated. The old man had brushed past him with a little chuckle that, as Ernie afterwards said, made his blood run cold.

Mr Sedeman was a surprising and unwelcome visitor. He came at odd moments, mooned around the house, asking no man's authority. In these days he lived in the vicinity of the creek; had a lodging with an attractive widow up in the Meadows area. Mostly he was to be found in the bar parlour of the "Duck and Goose," a man respected not only for his erudition but for his innumerable convictions. There was yet another reason for the awe in which he was held: in spite of his many years – he must have been nearer eighty than seventy – he was possessed of enormous strength. One sweep of his arm had sent Cosh Martin hurtling through the swing doors of the hostelry.

He was as mysterious as any man had ever been; hinted darkly of his friendship with Li, but refused absolutely to supply any information about the old man's movements. He alone had seen and conversed with him, according to his own account.

He was accepted as the oracle of Lady's Stairs; and the fact that on one evening, after a day's heavy libations, he had been picked up by the policeman on the beat and escorted to his own home, even though he had hurled the bitterest gibes at this representative of the constabulary, was placed to his credit, for he had not been pinched.

On the morning Mark McGill decided to call at Lady's Stairs, Mr Sedeman was seen making his way to the house, and there was about him such an air of importance that the creek-side people marvelled.

The refurbishing of Lady's Stairs was a slow and laborious business. Mr Shiffan was a great director, but, as his wife told him bitterly, she had only one pair of hands. She hinted that the work might go ahead better if he did a little work himself. Her shiftless young husband took some trouble to explain the need for adequate supervision.

She was staggering under the weight of a small table.

"Put it over there, Emma – that's right, somewhere about there," said Mr Shiffan kindly. He indicated the spot. "No, not there, my good gel – here!" He pointed. "That'll do."

She set the table down with a weary sigh.

"See what I mean? If you do things right you save half the work. Now put that coal-scuttle down near the door – when you go into the kitchen, all you've got to do is to pick it up – it saves a journey."

Mrs Shiffan shook her head admiringly.

"I wish I had your 'eadpiece," she said. Ernie's headpiece was much stronger than his hands. He had used it for many years to save himself the bother of working. It is true that his headpiece had landed him, on more occasions than one, in one of His Majesty's prisons, but during his enforced leisure he had had time to think up new methods of avoiding real hard labour – which is not the thing humorously described as hard labour by sentencing magistrates.

"Now push that table over there. Bring this chair here."

When she had obeyed, he looked at the iron-framed bed on which Li Yoseph slept.

"What about this bed? Shove it into that recess." He walked for some time about the room, saw the mark of the old trap, and beckoned his weary wife.

"That bit of carpet wants to be put straight," he said.

Mrs Shiffan sighed.

"You are a help," she said.

He smiled complacently at this.

"It's only a knack. What about dusting this table?"

She said she didn't know where she would be without him. Ernie smiled smugly. Once or twice he lifted the little flap and looked out into the street.

"Seen old Li this morning?"

She shook her head.

"I've only seen him once. He gives me the creeps. Where he sleeps I don't know. He was never on that bed last night."

"It's funny his coming back at all," said Ernie thoughtfully. "That old boy's crackers if ever there was one! Personally, I thought he was croaked – so did everybody else."

"Who'd croak him?" asked Mrs Shiffan curiously. She was the merest tyro in the criminal world, but was learning rapidly.

"McGill's lot would croak anything," said her husband.

It was at that moment Mr Sedeman arrived, a majestic figure.

"Look what's blown in," said Ernie admiringly. "Good morning, Sedeman."

Mr Sedeman fixed him with a basilisk glare.

"There's a 'mister' attached to my name, my good fellow," he said loftily, and Ernie made haste to apologise.

He had only met the old man once or twice, but he had some claim to a more intimate acquaintanceship.

"I saw you in Pentonville."

Mr Sedeman's eyebrows rose.

"I beg your pardon?"

"You was on the same landing as me," said Ernie ingratiatingly.

The old man shrugged, and stalked across to the little cupboard on the wall.

"I think there is some mistake," he said. "Pentonville? What is Pentonville?"

He opened the cupboard door and his face puckered in disgust.

"There's nothing there," Mrs Shiffan hastened to assure him. "You'll have to wait till Mr Yoseph comes."

Then, in a stage aside to her husband:

"That man thinks of nothing but his inside," she said.

But Ernie was intent on cementing their association. For nowadays Mr Sedeman was a man of importance, reputedly in tow with the police, and a very likely friend in trouble.

"I've only just come out," he explained, and again the old man's eyebrows rose.

"My dear, good man, I haven't the slightest idea to what you are referring. You've just come out – what do you mean? Are you a debutante or a chick? I am not interested in your comings out or your goings in."

Mr Shiffan was crushed.

"Have you seen Li Yoseph?" he asked, and, when Sedeman did not reply: "We've only just seen him. The missus got the keys of the house sent to her last week, and was told to get the place ready. We've been working for a week. You've no idea what a lot of rubbish there was – "

He looked up. Mark McGill was standing in the doorway, and one spoke warily in front of Mark. One did not speak at all, if the truth were told. He stood for the big mob, and men to whom it was wise to kowtow.

Mark McGill walked slowly into the room; Tiser sidled in behind him, a grin on his unwholesome face.

"Good morning, sir," said Mrs Shiffan.

"Where's the old man?" asked Mark.

"He ain't been in this morning."

She waited for some further question, and when it did not come she caught her husband's eye and they left the room together.

Mr Sedeman, pursuing his search for liquor, took no more notice of Mark than if he were not there.

"It makes things more real, Mark, doesn't it?" Tiser asked ingratiatingly. "By gad, there's nothing in this place that could frighten a man – I've been perfectly stupid; I hope you will forgive me."

Mark took no notice of him. He addressed Sedeman.

"I suppose you've come for a cheap drink?" he demanded.

Sedeman smiled broadly.

"I was at the speeding of the parting guest: I thought I should like to be at the welcome home." He shrugged his broad shoulders.

"You did, eh?" Mark smiled unpleasantly. "I suppose you realise you've lost a pension – you know that? I've paid you quite a lot of money since Li Yoseph disappeared. You may have to work for your living."

"Don't be absurd," said Mr Sedeman testily.

McGill walked up the room and stared out of the half-clean windows upon the shipping in the creek.

"Have you seen Li?" he asked over his shoulder.

"I've seen him, but we have not conversed," said Mr Sedeman gravely. "His conversation lacks point, if you understand me? In fact it lacks everything, including conversation. Is that an epigram?"

"Why are you hanging around here so much lately?" asked Mark. "They tell me you've got a lodging in the neighbourhood."

Sedeman ignored the question. With an elaborate gesture he brought up his arm, and Mark saw that he wore on his big wrist a ridiculous little watch.

"You will excuse me," said the old man. "The hostelries are just unlatching the gates of Paradise. I shall be in the 'Duck and Goose' if you want me – a ridiculous name, but they keep a good drop of stuff."

Mark waited till he heard the street door slam, and, looking through the little observation hole, saw Mr Sedeman stalking across the road in the direction of his favourite club.

"Mark, do you remember?" It was Tiser's anxious voice. "He didn't say a word that night he came to Cavendish Square?"

"No, he didn't say anything," said Mark, "if you're referring to Li Yoseph."

"There were no reproaches – I mean, nothing that would lead you to suppose that he was going to get nasty. He didn't give you the impression that he remembered anything – I mean about himself?"

Mark shook his head.

"It was a miracle that he escaped," he mused. "If I hadn't hit him I should have hit the floor."

He kicked back the carpet which covered the trap and made a close examination.

"There are no bullet marks here, not even old ones. I shot from this angle, and I couldn't have missed him."

"Is Ann all right?" asked Tiser fearfully. "You don't suppose she suspects – about Ronnie, I mean? That would be ghastly, wouldn't it, Mark? Naturally she can't be employed again. The sooner she is out of the country the better. I have always agreed on that, haven't I, Mark? You can't say that I've ever attempted to flaunt your views?"

But Mark was not listening. He touched the spring in the barrel table; the trap worked as sweetly as it had in the old days. Just a dull sound, and a square hole appeared in the floor. Beneath he could see the water lapping about the green piles that supported the room.

Dropping on to one knee he looked down, his hands clasped, his forehead puckered in a frown.

"Do you remember that day I dropped my watch through this trap?" he asked. "And we sent down one of the river mudlarks to get it? When we got him out he was only just alive – he said there was nothing but mud under there – mud that sucked him down and stifled him. A healthy man who fell in there would be killed – if he couldn't swim."

He looked slowly round at Tiser.

"Even if he could swim, he'd be sure to knock his head against that ladder."

Tiser's face went livid and he shrank back.

"Don't look at me like that, Mark!" he whined. "It makes my blood freeze!"

Again Mark seemed oblivious of his presence.

"Bradley will be here in a few minutes – I met one of my men in the street: he told me that Bradley would be here."

"Well?" quaked Tiser.

Again the big man's eyes returned to the trap.

"It would be terrible if an accident happened to Bradley, wouldn't it?" He was speaking half to himself, but Tiser knew what was in his mind and almost screamed in his terror.

"I'm not in this, Mark – I'm not in this! You can't monkey with Bradley. You're mad!"

McGill's eyes did not leave the lapping water below.

"Before witnesses," he said slowly, "I've nothing to do with this – you've nothing to do with it. What is there to be frightened about? A nice trap this, Tiser."

"Shut it up," whispered the pallid man. "It makes me sick to see it."

Very slowly Mark McGill rose to his feet, and taking up the square of carpet, stiff with dust and age, he laid it carefully over the gaping hole.

"Let me think about it, anyway," he said.

He walked slowly round the trap, his eyes on the carpet.

"It's one of my favourite dreams. Suppose he came in – suppose he put his foot on that carpet – "

"That's all right, Mark," said Tiser nervously. "It's a wonderful idea, but – "

"It's been one of the dreams of my life that I should mangle him, that I should see him dead, hear him screaming for help – "

There was a step on the stairs. Tiser guessed who was coming.

"Shut it up, shut it up!" he squeaked, and ran toward the barrel. Before he could reach it Mark had flung him back, and at that moment Bradley came in.

He was his old, smiling self, immensely confident, rather good-humoured.

"Good morning, McGill!" He halted within a few feet of the carpet.

Tiser, paralysed with fright, could neither move nor speak; his eyes were glued to the death trap, and he could not move them.

"Li Yoseph is back: you've come to see him, I suppose?" said Bradley. "I should like to have a little talk with you three people."

"Make it two," said Mark coolly. "He isn't here yet. The artful old devil! Fancy hiding himself! I'll bet you knew where he was. You're very clever, Bradley. I shouldn't be surprised if they promoted you over this."

The smile left Bradley's face.

"Don't be humorous at my expense," he said, and walked slowly forward, nearer and nearer to the carpet.

On the very edge of it he halted, and the scream that was rising in Tiser's throat was choked. Mark laughed.

"You're not in a police court now, you know, Bradley," he said.

He saw Bradley smile as he turned back towards the door.

"I'll talk to you in my own way – "

"When you've got about twenty policemen round you to protect you?" sneered Mark.

Bradley turned in a flash, and again came towards him. Mark stood in such a position that to reach him the detective must step on that carpet.

"Do you think I need protection from a rat like you?" asked Bradley scornfully.

"You're keeping a respectful distance," suggested Mark.

"That's because I'm afraid of you," said the detective sardonically.

"Afraid of having your face damaged?" asked McGill. "Your dear Ann wouldn't like to see you – "

"Keep her name out of it," snapped Bradley.

"I'll do as I damned well please!"

Bradley took two steps forward, and Tiser stood, his hands before his mouth to check the cry. And then the miracle occurred. The detective's foot dropped on the centre of the carpet – and nothing happened. The carpet did not sag. Even Mark was betrayed into an amazed stare. But it was the squeal which came from Tiser which attracted Bradley's attention.

"Hallo, what's the matter with you?" he asked, and then looked at Mark. "You're not any too rosy either, McGill. Is there any little joke?"

26

Mark McGill drew a long sigh. The tension of his face relaxed. Yet for the moment he was incapable of speech, and stood blinking at the detective, as though unable to realise what had happened. There Bradley was, in the very centre of the carpet, upheld by some mysterious force. Presently he found his voice.

"If there's a joke it's on me," he said, and went on, in a more even tone: "You asked me to come here and see you, Bradley. Am I to wait until Li Yoseph turns up, or haven't you let him out this morning?"

Bradley's face was inscrutable.

"Are you sure he will turn up?" he asked. "Isn't there a possibility that he doesn't wish to repeat his – unpleasant experience?"

He kicked the carpet aside and looked at the floor. And then Mark saw what he knew must have been the case – that the trap was closed. It had come noiselessly up into position, yet neither he nor Tiser had been anywhere near the controlling lever.

"Did you find any bullet marks?" asked Bradley. "I suppose you looked?"

He took from his pocket a small pill-box, opened and held it out.

"Take a good look at them, McGill."

"They hardly interest me," said Mark coolly. "Where is your friend Li Yoseph? You don't think I'm afraid of seeing him, do you? Or of what the crazy old devil may say about me? There isn't a jury in the world that would convict me on the evidence of a man who sees ghosts. Take that into court and they'd laugh you out, Bradley!"

The door clicked and the untidy Mrs Shiffan came in. She held a note, and seemed undecided as to whom it was for.

"A boy came with this to the back door; he said he came from Mr Yoseph."

Bradley took the note and read it.

"He'll not be here till eleven o'clock tonight," he said. "Presumably that was the eleven he meant. A curious hour."

"I don't see why it's especially curious," said Mark, and Bradley smiled grimly.

"It was about the hour he was killed, wasn't it – and about the hour that Ronnie Perryman was killed?"

Mark scowled at him.

"Killed! You're mad! I've seen Li Yoseph."

"You haven't seen Perryman, too, I suppose?" asked the detective. "*He's* not alive. I'll see you at eleven, then."

He turned abruptly and walked to the door.

"You still look frightened, Tiser." Bradley was amused. "What was it all about? Perhaps you'll tell me tonight?"

Tiser remained immovable, frozen stiff with the horror through which he had passed.

The street door slammed below, and Mark signalled to the woman to leave the room. When she had gone, he turned his attention to Tiser, who was staring at the trap.

"You saw that, Mark?" Tiser's voice was a thin wail of sound. "He put his foot on the centre of the carpet and he didn't go down!"

Mark snarled round at him.

"He didn't go down because the trap was closed, you fool! Who closed it?"

And then, as though in answer to his question, from somewhere outside the room, in which direction he could not gather, came the faint sound of a fiddle playing the "Chanson d'Adieu."

27

Mark McGill had four banks, and from three of these he drew within a pound of his credit. The fourth, which was the least important of all, he did not touch, knowing that the police were probably watching the banks or that somebody in the office had received instructions to notify Scotland Yard.

At five different points on the outskirts of London that night a powerful motor-car would be waiting for him. He had chosen them from five hiring companies, in different names, and had appointed a rendezvous for each. Through agents at Manchester and Leeds he had received two brand-new passports, and the portrait on each was different – Mark was something of an amateur photographer, and the necessary photographs had been taken at his leisure and in the privacy of his own room.

There remained only to decide upon the auspicious moment to make his get-away, and that decision had been made. Immediately after the interview that night he would pass into Essex. At Burnham he had a sea-going motor-boat, stored with all the necessities for a two-days' voyage. He had chosen Ostend. The motor-boat was registered in that country, and he might slip into the busy resort without attracting attention. Mark knew the value of the tricolour flag that was stowed away in a locker on the motor-boat.

He made no attempt to see Ann. His servant told him that she had gone out early in the morning. But Ann had passed from the status of factor to the most inconsiderable of quantities. He thought less of her than of Tiser – she was certainly less dangerous, though Tiser knew, or ought to know, that any attempt on his part at a squeak must end disastrously for him.

Bradley now had made no disguise of the fact that detectives were watching the house. Mark saw them lounging about the square, and when he went out into Regent Street to make purchases, two of them were at his heels. He would give them something to talk about, at any rate – he went into a furnishing house and made arrangements for the redecoration of his sitting-room, ordered a new settee and a Berger chair, and called at a tourist's agency to book seats on the Sud Express for the following Monday week. He not only did this, but paid by cheque, and spent half an hour arranging for his car to be sent across into France.

He might not deceive Bradley, but he would certainly puzzle him.

It was whilst he was out that Ann received a note from the detective. It began without preamble:

I am going to ask you to make a sacrifice for me, and submit to your feelings being rather harrowed. Will you come to Li Yoseph's house at Lady's Stairs tonight at eleven o'clock? You may say yes or no to the messenger, and I shall understand. I want you to come very badly. If you say yes, I will have a man meet you here and take you down with him in a private car. Perhaps you will never forgive me for what I am going to do, but it is a case of needs must. I will tell you this, that I am using you, not exactly as a bait, but for the psychological effect you may have upon somebody who also will be present.

She read the letter, folded it and put it in her bag, and went herself to the door to the waiting officer.

"Tell Mr Bradley the answer is 'Yes,' " she said.

Mr Tiser's summons came more urgently. Sergeant Simmonds called in the afternoon, and would take no denial when the servant told him that the master was out.

"I will wait till he comes back," he said, and planted himself stolidly on a chair in Tiser's sitting-room.

After a quarter of an hour that nervous man made his appearance.

"I want you at Lady's Stairs tonight, Tiser," said Simmonds; "and when I say 'I,' I mean Bradley."

"I'm not well enough to go out tonight," said Tiser.

"Then we'll send an ambulance for you," replied the unsympathetic Simmonds, "in which case you'll go down under arrest."

Tiser's panic was pitiable.

"But, my dear Mr Simmonds, what have you against me? You surely are not joining my enemies and believing these horrid things that people are saying about me? Do, I beg of you, my dear Mr Simmonds, listen to reason."

The sergeant stopped him with a gesture, and said something which he had never said before.

"Tiser, there's just a chance for you. It isn't much, and we can promise you nothing – but why not put up a squeak voluntarily?"

The only result of this suggestion was to make the man more fearful.

" 'Squeak'? You mean, give information to the police? About what, my dear fellow? I know nothing; I should be the poorest kind of witness the police could have on any subject."

Simmonds shook his head.

"You've got a chance," he said, "and if I were you I'd jump at it – you might get off with a lifer, though it's pretty sure you'd be condemned."

At the very hint of condemnation Tiser writhed.

"I know nothing – nothing, nothing!" he said rapidly. "You're altogether mistaken, and dear Mr Bradley is mistaken, if he imagines that I can tell him about poor Ronnie."

"I didn't mention poor Ronnie, but that's what I meant," said Simmonds, rising. "All right, I'll call for you at half-past ten tonight. If you're not here, I shall know where you are, because I've got a couple of men tailing you."

It was raining heavily when Ann and her escort went out into Cavendish Square. A closed motorcar, not the type usually employed by the police, was waiting for her, and she suspected that it had been procured by Bradley for her comfort.

"Who will be there?" she asked, as the car sped southwards.

"Tiser and McGill. They went away together ten minutes ago."

She thought she recognised the man when she had seen him in the half-light of the doorway. Now in the darkness she knew his voice.

"You're Mr Simmonds, the officer who arrested me, aren't you?"

"That's me, miss," said Simmonds cheerfully.

"Then you can tell me something. Is it about Ronnie – I mean, is that why I'm going to Lady's Stairs?"

But Mr Simmonds' favourite vice was reticence.

"Mr Bradley will tell you all about that, miss," he said.

It was not a particularly pleasant journey for Mark McGill. It was an everlasting misery to his quaking companion. In a burst of confidence Tiser had told him of the offer which the police had made.

"Naturally I turned it down, my dear Mark. Whatever are my shortcomings, I am loyal. The very thought of betraying you made me feel sick."

"You'd have felt sicker if you had," said Mark curtly. "I never dreamt you would – you value your own neck too much, my good man. They didn't tell you that you'd get out if you squeaked? That the Crown would withdraw any charge against you? I thought not. If they had put that offer into writing, I know just what you would have told."

"But suppose Li Yoseph tells – "

"Li Yoseph! What can he tell – about ghosts and spooks and little children? Is that the kind of stuff to bring before a judge and a jury? Don't be a fool. Now listen, Tiser: the one thing you've got to expect is that Li Yoseph *will* talk. He'll tell about Ronnie and about himself. And all you've got to do is to sit quiet and imagine that everything he is telling is a lie. Get that idea in your nut, and it'll be easier than falling off a house. That's Bradley's game – it's a new kind of third degree; and if he fails, I'm going to make it so hot for him that he'll be glad to clear out of the force. I've got a story all ready for the papers; tomorrow morning I'll see a reporter and tell him to come out boldly with the story – about Bradley and his persecution. If he doesn't completely fail…"

He did not go on. There was a boat at Burnham-on-Crouch, and the comforting weather report that North Sea conditions were favourable for a crossing – "Sea slight, misty, visibility poor."

He was puzzled as to Bradley's plan. A mere confrontation by Li Yoseph could not affect him – three parts of the value of surprise had gone when Li Yoseph came sidling into his drawing-room that night. His word, on oath or without oath, could make no difference either to himself or Tiser. He had gone over his past transactions with Li Yoseph trying to remember something that he might, wittingly or unwittingly, have placed in his hands, but could recall nothing that would support the old man's statement. He had been a fool not to have used the trap with Ronnie. That was a blunder, to throw the body from the window into deep water. He had never dreamt but that it would float out into the river.

Now that he came to think of it, the window of Li Yoseph's room had been Tiser's suggestion. Everything that coward touched went wrong.

They came to Li Yoseph's house and found the door closed. Mark knocked, and after a few minutes they heard the heavy feet of Ernie coming down the stairs to admit them.

"I'm glad somebody's come," he said shrilly. "This place is full of rats."

"Is the old man here?" asked Mark.

"No, he hasn't come yet, guv'nor. To tell you the truth, Mr McGill, I'm sorry I ever volunteered to stay here tonight. The place is 'aunted. Noises, noises, creaks and creepings. If I slept a couple of nights in this house I'd go crackers."

"Has anybody been here this evening?" asked Mark.

"That busy fellow."

"Bradley?"

Ernie nodded.

"Yes, he's been looking around for hours. I asked him if he wanted anything and he said no – I had to take his word. He walks in and out this blinkin' place as though it belonged to him."

Li Yoseph's room was a place of shadows by night; the one naked light which hung from the ceiling was no more than a dull yellow glow.

"Have you seen this, guv'nor?"

Ernie showed a little panel by the door where six green lights were.

"Funny idea, eh? What's that for?"

Mark was in a surprisingly amiable mood, and explained.

"There's a button beneath every third step," he said, "which operates one of these lights. It's a warning if anyone's coming upstairs."

"Good Lord! I'm glad you told me that. I got a fair fright this evening when my missus came up from the street."

There was a knock at the door below, and Mark went downstairs to open the door. Ann was standing alone. Her escort had left her with an assurance that she would be under observation.

"Come in, Ann." Mark's manner was geniality itself. "What the dickens are you doing down here? Bradley's idea, eh? Did you come alone?"

She did not answer, but preceded him up the stairs. The effect of her coming on Tiser was, for some strange reason, a cheerful one.

"My dear Miss Ann, how glad I am to see you!" He seized her hand in his two moist paws and shook it. "So they brought you here, did they? How disgraceful – "

"You'd better shut up, Tiser," snapped McGill, and, to the girl: "What is the idea?" he asked again.

"I don't know."

"Bradley sent for you?"

She nodded.

An interested spectator was Ernie. She remembered having seen the man at the police court.

"Is Mr Yoseph here?"

He shook his head.

"No, miss. They thought he was comin' this afternoon – there was quite a crowd to see him – he was very popular in the neighbourhood."

"Is Mr Bradley coming tonight?" she asked.

"I shouldn't think so, miss," said Ernie. "He told me to phone the Yard if anything happened. I've got his number somewhere." He took a paper from his pocket and handed it to her, but Ann was not interested in Mr Bradley's number. Besides, she knew.

"Are you sure Li Yoseph wasn't here the other morning?" asked Mark.

"No, guv'nor, as far as I know, he wasn't," replied the man.

"I thought I heard his fiddle playing."

It was the first news Ann had had that Mark had paid a recent visit to the house.

Ernie grinned.

"I've heard that lots of times – but I don't take any notice of it. Lord! the things you hear in this house! I wouldn't sleep here alone – "

Mark silenced him with a look.

"Are you sure, my dear Mr Shiffan?" asked Tiser nervously. "Are you absolutely sure there isn't another room of some kind where the dear old gentleman could be? Just think, my dear fellow."

"There's half a dozen rooms: they're all locked up. The police opened 'em when the old gentleman went away, but they found nothin' – full of rubbish by all accounts. Couldn't have more rubbish than this place had." He rubbed his chilled hands. "If you don't want anything, I'll go and make a fire in the kitchen."

He looked from one to the other, but had no encouragement to stay. An embarrassed silence followed his departure, which Mark broke.

"I don't know why you came, Ann."

"Why shouldn't I come?" she challenged, and Mark shrugged his broad shoulders.

"There's no reason why you shouldn't. What did Bradley tell you the last time you met him?"

She made no reply.

"And you have met him frequently of late. He's terribly keen on you, isn't he? That's rather amusing."

But still he could not provoke her, and again he asked her the blunt question.

"He said nothing that he hadn't told me before," said Ann.

She felt uncomfortable under the scrutiny of his keen eyes.

"You've been very cheerful lately. I even heard you singing the other morning as I came out of my flat. I wonder if your friendship with Bradley has anything to do with it?"

She smiled at this.

"I've been wondering that myself."

Again an uncomfortable interval, during which Tiser, tense and nervous, appeared to be on the point of saying something.

"I suppose you'll be going to Paris when this is all over?" said Mark. "I think perhaps it was a mistake to have kept you here at all. My original idea was that a woman driver would escape attention more than a man. That isn't the case, is it? You attracted a little too much attention in certain quarters."

Ann was silent.

"That fellow's still keen on you, eh? I was watching him that night he came to the flat. He never took his eyes off you. You're not getting soft about him, are you?"

Tiser moved to the window, and now his urgent voice called:

"Mark! Come here. What are those boats?"

"Boats?" McGill walked into the recess, and, rubbing one of the grimy windows, peered through. "They look like police launches — they're going up to the lock. The Thames Police have always got a couple of launches about here."

"They're turning," whispered Tiser. "Mark, they're patrolling the river front."

He clutched McGill's arm convulsively.

"I say, my dear fellow, need I stay…? I don't think I'm necessary. Will you excuse me, Miss Perryman?"

"You'll stay," rasped Mark.

Ernie had come in at that moment; he beckoned him.

"Is there any drink in the house?"

Apparently Ernie had a bottle of whisky in the kitchen. It didn't, he said, belong to him, but he did not explain its ownership.

McGill took his companion by the arm.

"What you want is a drink, Tiser. Do you mind if we leave you, Ann?"

Ann shook her head. Yet they had hardly left the room before she regretted her gesture. Even the presence of Mark was preferable to this eerie loneliness. There came from below squeakings and patterings; the wind was rising, and moaned dismally round the corner of the house. And then what had happened before happened again – the light went out. She heard the rattle of the trap, saw the square of light appear, and the head and shoulders of Li Yoseph emerge.

Ann shrank back against the wall as the old man came into the room. This time his face was visible in the light of the lantern he carried. She saw him close the trap and disappear into the recess. As he did so, the light went on again, and simultaneously Mark came in.

"There's no corkscrew – " he began, and then he saw her face.

"What is it?" he asked quickly.

Ann's mouth was dry.

"He's come," she said breathlessly. "Li Yoseph."

He pointed to the trap.

"Through there?"

"Yes; he went into the recess."

Mark walked quickly in the direction Li Yoseph had taken.

"Are you sure, my dear young lady?" asked Tiser tremulously. "It wasn't your imagination? Why should he come from below?"

"There's a door there," said Mark's voice, "just behind the bed. I never noticed that before. I wonder what – "

So far he got when there was the sound of a violin. Nearer and nearer came the music, and suddenly Li Yoseph appeared. He walked

247

to the window and sat down in the old place, his bow moving rhythmically over the strings.

"My God!" Tiser's teeth were chattering. "It is a man, isn't it, Mark?" He clung to McGill's arm. "It is something human, isn't it?"

Mark shook him off.

"Quite," he said. "You're not afraid, Ann?"

He saw the look in her face and knew that the question was superfluous.

The music ceased.

"Li, it's Mark speaking," he said softly. "Are you all right, Li?"

The old Jew put down his bow and fiddle, and came shuffling nearer, peering at him short-sightedly.

"Dat funny t'ing you say!" he chuckled hoarsely. "Am I all right, eh? Goot Mark…always t'inkin' about poor old Li." He lowered his voice to address his ghostly companions. "Now, Heinrich und Hans und Pieter, you go by your beds, eh? Dis is bad time for leedle chillun to be out of bed…shoo, shoo, shoo! Good night." He kissed his finger-tips to these dream children of his.

"The old craze," said Mark in a low voice. "Miss Perryman's here, Li – Ronnie's sister."

Li nodded.

"I see her fine. She isn't afraid by me, no?"

"I'm here, too, Li," said Tiser shrilly. "You know me – dear old Tiser."

But the old man did not heed him. He went to a cupboard in the wall and, unlocking it, took out a bottle and glass, and put them carefully on the overturned cask that served as a table.

"Why did you want us to come at eleven?" asked Mark. "Is Bradley here? Who is that wine for?"

"Heem," said Li, and nodded many times.

"Him? Whom do you mean, Li Yoseph?" asked Ann, controlling her voice with difficulty.

The old man looked at her from under his brows. In the shadowy light of the place she thought there was pain in his eyes.

"You will not be hurt if I say?"

248

"For Ronnie?" she asked, and the old man nodded.

"What do you mean, you crazy fool?" said Mark roughly.

"For heem," said Li Yoseph. "Every night he komm."

"Every night?" Mark laughed. "You haven't been here for a year."

He saw the old man smile; it was the first time he had ever seen Li Yoseph smile, and it was an ugly sight.

"You t'ink so? Yet here have I been."

Tiser was now in a condition of abject fear.

"I can't stand this! God! I can't stand it! Ronnie's dead, Li. He can't come here…"

"Every night at the quarter-past he komm," persisted the old man solemnly. "Up der stairs he komm und into dis room. Und to der table he goes and der wine he pulls toward heem, but never he drinks. He was going to drink dat night – you remember, goot Mark – when –"

"Stop, will you!" roared Mark. "Don't you see the effect you're having on this lady?"

But Ann signalled him to silence.

"Don't stop for me – living or dead, I am not afraid of Ronnie."

"You'll see nothing," said Mark contemptuously. "It's all in his crazy brain."

Old Li was talking.

"So, Ronnie, I give you your wine, eh?"

"What happens afterwards?" sneered Mark.

Li Yoseph turned slowly in his direction.

"Den he falls, und der chair she goes over, and he is dead all over again."

Ann was staring at Mark, wide-eyed.

"What is he saying?" she asked in a whisper. "Did Ronnie die here – here in this room?"

She felt somebody grip her arm so violently that she almost cried with pain. It was Tiser.

"Don't take any notice of him. Let's get out," he gibbered. "This place is full of ghosts…look at him!"

She wrenched her arm free.

"Ronnie was killed here in this room?" she challenged.

"You're as mad as he is," said Mark, and at that moment they heard a church clock strike eleven, and waited, every one of them, for what would happen. There was no sound.

"Well – " said Mark.

Even as he spoke, there came a slow knock on the door below. Nobody spoke. They heard the door slam, and then Tiser uttered a thin scream of terror. The lower green light was burning – somebody was on the stairs; and then the second, the third, the fourth.

They were all alight now. The door was slowly opening. Nobody saw who it was who had opened the door. Apparently nobody but Li.

He went forward; to him, it seemed, the visitor was a real presence.

"So, Ronnie, you komm, eh? You komm to talk mit old Li... There is der wine, Ronnie. You sit down, no?"

Nobody had come into the room, yet the door closed of itself. And there was Li, walking with his arm about an unseen shape. Ann watched, fascinated, as Li Yoseph guided the thing he saw to the table.

"It is goot wine, Ronnie, der best for you!"

And then, to her horror, she saw the full glass of wine moved by some mysterious agency across the table. Nearer and nearer it drew to the edge, and then she heard a cry from Li.

"Look out for Mark, Ronnie!"

At that moment the chair by the table was overthrown. There came a scream of terror.

"I can't stand it! You killed him, Mark!"

Tiser's face was livid; his trembling finger pointed to his companion.

"I'm going to the police to tell them! You killed him, you butcher – killed him in cold blood! I can't stand it, Mark I've got to tell."

Mark gripped him by the collar and swung him round.

"You're mad, too, eh?"

But now Ann knew.

"He's speaking the truth – you murderer!" she breathed.

"Truth or lie, it's all one to me," said Mark. "You don't get out of this house till I've got your mouth shut some way or the other."

And then, his face demoniacal in its rage, he turned upon the bent figure of the man who had wrung the confession from Tiser.

"I'll make no mistake this time," he said, but even as he jerked out his automatic, Li Yoseph's hand closed on his wrist, and, with a jerk which almost dislocated his elbow, sent Mark sprawling.

With a howl of rage he leapt at Li Yoseph. Two hands of steel gripped him again and flung him into the arms of the detectives who, unseen and unheard, had entered the room.

"Who are you?" said Mark breathlessly.

There was no need to ask. With one sweep of his hand, the yellow face, the great chin, the big, ugly nose had vanished, and he looked into the eyes of Inspector Bradley.

"You!" he croaked.

Bradley nodded.

"We found the body of Li Yoseph a little time ago, under here. I showed you the bullets that were taken from that body – oh, yes, you killed him all right. It took us a long time to get him up from the mud, but we got him at last. And then it struck me that I might scare Tiser into confessing. I play the fiddle a little – and Li Yoseph was about my build." McGill's extraordinary self-possession did not desert him. He could even laugh.

"You'll want two witnesses to a confession: that's the law, isn't it? They'll not accept you. I doubt if they'll accept Ann. Who's the other?"

Bradley pointed.

"Underneath this tub there's an ancient gentleman – didn't you see him work the glass? It had a steel plate at the bottom, and he manipulated the magnet that made it move."

He unlocked a door of the cask and Mr Sedeman staggered forth, a very dishevelled old gentleman, strangely sober. Keeping Mr Sedeman sober had been one of the greatest difficulties that the case presented.

Bradley had been remarkably insistent upon Ann taking a sea voyage.

"I want you to get used to the climate of Brazil," he said, "and I'd rather you didn't read any English papers until I come out to you, darling. No, I don't think your evidence would be worth much, and, anyway, we'll get on very well without you. Tiser's made a written statement."

So Ann sailed on a luxury liner to Brazil, and read nothing of that sensational sight in the dock when a half-crazy Tiser leapt at the man who had encompassed his ruin. Nor did she read of those strange execution sheds. The day McGill was hanged, the Flying Squad lost one of its most valuable members.

EDGAR WALLACE

BIG FOOT

Footprints and a dead woman bring together Superintendent Minton and the amateur sleuth Mr Cardew. Who is the man in the shrubbery? Who is the singer of the haunting Moorish tune? Why is Hannah Shaw so determined to go to Pawsy, 'a dog lonely place' she had previously detested? Death lurks in the dark and someone must solve the mystery before BIG FOOT strikes again, in a yet more fiendish manner.

BONES IN LONDON

The new Managing Director of Schemes Ltd has an elegant London office and a theatrically dressed assistant – however, Bones, as he is better known, is bored. Luckily there is a slump in the shipping market and it is not long before Joe and Fred Pole pay Bones a visit. They are totally unprepared for Bones' unnerving style of doing business, unprepared for his unique style of innocent and endearing mischief.

EDGAR WALLACE

BONES OF THE RIVER

'Taking the little paper from the pigeon's leg, Hamilton saw it was from Sanders and marked URGENT. *Send Bones instantly to Lujamalababa… Arrest and bring to headquarters the witch doctor.*'

It is a time when the world's most powerful nations are vying for colonial honour, a time of trading steamers and tribal chiefs. In the mysterious African territories administered by Commissioner Sanders, Bones persistently manages to create his own unique style of innocent and endearing mischief.

THE DAFFODIL MYSTERY

When Mr Thomas Lyne, poet, poseur and owner of Lyne's Emporium insults a cashier, Odette Rider, she resigns. Having summoned detective Jack Tarling to investigate another employee, Mr Milburgh, Lyne now changes his plans. Tarling and his Chinese companion refuse to become involved. They pay a visit to Odette's flat and in the hall Tarling meets Sam, convicted felon and protégé of Lyne. Next morning Tarling discovers a body. The hands are crossed on the breast, adorned with a handful of daffodils.

EDGAR WALLACE

THE JOKER
(USA: THE COLOSSUS)

While the millionaire Stratford Harlow is in Princetown, not only does he meet with his lawyer Mr Ellenbury but he gets his first glimpse of the beautiful Aileen Rivers, niece of the actor and convicted felon Arthur Ingle. When Aileen is involved in a car accident on the Thames Embankment, the driver is James Carlton of Scotland Yard. Later that evening Carlton gets a call. It is Aileen. She needs help.

THE SQUARE EMERALD
(USA: THE GIRL FROM SCOTLAND YARD)

'Suicide on the left,' says Chief Inspector Coldwell pleasantly, as he and Leslie Maughan stride along the Thames Embankment during a brutally cold night. A gaunt figure is sprawled across the parapet. But Coldwell soon discovers that Peter Dawlish, fresh out of prison for forgery, is not considering suicide but murder. Coldwell suspects Druze as the intended victim. Maughan disagrees. If Druze dies, she says, 'It will be because he does not love children!'